I AM THE SEA

Matt Stanley

Legend Press Ltd, 51 Gower Street, London, WC1E 6HJ
info@legendpress.co.uk | www.legendpress.co.uk

Print ISBN 978-1-80031-0-056
Ebook ISBN 978-1-80031-0-063
Set in Times. Printing managed by Jellyfish Solutions Ltd
Cover design by Sarah Whittaker | www.whittakerbookdesign.com

Matt Stanley was born in Sheffield and achieved a first-class degree in English and American Literature from the University of East Anglia. He is the author of a number of detective novels for Macmillan and has previously taught an MA in Creative Writing at Sheffield Hallam University. *I Am the Sea* is Matt's eleventh novel.

For Javier Mustieles Renales,
unexpected son

For now I stand as one upon a rock
Environ'd with a wilderness of sea
Who marks the waxing tide grow wave by wave
Expecting ever when some envious surge
Will in his brinish bowels swallow him

Titus Andronicus

ONE

The corpse has been tied to the balcony railing for five days, enshrouded in a bed-sheet cerement. Five days and five nights out in the sea air, dampened by drizzle and spray, soiled by seabirds, lit intermittently by a beam that could not ignite life even as it prevents death. Gust buffeted. They say the torso rocked in the gale of the second day, as if the thing was struggling, Lazarus-like, to escape its wrappings.

I have watched it through the telescope these last two days from the shore station but it hasn't moved for me. I don't know why I gaze at it so. Perhaps because that pale pupal form, limbless, faceless, has altered *my* fate. But for this death, my first posting would have been some other house than Ripsaw Reef.

Spencer was his name. There's no notion, as yet, of how he died – only that Principle Bartholomew and Assistant Keeper Adamson were seen lashing him to the bars on the day they signalled for aid.

I understand it is not official Commission practice to expose the body in this way. Nor is it a simple matter to hoist a deadweight vertically up the tower. But keepers around these isles have learned that a cadaver soon becomes noisome if confined, and accusations of foul play may be avoided only if the dead man is available for autopsy. He cannot simply be tossed into the sea with the day's ashes. Better that the gulls settle on him, not knowing that a skull sits beneath their delicate webbed feet. There's no ignominy in it. The hero

Lord Nelson bears the same fate with equanimity in Trafalgar Square – he, too, supported on an imperious column almost the same height as Ripsaw.

I feel no dread or repulsion – only curiosity. Still, the station officers here have tried to frighten me with tales of the perils faced by keepers on a rock house like Ripsaw. They say there was a fellow at Bell Rock or Haulbowline who, through unbearable monotony or vertigo of the abyss, stabbed himself in the breast rather than tolerate another day. He couldn't be taken off the rock for two days due to the weather. He died on shore.

Then there was the new keeper at Longships or Skerryvore whose hair went completely white during his first storm. He was offered a generous pension but elected to stay on the rock. The keeper before Adamson was washed off the rock while emptying the ash bucket. Three months previous to that sorry occurrence, another man simply disappeared, either swept from the balcony in a gale or sucked from the doorway by some immense billow. No trace of either was found. Ripsaw, so they tell me with exaggerated gargoyle contortions, is the "most fatal" house run by the Commission.

I've read that the keepers in France live with their families so that the desolation is mollified by the comforts of a common hearth, by the sound of childish laughter, and by love. No such sentiment for the Commission. Men alone is their approach. Emotion stays on shore.

* * *

On the sixth day, the tides and winds were judged propitious and we finally departed for Ripsaw in the cutter. I myself saw little difference in the weather. To the naked eye, the lighthouse remained a pale finger bisecting a plumbeous sky and a sea of slate. Even through the telescope, the waves about the reef had no fearful aspect. Their silent white was merely hoar frost or lichen on the sea's surface.

My uniform was still stiff with newness. Drizzle and spray beaded on the woollen greatcoat and I worried that the salt would ruin its smart brass buttons. With my cap and my epaulettes, I felt more like an actor about to walk on stage than an apprentice keeper about to take his first position. The cork lifebelt was my Yorick's skull or my papier-mâché helmet.

I expected that the sailors – rough sorts and vulgar – would snigger or mock, but rather they deferred to my tall black figure as if I were a policeman or curate. The trip is but twenty miles, but the men were as sombre as Magellan's setting sail for the Horn. Perhaps because they knew they had to bring a body back, rather than for some other subtle augury.

Perspective is distorted at water level. For the first hour, it seemed that the lighthouse was no closer, forever distant as the moon. But as the tide ebbed, it grew larger, its dark pedestal of rock emerging so that the column stood naked but unashamed above the waterline – an elegant and fragile figure amid the brute elements.

Waves that had seemed so flatly passive from ashore were heaving hills of glass afloat. I confess I was weak with nausea. Midway between station and lighthouse, there was a moment when I measured the scale of our tiny vessel against the blackness below, the chiaroscuro vault above, the horizon's hard demarcation and the scrap of coast blurred imaginary by mist and spray, and I gripped the gunwale for the consolation of something physical and solid. It was a moment only. A brief and fleeting moment only.

Some miles later, I sensed the place. First, the rushing reef: the skirring plash and suck of boiling spray across the thousand feet of jagged saw-tooth gneiss around the lighthouse. Then the screams and shrieks of circling birds around the lantern. Then the salty iodine tang of gurgling, molluscous nooks and cavities. It was not land. It was not sea.

Out here among the furious eddies, between the twenty-fathom abyss and the limitless sky, man had built this adamantine tower of granite – totally solid for its first thirty-five feet of interlocking, double-dovetailed, masonry – as an imposition of light and order on chaos. The waters were perpetually about its throat like strangulating hands but the structure stood tall.

And suddenly we were at the foot of the monument, whose exposed rock was choked with swaying henware and bladderwrack. A long gunmetal ladder descended some fifteen feet from the doorway to a small patch of rock where a metal grille formed a rudimentary landing platform. The tower's weather side was green with algae and speckled with barnacles to a surprising height, while the lee side was as pristine as the day it was built. I squinted up its tapering immensity, at the windows, at the balcony's curled lip, above which poor dead Spencer was lashed.

All was now activity on the cutter as we came around to the landing stage. Ropes were readied. Tarpaulins were hauled from barrels and chests. Sails were reefed. Close to the rock, the waves seemed even greater. The little vessel tipped and rocked as if in a tempest and it seemed inconceivable that any person or thing could be landed from such instability.

A beam emerged from an aperture above the great iron-bound door – the lighthouse crane. Then the door itself opened and I saw for the first time my new colleagues, Principal Bartholomew and Keeper Adamson, both in uniform.

My impressions from a distance: Principle Bartholomew looked like an elderly clergyman with his white mutton-chop whiskers and his pale, ascetic countenance. Mr Adamson was shorter and more muscular, resembling a coal-heaver to my mind rather than an officer of the Commission. His uniform seemed not to fit him. It was he who carefully descended the ladder to receive and secure ropes thrown from astern and from the bow. He appeared not to notice me. Rather, he ascended to help with the resupply.

I held tightly to a beam and tried not to slip on the wet rope matting as the sailors prepared the supplies for the crane, swinging them out over the waves and up to Principal

Bartholomew at the doorway. Oatmeal, small beer, butter, beef. Newspapers. My own trunk of clothes and few possessions. My journal was safe inside my greatcoat.

When all had been winched to the house, the body of Spencer was swung out from the beam and swayed precariously above the depths as it approached the cutter. The sailors were efficient but subdued, not wanting the bad luck of a body on-board. In its gull-stained shroud, it was a disturbing, amorphous chrysalis, its head lolling oddly as if the neck were broken.

Finally, it was my turn – I, the least important item of cargo.

"What's it to be, then: rope or jump?" said one of the sailors.

My choice: be attached to the same rope that had just delivered the corpse and be hoisted, pendulous, fifteen feet above the hungry sea, or jump from the madly tilting bow to a slippery platform. I saw that Keeper Adamson was descending the ladder once again to loose the ropes. I decided to show my valour.

They positioned me at the prow, which was plunging and soaring and twisting to be free of its restraint. The platform seemed both too far and too low to permit a safe leap. A slip or a mistiming and I'd simply topple into the water where it churned against the rock. My heavy greatcoat would soak in a fatal embrace and the weight of it would draw me down to darkness.

Ropes were tugged. The boat was brought about.

"Keep hold of the stake! Jump only when you're told!"

I bent my knees and gripped the stake until my fingers ached. Each jerking prow rise threatened to toss me. Each complementary fall made me almost weightless. Keeper Adamson was watching keenly and I saw in his eyes that he was hoping for a slip, a fall.

"Now!"

The prow was in a trough, about to rise. I allowed my hand to ungrip the stake and fall forwards, springing my knees as if I were to vault the tower itself. The deck raised beneath my soles, lifting me through the air, over the void and on to the metal grillwork. I landed squarely, my boots clanging on the metal. I flexed my legs to minimise the force and held out my arms for balance. Perfect athleticism.

Mr Adamson merely nodded and set about casting off the ropes. I turned to look back at the boat and noticed one of the sailors looking furtively up at the door as if to check whether Principal Bartholomew was watching. On verifying his chance, he whistled to Adamson and tossed a package.

The assistant keeper snatched it from the air and thrust it inside his coat before throwing back the last coil of rope. He glanced at me and saw that I had seen.

"Newspapers," he said. "Come on. The tide."

I followed him to the foot of the ladder and climbed the cold, wet rungs until the rock and the sea seemed very far below us. A fall from here could be fatal, though at high tide half of the ladder would be submerged.

Principal Bartholomew was waiting with a dry hand to draw me level with the doorway. The supplies were stacked behind him, just inside the brass threshold, and would need to be taken within for safe storage. He looked at me critically, as if assessing a slender walking cane that he feared may not take his weight.

"Welcome to Ripsaw," he said. "Meakes, is it?"

"Yes, sir. James Meakes, sir."

He nodded. The conversation was over. He gestured to the supplies.

I caught just a brief glimpse of the departing cutter before the great oaken door swung closed and its copper bolts were shot. Perhaps my eyes had not adjusted, but everything within seemed darkness.

TWO

Moving the supplies within was accomplished in no time, though they would be further distributed later to their respective stores. The barrels were rolled and the boxes or bags carried by Mr Adamson or me, or by both together if the weight warranted. Principal Bartholomew directed us where and in what order to carry the things and I was soon perspiring inside my greatcoat.

"Leave your trunk here," said the principal, finally. "You can collect it later. Accompany me now directly to the lantern."

We were in the windowless and lamp-lit lower storeroom, where four enormous cast-iron water cisterns followed the circle of the walls. The air was damp and smelled of stone, rust and the privy located there. It was like a castle dungeon, with granite walls seven feet thick. A second door with a thick glass pane closed the vestibule to the great exterior door.

The ascent was a rush of impressions and sensations. Though I had studied the construction of lighthouses and the minutiae of their operation, this was my very first experience inside one, and I felt the urgent excitement that a historian must feel when he closes his book and enters the actual tumbled temples of antiquity where orators and philosophers once congregated.

We passed first up a stone spiral staircase with a smart brass handrail to another store, whose strange perfume was like a steamship engine room. In the dim light of two windows, I saw glinting copper containers and the glisten of accumulated coal.

The next staircase was of wood and at an angle almost vertical, so that one had to hug close to the steps in order not to fall and so that one could pass through the narrow manhole hatch into the next chamber. There, I saw baskets, more shelves, and the japanned metal lockers that stored food and drink away from the chill damp of the lowermost chamber and the oleaginous odour of the other.

The staircases continued thus through hatches, past the kitchen with its smell of fried bacon and baking bread, past a number of bedrooms behind wainscot partitions and a library whose doors were closed. I saw the sea recede ever lower through windows in the stairwells and I fancied I could feel air rushing silently about the house, imagining myself not so much in an earth-bound building as in a vivid dream.

The light-room was a bare and utilitarian space with a ceiling of metal mesh rather than vaulted stone. Here was the mechanism that turned the light and the great cast-metal column that supported its weight. Here were the logbooks and the weather instruments, an iron stove, a solid oaken table and three telescopes stored in a rack.

The principal did not stop but continued up a gunmetal spiral staircase that led into the lantern: the altar where the enormous lens was enthroned. We rose into the very lens itself and I admit I could not breathe for the beauty and the majesty of it.

Twice the height of a man, this crown-glass jewel fully enveloped us in multiplicitous blue-green rings of prism and lenticular bullseye magnification. Spectral sparks glinted red and violet among the annular sections. Sea and sky and light itself were here concentrated. It was a wonder of science and modernity, true, with its collective genesis in the brilliant minds of Faraday, Newton, Argand, Teulère and Fresnel. But it was more than optics, more than mere refraction. So much more. The diagonal black astragals of the lantern panes were warped and crazed by the distorting lens, as was the horizon, as were the flitting sparks of gulls about the dome. Rigid linearity was but a myth inside this divine kaleidoscope.

And there was the noise of the ventilator, the tower's glass and metal throat that conveyed all effluvia to the upper atmosphere, even as the outside air enviously attempted entry. It was a deep, low moan, interrupted by pneumonic coughs and gasps. A consumptive deity rising in the morning.

And there was the lamp itself, extinguished now, its circular maze of wicks, its network of brass tubing, its elegant glass chimney protecting pristine perfection like a museum display case. I was like a child wanting to touch every gleaming surface.

Principal Bartholomew, guardian of this sacred light, was observing my awe. In the limpid illumination of the lantern, I could see that his eyes were a smoky blue and that his pale skin had a luminous quality that, with his white whiskers, made him almost an apparition trapped inside an exquisite jar.

He saw that he had my attention. "Very well, Mister Meakes. Do you have something for me?"

"Sir? Oh, yes, sir."

I took the letter of presentation from inside my greatcoat and handed it to him. He appeared to read it all, though he must have seen the same thing many times.

"Hmm. All is in order. I welcome you officially to the first-order dioptric lighthouse of Ripsaw Reef. You will spend the first six weeks of your apprenticeship here and learn the duties of a keeper. If your conduct is satisfactory, you will move on for a further six weeks at a catoptric house before receiving your certificate of satisfaction and being added to the expectant list. Thereafter, you will be assigned a lighthouse according to availability and necessity."

"Yes, sir. These things have been explained to—"

"Your duties. You will be instructed in the full duties of the light-room, lantern and other parts of the house. You will learn to light the lamp, trim the wicks, replace valves, clean the lens, replenish oil and maintain the lantern glass. When on duty, you will record relevant information in the ship log, the daily log and the weather log, using the barometer, thermometer and rain gauge. If your watch finishes in the morning, you will raise the signal ball between the hours of eight o'clock and ten o'clock to assure the shore station that all is well. You will also write a monthly report. Until I am assured that you have learned and executed these duties well, you will not be permitted to be alone in the light-room during any night watch. Either I or Keeper Adamson will accompany you.

"You must be cleanly and well-dressed at all times, though your uniform is obligatory only on Sundays and for visits. Any and all infractions will be noted in your record and a copy of the regulations can be found in the library for your reference. Two rules, above all, are utterly inviolable. First: you will report to the light-room five minutes before your watch starts or when called at any time by the air-whistle. Second: it is forbidden to sleep while on duty in the light-room. Either one of these infractions will result in immediate dismissal and removal from the house on the first available boat. Your work here is of the utmost importance. Your diligence and attention to the light saves lives. Indolence and lethargy on your part will leave the deaths of dozens upon your soul. Do you understand all that I have said, Mister Meakes?"

I would appreciate only later that this was the most he would ever say to me at Ripsaw.

"Yes, sir. I understand."

He took a folded paper from inside his jacket. "Then sign this letter of acquiescence, which contains the details of all I have said. Read it prior to signing if you wish."

I read the letter quickly, noting that Principal Bartholomew had repeated almost verbatim what was written therein, including the question of whether I had understood. I took out my silver pen and signed, handing the letter back to him.

"As this is your first posting," he said, "I will give you one piece of advice: do not be idle. When not cleaning and maintaining the house, occupy your time well. There is a library. There is a workshop. You may fish from the rock when the tides permit. Write a diary if you are accustomed to it. This is a profession of habit and routine, not of contemplation. We are not monks in a hermitage, nor poets, nor prisoners in an oubliette. We are servants of the Commission doing important work."

"Yes, sir."

"There are other duties to describe, not least the cleaning of the lantern, but those tasks have been completed today. Your first watch will be tonight, when you will learn how to light and maintain the lamp. Until then, you may consider yourself at liberty. Lunch is at one o'clock and tea at six o'clock in the kitchen. We eat together always. You have missed breakfast but Mister Adamson has reserved something for you if you are hungry. I suggest you spend your time profitably until dusk by accustoming yourself to the house. Unpack your chest. You are rooming with Mister Adamson. Will there be anything more?"

I wanted to ask about Keeper Spencer, about the cause and the manner of his death, but the moment did not seem appropriate.

"No, sir."

"Very well."

I waited for a handshake and for a moment it seemed the principal would offer one, but he turned and walked silently down the metal staircase, leaving me alone in the lantern.

I admit in that moment I was caught between euphoria and the weight of expectation upon me. I would have preferred the lighthouse to myself, but it seemed Principal Bartholomew was no enthusiast of social intercourse. Keeper Adamson, meanwhile, had barely exchanged two words with me.

I descended to the light-room, which now appeared a dim and gloomy place despite its four windows, and opened the door to the balcony that circled the column beneath the lantern. Sea air burst in upon me and I heard the ventilator groan in complaint. I closed the door behind me, dropping a floor bolt into one of four holes to hold the door securely ajar.

The sea was a hammered pewter plate extending to the horizon all around. Land was just a green-brown smudge, the shore station invisible without a telescope. I was a sailor keeping watch atop a ship's main masthead. I was a stonemason affixing the cross to a cathedral spire. The Earth's curvature bowed before me.

I hardly dared cross the short, iron-studded parapet to the railing where poor Spencer had been lashed, but I gripped the metal and looked down into the abyss. The tide had risen and the rock was now submerged in foaming white. Birds circled raucously. Though the sky was grey, the weather was calm. What must it be like to stand on the balcony during a tempest, with every raindrop a needle and every gust an angry hand attempting to sweep one into the void?

I saw the signal ball (now lowered) and the fog bells dormant. I looked up and saw the metal parapet around the lantern base, which I would have to tread to clean the panes. There was some manner of measuring device fastened to the railings on the weather side. I remembered that at Bishop Rock the fog bells had once been ripped from their fittings by a wave of over one hundred feet in magnitude, and suddenly I was hungry.

* * *

Keeper Adamson was seated in the kitchen, an admirably efficient arrangement of wainscot cupboards following the circle of the house. He didn't look at me, but merely jerked his head at the pot on the stove.

"More coffee there. Bread. Bacon and eggs cooked if you want them, but they're probably cold."

"Thank you."

"We heat the stove only three times a day so you can't warm anything now."

"That's all right. I can—"

"And you'll have to take the ashes out when you've finished. That's your job."

He had still not looked me in the eye.

I put the eggs and bacon on a plate and sat opposite him at the table. I said, "Principal Bartholomew tells me we are sharing a room."

He snorted derisively. Whether at the principal's name or at my statement, I wasn't sure.

"You'd better not snore," he said.

"I'm sure I don't. But… May I ask if I have offended you?"

He fixed me with a baleful gaze. "You look like a poet. You have that cast. I know it when I see it. Pale. Sickly."

"I assure you I am not a poet. And I am in very good health."

"A lighthouse is no place for the contemplative."

"I fully intend to apply myself to my duties with all diligence."

"You talk like a poet. Like *him*. Too many words."

"Forgive me, Mister Adamson, but I was taught that one should know a man before judging him. That is the educated way. We are obliged to work togeth—"

"Are you telling me I'm uneducated?"

"I… I'm afraid I simply don't understand your displeasure."

"Of course you don't. Thanks to you, I'm going to lose sleep. You can't be left alone in the light-room so I'll have to do longer watches."

"I am sorry for that, but it is not my choice. It will be temporary while I learn, and I'm sure there is time during the day to sleep if you are tired."

"Time to sleep, you say? With the incessant cleaning and cooking? Old Bartholomew's a tyrant. Twelve years he's been here and he considers Ripsaw his home. He can't tolerate life on land. As soon as he gets soil under his feet, he starts drinking. Two days ashore and he's insensible with whisky.

The Commission would like him to retire or at least take a posting at a shore station, but he won't do it. He can't. And they let him stay. Why? Because he's more of a machine than the revolving mechanism. The copper and brass and glass must be polished. The lamp must be lit. Men may die, but the sacred beam must keep on shining!"

I waited for the tale of Keeper Spencer, but...

"Do you want my advice, Poet?"

"I am not a poet, but I acknowledge your greater experience."

"Spoken like a poet. Well, here it is: visit the privy before you go to bed. I don't want you waking me by getting in and out of your bunk at all hours. Also, you don't want to be descending stairs half-asleep in darkness. That's the way to break your neck. In fact, avoid all and any injuries while you're in this house. The shore may be twenty miles distant, but the winter's coming. We might as well be on the moon when the bad weather starts. No boat'll be able to approach. Your duty is supposed to be just six weeks, yes? Well, the sea will decide that."

"But there has been bad weather for the last week and yesterday—"

"You think that was bad weather? That was only the moon tide."

"Well, I thank you for your advice."

"And never go out on the rock alone. I expect you've heard about the others?"

"Yes. They told me at the shore station."

"Are you going to eat the bacon or not? I won't see it go to waste."

"Please. Help yourself."

He moved the plate in front of him and started to eat with his fingers. "I like to sleep at three o'clock. Make sure you're not in the room."

"I will."

I watched him eating for a moment and thought about

mentioning the package the sailor had thrown to him. Clearly, it had not been newspapers. Perhaps that was why he'd been so short with me – because I'd seen what I shouldn't have. I also wondered to whom he'd been referring when he said I use too many words like "*him.*" Had he been referring to Keeper Spencer? I did not ask. Evidently, this was how it was going to be with Mr Adamson.

THREE

I have unpacked my trunk into the drawers beneath my bunk
and put my few possessions in one of the two cupboards.
Keeper Adamson's bunk is above my own, both of them
curved to conform with the house's circular walls. It is a neat
little room, like a ship's berth, with a waxed cloth on the stone
floor, a small stove for warmth and two oak stools. The ceiling
is vaulted stonework and there is sufficient light to read or
write from the three windows. For the evenings, an oil lamp
and a candle are provided.

I now sit at the small circular table in the room. I should
be calm, having described everything since leaving shore. My
hand aches with writing it. Yet I am nervous and unsettled.
Remembering the words of Mr Fowler, I tell myself that this
is to be expected under the circumstances.

As he would have advised me, I have opened the windows
and allowed the outer air to enter, along with the cry of the
birds and the swirling rush of the reef.

The view, however, does little to calm me. These isolated
squares of sea and sky disorient me with their bright vacuity.
I feel airborne, as if the house were rushing through the aether
with me its passenger. Or as if I were in a cell and being
watched panoptically. It is different in the lantern. There,
one feels a king upon his battlements, surveying all that he
possesses.

Perhaps something of the previous keeper's spirit still
lingers here. Poor Spencer was sleeping in this bunk barely a

week ago. His watch-cloak still hangs on a hook just inside the wainscot partition. He sat on this stool at this table and looked through these windows.

Mr Fowler always said to find a quiet place – a space of one's own. This room is no such space. I would like to visit the library, but Mr Adamson has told me that he will be there reading the latest delivery of newspapers and that he will not be interrupted. I wonder what manner of misanthrope elects life on a rock lighthouse twenty miles from shore and even then feels crowded by two other men.

Do I really look like a poet? I see none of the pale and sickly cast that he claimed to see in me. Indeed, I have gained weight these last few weeks, having eaten well. Nor have I ever written a line of poetry, though I have read perhaps more than most men.

Principal Bartholomew is the model keeper. I may learn much from him about a life of quiet habit, untainted by contemplation.

My interview at the Commission's offices showed me other men like him. Everything was order, everything ritualised. Their questions were carefully read verbatim from a list and my replies noted word for word. Sombre men. Careful men. Watchful men.

I believe I answered honestly, even as I speculated on the reasoning behind their questions.

Are your parents alive?

I was sorry to say they were not. They had died some time previously and I had been living with my guardian, Mr Fowler. Did the Commission prefer keepers *with* parents (because that suggested a stable home and a healthy bloodline) or *without* (because that suggested an independent spirit and nobody to mourn them)?

What is your most recent employment?

I said that I had recently been without work, though I had been advised that I would make a competent schoolmaster. I suspect that they were looking for professions known for their diligence, practicality and reliability. Printers, perhaps, or craftsmen used to working with tools.

Are you married? Do you have children?

Neither of these. Again, I could not and cannot decide if the Commission would prefer a family waiting on shore. Would a husband and father be more regular and dependable in his work, or would he miss his beloveds and pine for them during months trapped at sea by winter weather?

Where were you educated? What branches were taught? Do you have certificates?

I attended Mr Bond's Boarding School, where I was instructed in penmanship, classics, arithmetic, bookkeeping, navigation and astronomy, French, drawing, dancing and general science. I did not mention the classics and the dancing to the Commission. Something in the demeanour of the interviewing board suggested to me that these disciplines were unnecessary to the life of a keeper.

What is your present state of health?

I was, and remain, in the very best of physical health, despite Mr Adamson's comments. I believe there was nothing in my appearance or behaviour that day to contradict my assertion and I am sure that the Commission accepted my word.

Have you ever been subject to spitting blood, rupture, fits or severe illness?

None of these. I am physically without fault. Nevertheless, I understand the concern. A man with such complaints may be subject at any moment to a sudden and grave attack of ill health that could kill him on an isolated lighthouse.

Have you ever been subject to a complaint in your eyes?

An understandable question given the requirement to note passing ships and to read weather instruments. Fortunately, my eyes have always been excellent.

How long have you known the person who forwarded your recommendation?

I have known Mr Fowler my whole life, he being my paternal uncle. I have lived with him these last two years. Naturally, a recommendation for any position of importance must come from a trusted source.

The work you are applying for is arduous and responsible. It requires great steadiness and resolution. Why do you want to be a lighthouse keeper?

A fair question. Every man has his reason, though those reasons are often better concealed. We may be in no doubt that the houses surrounding these isles harbour their share of men who do not wish to be on shore. There are the romantics who dream of dramatic solitude, not realising that true isolation may be an asphyxiating weight. The idle, meanwhile, believe that they may sleep their way to a pension with food and bed provided. No doubt there are some sailors, too, who prefer to be at sea without the peril of a wreck before them. They, more than most, appreciate the safety of the coastal lights. As for myself, I believe I told the truth when I said that I was seeking employment with a certain regularity and repetitiveness, as this manner of work suits my temperament. My answer was well received.

I was also advised in the interview that my employment would be on a day-to-day basis, contingent always on my behaviour and on the effective execution of my duties. I could be dismissed instantly with no wages past or future. If certified as a keeper after my apprenticeship, I would be obliged to go wherever and whenever the Commission posted me. I would be required, furthermore, to give constant obedience to the principle keeper and to the assistant while an apprentice.

Evidently, my interview persuaded the Commission of my suitability, because they sent their list of standard questions to my recommender, Mr Fowler. I cannot say whether I was supposed to see this letter and its responses, in Mr Fowler's best copperplate writing, but I did.

Is the candidate sober, honest, obliging, obedient and cleanly in dress and person?

He is all of these things. I believe I have not known a more reliable and trustworthy man. His steadiness, resolution and sense of responsibility mark him as an exemplar to other men.

What character do his parents have?

His parents, now deceased, were paragons of morality, generosity and fortitude. James' father, George, was a librarian of many years' trusted service. His mother, Anne, was a faithful congregant and modest lady.

Is the candidate able-bodied and free from deformity?

Though he may appear slight of build and pale, James is vigorous and hardy. His sight is quite perfect and has always been so.

Do you know if any near relatives, he or his parents have ever displayed any symptoms of insanity or eccentricity of character?

I can assure the Commission that Mr James Meakes is entirely without mental impairment and that neither he nor any of his family has ever shown the slightest indication of such ailments.

And barely three weeks later, here I am at Ripsaw Reef.

I think much of Mr Fowler. Indeed, it is his words I recall when I fetch the phial from the back of the drawer and take my muriate of morphia. Just a half a minim, as he recommended. Just to fend things off. Just to help me sleep until the first watch.

FOUR

I woke to a strange metallic whistling in the room – a hollow sound that seemed to emit from a tube.

"That's Bartholomew calling," said Adamson from the bunk above. "He's going to be angry."

I hurriedly stood and tried to brush the creases from my uniform.

"And didn't I tell you to be absent when I came to rest?" said Adamson.

"I'm sorry. I just fell asleep and…"

"Next time, I'll wake you."

The whistle was still sounding. I climbed the five sets of stairs to the light-room and arrived quite out of breath.

Principal Bartholomew was standing and staring fixedly at his pocket watch. He said nothing, looking at my crumpled uniform with a downturned mouth. I had not changed into my everyday clothes. He, too, remained in uniform, even to his cap, but this was clearly his choice.

"Forgive me, sir. I… It will not happen again."

"I assure you it will not, Mister Meakes."

Though it was still bright outside, twilight was approaching. The ritual of lighting the lamp for the first time lay before me – something that had attained the status of a great mystery in my imagination. It was initiation into the Eleusinian Rites or entry into the Holy of Holies in Jerusalem. Fewer men had ignited and maintained the beam of a first-order rock lighthouse than had been accepted into the secret ranks of the Masonic Temple.

"Very well, let us ascend to the lamp," said the principal.

I followed him up the metal spiral, my own shoes clanging as his trod noiselessly. Truly, he was a spirit haunting this house.

Inside the crystal oval of the lens, his gaze took on the watery transparency of the glass. He gestured to the lamp and I saw that it was different.

"Note, Mister Meakes, the exact position of the lamp. You see that the lead plumbet hanging above the wick denotes that the lamp is in the exact centre of the lens. Likewise, you see that the bubble in the circular spirit level resting upon the wick is absolutely central, denoting absolute levelness in every azimuth."

"Yes, sir."

"These tools are used to reposition the lamp each morning after cleaning. I have placed them here now only for your tuition. We may now remove them." He put the tools in his jacket pocket. "Now observe."

He turned a brass screw and the four concentric circular wicks raised smoothly as one. He turned the knob on the fuel inlet and I watched the colza oil rise and brim around the wicks. It was mere science, but seemed alchemy to me.

Next, he lighted the wicks and a weak but pure flame rose straight up – a timid thing that cowered uncertainly. How could this small candle throw a brilliant beam to all horizons?

The principal then took the glass chimney from where it rested on the floor, inserted it partially into the sheet-iron chimney above, then gently over the lamp itself, so that the flame was protected from any breeze or accidental contact. A low, echoing moan now began as the hot breath of the lamp passed up though the cupola and out through the cowl.

"Watch carefully how the damper works," he said, reaching for a cord that was attached to a weighted lever higher up in the metal chimney. Restricting the air-flow through the ventilator caused the flame to shrink but increase in brilliance. Opening the vent stretched the flame but reddened it. Evidently, a delicate equilibrium was required to feed the light.

"In twenty minutes, the flame will be at full strength: four inches high. Then we will increase the flow of oil so that it floods the wicks and stops them from carbonising. Thereafter, we check periodically that the oil supply remains constant. A valve may fail in the pump and need replacing. Do you have any questions?"

"No, sir."

"Very well. Tomorrow, you will do it. Accompany me below."

We descended the stairs and he indicated a latch in the clockwork mechanism below the great black pillar supporting the lens frame. He unlocked the latch and wheels started to move, gears intermeshing with a low murmur. A bell began to ring at the same moment: a constant high-pitched trilling.

"Now the lens is turning," said the principal, "driven by the weight of a chain through the mechanism. Four beams of light are shining forth from the lantern, flashing a light every thirty seconds at all points for twenty nautical miles. The lamp is lighted."

I heard the pride in his voice, as if he himself had built this wonder of the modern age. No doubt he understands it all as well as its own creators do. But unlike them, he has cleaned it daily, fed it with oil, nursed it when its pump valves coughed or dribbled, oiled its parts and loved it with linen rag and chamois cloth.

The lamp is lighted. *Fiat lux.* On land and out amid the stalking waves, our point of light protects from peril. Is our beam also visible to other shore houses, rock houses, lightships and light buoys, so that an illuminating ring passes all around these isles as signal fires were once lit from peak to peak in eons past? But those flames prefigured invasion and imminent destruction. Ours is pale like the moon, like the stars. A singular constellation.

"Mister Meakes – are you listening?"

"Yes, sir."

"Then come here. Note the barometer and thermometer. We log the readings in this book at the beginning and end of each man's watch – more regularly if the weather is changing rapidly. During the day, I take all measurements myself."

"And this device, sir? This glass tube?"

Principal Bartholomew smiled for the first time since I had arrived. "It is a storm-glass – an instrument of my own. The white substance lying dormant at the bottom is a mixture of camphor, nitrate of potassium and muriate of ammonia partially dissolved in alcohol and with some water. As the weather changes, so the substance metamorphoses. You will see. For now, the weather is calm, but look here at the mercury in the barometer. Do you see how the upper limit is concave? That suggests an imminent drop in pressure, though nothing has been registered today."

Weather, then, was his whisky while on the rock. Its changes. Its varieties. Its subtleties. Its sleights of hand. Here in the light-room, he had his own laboratory of wind and rain and temperature. In place of emotion, he had barometric pressure, velocity and hydrography. His pulse was the waves.

We ascended again the spiral staircase to raise the wicks, and I experienced the lens moving around us, its prismatic glints winking and swooping through circular sections. The lamp itself was not the blinding white light I had imagined but rather the kind of illumination that a handful of candles might collectively produce. Only outside the slowly circling lens would the beam be something brilliant, its light magnified and focused on the distant sea. I hoped to experience it later, but the principal had not finished his instruction.

He showed me the various telescopes in their stand: the long and heavy night telescope, the Dollond achromatic for viewing the shore, and another whose function I cannot currently recall. Any ships seen from the house must be recorded in the log without fail because these figures serve to show and justify the Commission's work.

There was also the watch journal in which each keeper on duty would record anything of note. I could not imagine anything of note occurring, save perhaps an accident or some dramatic weather event.

And thus my first watch began. It consisted simply of sitting in the light-room, listening to the drone of the mechanism, the moan of the ventilator and the maddening trilling of the bell that indicates all is well, while also being an insistent preventative against sleep.

In such ways, I thought, does the Commission's lack of faith extend itself across the waters. The engineers could have built a mechanism that chimed only if it stopped, but that might have led to lassitude or complacency. Clearly, the too-mortal keeper cannot be trusted to remain awake by his own diligence. He must be tortured into wakefulness by the constant supervision of the bell. Even holy monks are jarred from contemplation only every two or three hours by the ringing of matins, lauds, prime, terce, vespers, compline.

So we sat with nothing more to do than wait for Keeper Adamson to relieve us, standing occasionally to look through the four windows for any ship or notable occurrence. Principal Bartholomew had brought a book with him and commenced to read it by lamplight, as if I did not exist.

I looked at the clock: four hours more of simply sitting with nothing but the prison of one's own mind to occupy. I realised I was cold despite my watch-cloak. The iron stove was cold and empty and I did not yet feel bold enough to ask why. All of the windows were open because air must rise through the metal mesh ceiling to ensure that no condensation forms upon the lantern panes or lens. How ironic to be seated in a light-room that in fact was as dim as any cellar. The lantern was heaven; the keepers were sooty demons hunched below.

I watched Principal Bartholomew reading – an absurdity in itself. Like watching a man thinking. His eyes followed lines across the page. His lips moved almost imperceptibly. He was in another place.

I thought about raising the subject of Keeper Spencer and his cause of death. Spencer, who had sat in this very same chamber and in this same seat for hours on end. I weighed possible phrases that I might use insouciantly. *A pity about Mister Spencer... Did you know Mister Spencer well?... I hear that a number of keepers have unfortunately...*

But I said nothing. Sometimes, it is necessary to wait for the opportune moment. Perhaps Spencer's death was still a grievous sorrow in this house. Perhaps there was some aspect of lighthouse lore that forbade mention of a colleague's death. I resigned myself to more hours of nothingness and worried at the prospect.

But something did happen.

Initially, I thought the principal had coughed gently, but the sound repeated itself as I was watching him: reverberating soft thuds as if tiny hands were patting at the panes above us. Sometimes there was a sharp tap, like an ember cracking in a fire.

"Ascend," said the principal without looking up from his book. "See for yourself what it is."

I took the staircase with trepidation as the sounds continued. All was well inside the lens, but when I passed into the area around it – the metal grille floor that circled the lantern – I saw the reason for the morbid percussion.

A hundred birds were wheeling and swooping about the false sun of the house, maddened by the beam and drawn to it by fatal instinct: flitting black-and-white sparks darting though the light. I saw them in flashes, momentarily illuminated: crows, magpies, larks, blackbirds, ducks, a raven, petrels, ptarmigans, terns and herring gulls. All were orbiting insensate.

Every few minutes, a land bird would overcome its better impulse and hit a pane with feathery thud or splintered beak. Some dropped immediately to lie still or twitching on the lantern parapet. Others returned dazed to the air and began their hectic charge until exhaustion or further impact killed them. The seabirds were more intelligent, however, swooping close but ever dubious. I caught their piercing garnet and citrine eyes staring at me: a human shadow within the infernal tower.

And I could not help but reflect that man, too, is often like these poor deluded birds: drawn inexorably to what destroys him, though it looks like justice or virtue or light. Some rush willingly to immolation; others do so unwittingly; others retain some innate sense that tells them to beware. I am sure Plato was not the first to think that not every light is as true as the sun.

"Mister Adamson makes them into pies or stews."

I jerked in surprise at Principal Bartholomew beside me. The man moved like a phantasm about this space.

"Pies, sir?"

"Indeed. He collects the bodies from the balcony, plucks them and cooks them. Duck and magpie are his favourites."

"And it is like this every night? With the birds?"

"Every night. There may be more or fewer depending on the season. Tomorrow morning, it will be your task to clean their bodies from the parapet and balcony. If not, they will accumulate and putrefy."

As the body of Keeper Spencer had threatened to putrefy?

The thought of venturing out on that naked parapet to sweep bloody feathers from the metal was something that would not let me sleep. I thought about it until Principal Bartholomew looked up at the clock and closed his book. He stood and went, tutting, to the wall-mounted whistle near the weather instruments. Evidently, Mr Adamson was running late.

Three minutes later, Mr Adamson ascended into the light-room. He appeared tired and sluggish. He did not look at or speak to me, or the principal, but went directly up to the lantern to begin his watch. It occurred to me only then I had not seen either of the men exchange a word since I had arrived.

The principal went directly to his bedroom, but I – remembering Mr Adamson's advice – continued my descent towards the privy in the lowermost chamber of the lighthouse.

It was warmer down there because the coal stove had been ignited. Red embers gleamed through its cast-iron doors. A pair of candles were the only illumination, throwing distorting shadows and dark reflections among the water tanks.

I sat there on the cold copper seat and I could hear the sea swirling at the tower's flared foot, hissing over Ripsaw Reef. Indeed, I fancied could feel the pressure of the high tide even through seven feet of solid interlocking granite. I looked to the twin doors and imagined a colossal billow filling the corridor with its green-glass immensity. Would I be smashed against the water talks, or lifted like a cork to the higher storerooms?

The darkness became suddenly oppressive and I finished my business in haste. It was as I was rising to leave that I saw the tiny words scratched into the stonework by the privy:

"Lord, deliver me from this windowless pit."

FIVE

I write at the small table in the bedroom, having barely slept a wink and yet having suffered all the same from tormenting dreams. I dreamed of suffocation, my face muffled in some feather mass, my arms lashed tightly across my chest. I was absolutely certain at one moment that water was slowly dripping, one drop at a time, on to my forehead but I could not raise my hand to cover or to wipe that spot. Pain burned in my shoulders and in my elbows. It seemed that I had been bound like Keeper Spencer, mummy-like, from head to foot and could only wriggle.

Later, I heard the wind around the lighthouse. Perhaps there was a window ajar, or perhaps air was rising up the great stone flue of the house – I am not yet accustomed to its sounds – but I thought I heard voices whispering, weeping, shouting, keening. The words were indistinct and the voices many. I tried to concentrate on just one to make sense of the cacophony, but they wove and blended and evaded my interpretation in the moment when I thought some sense was present.

I believe that during some brief tatter of sleep I was woken momentarily by a tremendous impact. It seemed to make the entire tower quiver. Some vast black leviathan colliding with the pedestal? A monstrous gust of wind? A giant billow slapping at the granite column? I told myself, full-drowsed with sleep, that it must have been the burly form of Mr Adamson moving in the bunk above me.

I was woken once again as dawn was breaking by the rattle of the lens-rotating chain being winched up link by link. The seabirds were already screaming at that moment, but I was so fatigued I must have fallen back to sleep.

Incredible as it may seem, I was finally jarred awake by the sea itself. Salt spray speckled my face from the nearest open window, though the bedroom must be seventy or eighty feet above the surface. I noted that Mr Adamson was not in his bunk as I went to the window in my nightshirt.

What yesterday had been an undulating plate of grey is now a cauldron of angry surf that spits and boils about the reef. White-flecked waves are charging upon the house from all directions and dashing against it alarmingly, each impact a *whump*, a *whump*, a *whump*. Not the friendly rolling waves of yesterday, but jagged angles chipped from flint. The structure is definitely trembling. Spray strikes the glass, driven by the vaunting power of the surf and carried higher by the wind.

I am afraid. I will go down to breakfast and speak with the other two.

* * *

Keeper Adamson was sitting alone at the kitchen table with his plate of bacon and eggs and his cup of coffee. He did not look at me when I entered and bade him a good morning.

"You were mumbling in your sleep, Meakes. You kept me awake."

"Excuse me, but I am sure I was not."

"Babbling. Moaning. I know what I heard."

"I, too, heard voices. Perhaps—"

"What voices? Bartholomew doesn't speak and I was the only other person in the room. You heard yourself."

His logic seemed incontestable. Or, more likely, he is accustomed to the sounds of the sea and of the house. He is clearly not a man of much imagination.

"And it was your turn to make breakfast today," he said.

"I've made my own because I was hungry. There's a list of duties on the cupboard there, see?"

"I… Forgive me. I have not yet…"

"You know that there's a spare bedroom above Bartholomew's? It's for the commissioners when they visit once or twice a year. It's locked, but I've seen inside. Carpets. Curtains. Mouldings. A regular *boodour*, it is. I could sleep there to escape your babbling, or the swinish snoring of Spencer, God rest his soul. But, no. It's *reserved*. Not for the likes of us who sit here exposed to peril at every moment. We must make do with bare stone, wax-cloth floors and creaking bunks. There is an actual *bed* in the commissioners' room. Can you imagine?"

"I suppose they deserve their comforts."

"*Deserve*, you say? I know what they deserve, Poet. Well, I can't take the commissioners' room so you'll need to stop your babbling. If not, I'll have to report it to Bartholomew."

I went to the stove to pour myself coffee and was surprised to see the washbasin full of avian corpses. The feathers were silky black and chalk white: magpies, crows, possibly a blackbird – it was not easy to discern all types. There were only eyes and beaks and flecks of blood. Heads lolled on broken necks. Wings jutted at angles.

"Principal Bartholomew told me that *I* should collect the birds this morning," I said.

"Aye, but have you seen the wind? I took them last night before it started gusting."

"Thank you."

"No. I did it because otherwise the wind would have carried the bodies off into the sea. I wanted another blackbird pie."

Spray lashed the kitchen window on the weather side and another *whump* reverberated up the tower. Cups and plates rattled in the cupboard. I glanced at Mr Adamson but he seemed not to have noticed. He was attempting to lick a drip of egg yolk from his chin with a grease-glistening tongue. It soured my stomach.

Lord, deliver me from this windowless pit.

It was not beyond presumption that Mr Adamson had scratched the words by the privy merely to unsettle me. For that reason alone I did not mention that I had seen them.

"Have you prepared breakfast, Mister Meakes?"

Principal Bartholomew's face was red and his white hair had risen like a halo around his head. Evidently he had been out on the balcony. He was still in uniform.

"Not yet, sir. I have just now been advised of the duty list by Mister Adamson."

"Very well. It will be buttered toast and porridge for me. Make a pot of good, strong tea."

Fortunately, I had spent time in the kitchen at Mr Jerrold's house. I have no fear of the stove or the pan. I cut the bread into slices of equal thickness and put them in the tin toasting rack. I measured out the oats and added a proportional amount of water and sugar. I filled the copper kettle with cold water – noting how the condensation beaded on the metal – and set it to boil.

All the while, I was aware that the two others were sitting behind me without exchanging a single word. The scrape of pan on stove and clanking spoon seemed greatly magnified in that small semi-circle of cupboards. Every now and then, the reef would spit at the window and a billow would boom.

"The lighthouse quivers much during a storm," I said.

Both laughed. Mr Adamson's was a derisive bark, Principal Bartholomew's a dry chuckle.

"A storm, Poet? You call *this* a storm? It's not even a gale!"

"Mister Meakes," said the principal. "This is normal weather here at Ripsaw. You arrived during an unusual calm, hence the cutter coming out with supplies yesterday."

"A storm!" scoffed Mr Adamson. "How precious!"

"When we have finished breakfast," said the principal, "I will ask Mister Adamson to show you how to empty the ash bucket at the door."

"Sir? At the door below? But the waves are beating about the pedestal."

"Indeed. You need to lose your fear of the sea. It will do you good to make acquaintance with the reef when it is lively."

A *whump*. A splutter of spray at the window.

"The toast is burning," said Mr Adamson with some evident satisfaction.

I turned and saw skeins of blue-grey smoke rising from the toaster. One side of the bread was quite blackened. I watched briefly fascinated as the smoke sought the kitchen door and rose suddenly towards the lantern, borne on the upward rush of air from the lowermost chambers.

Principal Bartholomew said nothing but rose to close the kitchen door.

"'I wandered lonely as some toast,'" said Mr Adamson with exaggerated poetic projection.

I threw the burned bread into the wastebasket and started again. That's what Mr Fowler always used to tell me. Don't worry. Start again. There is always another chance to get it right, to be good, to be better.

* * *

Mr Adamson later stood over me as I emptied ashes from each of the lighthouse stoves into the ash bucket. There is a grave necessity to do this slowly and carefully lest the particles fly into the air and rise up the house to contaminate the lens and its mechanism. Not even the merest speck must mar the immaculate transparency of the lantern's eye.

When the bucket was full, I closed its lid and followed Mr Adamson down the precipitous stairways, tremulous at the booming waves and the idea of opening the great door into such a maelstrom. By the time we had reached the water store, it was almost impossible to be heard with the constant buffeting of the waves. I could see through the window in the first door that the vestibule floor was wet. The sea was coming in. Perhaps the level of the water was midway up the door or even above it. Releasing the bolts now would allow tons of water to rush in.

Mr Adamson appeared to relish my fear. He opened the first door and bade me follow him. Here in the vestibule the volume was something fearful: the detonating waves, the hissing reef, the gulp and spit of swirling eddies, the spatter of spray against the door. Beyond those four inches of iron-bound oak, a veritable tempest was raging, whatever they would have had me believe.

He unloosed the copper bolts with a great show of trepidation and grasped the doorknob with a theatrical deep breath. He beckoned me closer, as if together we were to view a sleeping lion. He wanted me right by his side.

He opened the door just a crack and peered out, waiting, I assumed, to see if the sea would inundate and sweep our feet away. But he had another plan: to startle me. He was waiting for the next wave to strike the weather side.

At that moment, he swept open the door and simultaneously I felt the boom of the wave on the house's opposite side. A great green claw of water curled around each side of the tower, almost at the upper lintel of the door, and seemed to hang there in all of its immense density before the two parts joined foaming fingers in the very air before us and vaporised with an explosion of spray. Miraculously, no water entered the house.

The wind then carried tendrils and filaments horizontally, gasping and sighing from the stonework, but again, these did not enter. I understood why the door was on the lee side and how the circular surface of the lighthouse fools the waves, dividing them as a ship's prow divides the water. A colossal billow may strike, but there is no flat surface to assail. The wave must fold, cleave in twain and meet upon the other side, surprised and frustrated, to destroy itself.

I looked down and saw the sea convulsing and writhing about the rock like a man in the throes of a terrible fit. Lurching and charging, twisting and falling, it had worked itself into an exhausted lather of spume and spindrift but it would not cease. It could not. It was driven mad by wind and by eddies that tormented it without mercy. Further afield, the reef appeared to steam and boil, the waves breaking upon each other from all directions in their blind rage. And this was not a storm.

It was a mesmerising sight. Waves charged at the house with seeming intent, offended by its stubborn strength. Their choking hands tried again and again to close around its pale throat, but all were blown to spray. Man's ingenuity was imperious. Our science and engineering could mock the very fury of the ocean. For there we stood at the open door with barely a drop upon us.

I cannot guess how long I gazed at it, but my reverie was halted quite suddenly when I felt Mr Adamson's hand, firm and flat, between the shoulder blades.

In that instant, the hairs bristled at my collar and I was seized with the certitude that he was about to push me from the parapet into the thrashing maw below. I believe I cried "No!" and thrust out my hands to the doorjambs left and right.

He may have laughed (I could barely hear a thing with the roaring of the waters), but he removed his hand from my back and I turned to face him.

"You tried to push me!"

"Ha!"

"I felt your hand! You were about to…"

He was laughing. "Becalm yourself, Poet! I was not trying to push you. I told you that it was time to close the door, but you didn't hear me. The sea has bewitched you. I've seen it before."

It was true I could see no malicious intent in his eyes, but I still remember the firmness of his hand. I feel it still, burning there between my shoulders. Had I not buttressed myself against the doorway, I feel sure he would have launched me from it. For what motive, I cannot say. I only know what I felt.

He nodded towards the ash bucket by my side. "Well? Are you going to empty it? Or do you want me to take a few paces back lest I push you into the sea?"

"I would prefer if you did step back."

His eyes changed then. He was no longer laughing at me. He took three or four exaggerated steps back and gave a mocking bow.

I very quickly bent to the bucket, opened its lid and felt for the brass sole of the door without once taking my eyes from Mr Adamson. Holding tightly to the jamb, I emptied the ashes on to the parapet, rather than into the waves, knowing that this was very likely unacceptable to Principal Bartholomew.

"Bolt the door!" shouted Mr Adamson, before turning and ascending the stone staircase without me. Was he going to report me for not disposing of the ashes correctly?

I found that my legs were shaking. I closed both doors and paused briefly in the water store, where, despite my best efforts, I could not find the message I had seen scratched on the wall the previous night. Had Mr Adamson abraded it from the stone before I awoke?

I had heard about this kind of thing from the men at the shore station: jokes played upon new keepers by experienced lighthouse-men. I had resolved to greet such attempts with good grace and humour, knowing that safety was the first rule in any house. I would be in no danger if I could merely tolerate these initial trials.

But, still. A man died here not ten days ago.

* * *

Though I am excused from cleaning the lantern and light-room today because I made breakfast, I thought it a fine idea to volunteer my services to Principal Bartholomew all the same. Besides, the words of Mr Fowler are always with me, and his advice was constantly to occupy myself with mechanical or repetitive tasks.

I found the principal in the light-room store, where he was using a funnel to fill two half-gallon canteens from a one-gallon canteen. Here are also stored spare lantern panes (each already mounted in its astragal), spare glass chimneys, oil for the revolving mechanism, coils of rope, a press for leathern valves, a box of medical supplies, and cloths and chamois rags for polishing. I also noticed a litter leaning against the wall, presumably for serious accidents. Every locker or shelf or can was clearly labelled.

"Mister Meakes. How did you like the rock and the reef?"

"It is fearsome and beautiful."

"Is it?"

"You don't think so, sir?"

"It is a great body of water subject to tides, winds, pressure, temperature and the season. I will grant you that it may be perilous, but that is why we are here. We impose efficiency and order upon the deep."

"Yes, sir. To that end, I have come to help with the cleaning."

"Very good. Select two linen cloths, two chamois rags and some spirit of wine – the bottles are on that shelf. I have already carried the other materials aloft."

Before ascending, the principal noted precisely in the inventory log which supplies we were taking from the store, so that in one month, in six months, a clerk at the Commission offices can corroborate his columns and confirm that not a single rag nor drop of colza oil has been wasted or misappropriated on an isolated rock hundreds of miles distant. Efficiency and order.

In the light-room, he showed me how to polish the brass and copper of the lamp to a flawless sheen, though to my eye it was already perfect. The lens we caressed with voluptuous and fragrant chamois, I within and he outside. I watched his silhouetted form rippling through the rings of glass, his torso curved, his limbs tentacular, his head variously deliquescent, variously convex through bulbous bullseyes. He seemed a shadow trapped inside the glass and swimming in its vitreous angles. No doubt I appeared just as strange to him, except that Principal Bartholomew is evidently not a man much given to fancy. For him, the lens is nothing but an instrument we serve as eunuchs serve a sultan or as monks preserve reliquaries of sacred bone.

The lighting apparatus thus polished, he handed me the stiff-bristled broom and sent me to the balcony to sweep the droppings and the feathers that had accumulated overnight. The wind and rain would have scoured these in time, but a lighthouse does not function in such a way. A keeper must be occupied in almost every waking moment with the house's constant maintenance, lest the tower act conductor for his thoughts and blast him with a bolt of emptiness.

This Mr Fowler instilled in me. Work, work and work some more.

Truly, it is invigorating to be upon the balcony and, like Hamlet, to contemplate the precipice. *The very place puts toys of desperation / Without more motive, into every brain / That looks so many fathoms to the sea / And hears it roar beneath.* The wind is brisk and tugs insistently at cloak and trouser leg, while all around the congregated waters whisper. Perhaps only they know what happened to Spencer. Perhaps they spoke with him as he nodded here inside his shroud.

"Mister Meakes? That broom will not push itself."

I looked up and saw the principal on the narrow parapet that circled the lantern. He was holding on to a metal ring between the astragals and using his free hand to clean the glass of salt. A slip, a lapse of concentration, and he could tumble past me two hundred feet into the surf. What man could survive such a fall? If he was not pulverised by the rock, he would certainly be stunned by the sea's slap and subsumed within its cold embrace.

He was gazing at me quite fixedly. For how long had he been watching? I applied myself with fresh diligence to my sweeping.

In the ceaseless washing of the reef, I could hear the words of Mr Fowler: "What shall we do with you, James? What shall we do with you?"

SIX

Mr Adamson served his blackbird pie for lunch in the kitchen.

"Not every bird in it is a blackbird, but every bird in it was black," was his apparent attempt at humour.

The principal did not laugh. Indeed, I had overheard the two arguing about the pie earlier while I was in the bedroom. I listened only because it was the first time I had them converse at all. Mr Adamson had begun it.

"Mister Bartholomew – may I have the key to the lock box? I need a little wine for the pie."

"No, Mister Adamson, but I will fetch a cup of it for you. How much do you need? Will a glassful be sufficient?"

"I can't say, sir. I don't measure when I cook. I go by sight only." (The word "sir" seemed like vinegar on the assistant keeper's tongue).

"Then you will make do with a glassful."

"You don't trust me."

"Assuredly, I do not."

"And you are a paragon of sobriety, to stand in judgement of me?"

"One more word of insubordination and I will write a report to the commissioners. You know what that will mean."

Mr Adamson murmured something I could not hear.

The two now faced each other across the table and ate without exchanging looks. It was a very good pie and I marvel that such a thing is possible with the meagre larder of a lighthouse. I raised this question as we were finishing and Mr Adamson gave his derisive snort.

"Aye, there's onion and carrots now, but let's see what you think of the fare in two or three weeks when the fresh produce has been exhausted and the supply boat can't come out for weeks. I hope you like salt beef and hard tack."

"We often catch fish, Mister Meakes," said the principal. "The rock furnishes us with crab, lobster and mussels. With a line and rod, we may feed from the ocean each day the tide favours us." He looked at the kitchen clock. "Why don't you both go down to the rock this afternoon and see what you can catch for supper? The wind will have lessened by then."

"He's afraid of the rock," said Mr Adamson.

"Then here is another opportunity to overcome that fear," said Principal Bartholomew.

He would soon be proved quite wrong about that.

* * *

"Don't worry, I won't push you," said Mr Adamson, as we approached the main door. "If you prefer, I'll go down first."

We were carrying a crab basket, a rod and a copper bucket for collecting cockles. The ebb tide had almost fully revealed the metal grille of the landing platform and a few metres of reef were exposed around.

He descended the ladder and I lowered the equipment to him on a line before climbing down myself, gripping each wet rung with great concentration.

The rock was still awash and pungent with the smells of the sea. Flaccid seaweed lolled in crevices and lapped at the lighthouse pedestal. Rock pools were dozens of tiny mirror shards that rippled or bubbled with life. I could hear the click and scuttle of shell and claw.

Mr Adamson tied an avian corpse of white-needle bones and purple flesh to the crab basket and tossed it into the sea, securing its cord to an outcrop.

"To work, Poet!" He was grinning. "Fill your bucket with cockles and mussels and whatever else you can find. I will cast a line."

I believe it is the first time I have seen him contented. He is a man of the land in his soul.

"And watch where you step!" he called. "You know what happens to keepers on this rock!"

I moved with special care towards the reef's black incisors, aware of the sea yawning all around us, licking impatiently at the edges of this sanctuary in anticipation of a slip, a fall. The tangle of glistening kelp, the bladderwrack's obscene yellow eggs and the clinging dulse seemed almost to writhe about my feet, colluding with its briny master to trip me.

I should not have been surprised by the amount of debris strewn about. So many ships have foundered here. Timber fragments, cordage, rusting nuggets of conglomerated nails. Sundry cargo semi-digested by the sea until barely distinguishable: scraps of cloth, a mass of jellied soap, a sodden hat. Even a cannonball turned red with flaking corruption. How does an iron cannonball arrive here when, all about, the abyss descends to twenty fathoms?

I saw the body near the cannonball.

It first appeared to be just a heap of kelp, but then I saw a pale upper arm and shoulder. An ear. I don't know what made me think it could possibly be alive, but that's what motivated my cry.

"Mister Adamson! Help! Help! A body on the rock!"

I was drawn to it despite my fear and revulsion. The corpse was quite naked, stripped by the interminable surf. Wet hair covered one eye, but the other was a mere ragged socket – victim first of crabs and then the fishes. The private parts, too. His limbs were all horribly broken and as twisted as the rubbery seaweed stripes around him. Skin had been abraded from knees, elbows, shoulders…

"What have we here, then?" said Mr Adamson, now at my side. He appeared not remotely shocked or surprised.

"A body – look."

"I told you to look for cockles and mussels, not for cadavers."

"But... Should we not reclaim the body and signal the shore station?"

"Look at it." He grimaced. "It's been in the sea a while. Who knows where it came from? A fishing boat. A wreck further out to sea. A suicide on shore. There's no saving him now."

"Could he be... Could he be the keeper who was washed from the rock before you came to Ripsaw?"

"How would I know that? I never saw the man."

"But are we to just leave him here?"

"The sea is full of men, Poet. He's not the first on this rock. He won't be the last. Here – help me."

He strode towards the corpse and began pushing at it with his boot, his mouth twisted in disgust.

"What are you doing?" I said.

"The dignified thing."

Grunting, he rolled the body towards the edge of the reef.

"You're just going to throw it in the sea?"

"That's where it came from!"

I took a few steps towards the body. "But..."

With a final tremendous shove, Mr Adamson sent the tangle of lifeless limbs rolling into the sea. I watched it sink, a pale spirit that seemed to wave as it was swallowed into blackness.

'And are you happy now?' said Mr Adamson. "We have wasted time on this nonsense when I could have been catching fish for supper. No more games. Fill your bucket."

But I could not concentrate on my task. The reef now seemed a place of horrors to me. What else might I discover hidden amid its rotten fissures? A sailor's finger? Waterlogged bird corpses? Some gelatinous monstrosity from the deep? We could not feed ourselves from this pestilential outcrop.

I didn't hear him when Mr Adamson first attempted to call me, perhaps due to the noise of the waves breaking further along the reef. Indeed, it may have been his second or third attempt to rouse me.

I saw his urgently pointing finger. I turned to look in that direction but too late. The wave announced itself behind me with a great explosion of spray, breaking over the reef and rushing towards me at quite the height of my knees.

I braced and willed myself heavier as the inundation raced at my legs. The fugitive thought occurred that if a timber was hidden somewhere in that flow, it would snap my bones like twigs and I would be carried off into the deep.

Instead, I merely crouched impotently and the water struck my legs as it strikes the lighthouse, rising up my thighs and attempting to push me over. I dropped the bucket lest it overbalance me as I felt the immense weight of the wave tugging at me. It seemed to go on forever before diminishing, leaving me soaked and shaking.

"Where… Where did it come from?" I suppose I was asking myself.

"You're lucky!" said Mr Adamson, splashing to my side. "If you hadn't turned when you did, it would have swept you off."

I was dumbfounded.

"*Always* keep your wits on the rock, Poet. A wave may come at any moment from any direction."

"I am soaked through."

'I see that. And the copper bucket will come out of your wages. Come, let's go back inside. The tide is rowdy today. Besides, I have a crab and a fish."

* * *

It is only now as I note this incident in my journal that I question why he didn't tell me *before* descending to the rock that an unexpected wave may come. It is true that he warned me of its arrival, but it wasn't only the waves interfering. He called out in a subdued voice I almost didn't hear. If

Principal Bartholomew had been watching from the balcony or a window, my death would have looked entirely credible and Mr Adamson even something of a would-be saviour.

I am wearing dry clothes and have calmed myself a little thanks to a minim of morphia. I know I must be sparing with it, but the if experiences of this afternoon don't warrant a small dose, then surely nothing does.

I have finally been able to find time to spend in the library, where I currently write – perhaps the most unusual room in the lighthouse. It is clearly designed to be a home from home, with its carpet, its dark furniture, bookshelves, a panelled wooden dado, and stucco decoration in the dome. There are watercolours and a marble-topped table. A classical geometric frieze is painted around the base of the dome and there is even a wooden-framed bed, presumably for guests.

Indeed, its strangeness in contrast to the stark utility of every other room reveals too obviously its function here at Ripsaw. It is a space to pacify, calm and civilise. Out here on the rock, we are clearly regarded with great suspicion by the Commission. The tower, the oil, the lens, the shore-station and cutter – all represent a colossal investment of time and money. Lives depend on the faithful lighting and extinguishing of the lamp. Can three men – three mortal men with the seeds of weakness, dissipation and destruction in their souls – be trusted with their duty, so alone and distant?

Hence the library with its books and newspapers and paintings. It represents the promise of home and safety. A placebo for comfort, as Mr Fowler would have said. I wonder why the Commission's lighthouses do not contain chapels instead of libraries, but each and every Sunday the principal holds a service here. Attendance is compulsory. So it *is* a chapel of sorts.

But the motive is rather in the books. Knowledge is a palliative. It distracts the mind from evil and elevates it to morality, rationality, order. If a man is reading improving material, he maintains his dignity and remains on an intellectual plane. Such is the theory.

The small catalogue (not more than fifty titles) is thus well chosen. Nothing to agitate or disturb. Sundry Walter Scott. Various Charles Dickens. There is a Bible and a Book of Common Prayer. The newspapers include *The Penny Illustrated Paper*, *The Illustrated London News* and *The Scotsman*. There is a dictionary to negotiate the rocky reefs of lexis. As for the books, they are a mixture of predictable and incongruous, the latter no doubt left by visitors and previous keepers. I note the titles on the shelf immediately before me:

* *Stevenson's Account of the Skerryvore Lighthouse*
* *Some Enquiries into Lighthouse Construction*
* *Robinson Crusoe*
* *Gulliver's Travels*
* *Pilgrim's Progress*
* *Chambers Cyclopaedia of English Literature*
* *The Edinburgh Encyclopaedia*
* *The Iliad (trans. Alexander Pope)*
* *The Principles of Geology*
* *The Monument to the Great Fire of London: A Visitor's Guide*
* *The Works of William Shakespeare*
* *Paradise Lost*
* *The Narrative of Arthur Gordon Pym of Nantucket*
* *Antiquities of Greece and Rome*
* *Bottle Messages: Their History and Some Remarkable Accounts*
* *Anderson's Compendium of Weather Predictors*
* *The Chronicles of the Stylites*

They are, perhaps, the books one would not choose to read unless trapped inside a lighthouse for the winter season. Under that circumstance, there is much to be recommended and I anticipate reading most of what is offered.

There is also a book log in which one has to sign out each item, noting the title, the borrower's name, and the dates taken and returned. This seems to me quite absurd in a virtually hermetic space inhabited by only three men, but I see in it the Commission's *imprimir*. To not return a library book may be the first small step in a catastrophic failure of responsibility. (I note, however, that Keeper Spencer apparently left this world with his copy of Brown's *Urn Burial* unreturned and possibly unread).

In addition to the paintings, there is also a detailed etching of the Ripsaw Reef Lighthouse done in cross-section. Every chamber is shown with admirable clarity.

There is the main door and the water store with its single window and privy. Next is the oil and coal store with its rough industrial perfume and its tinned-copper cisterns circling the room. Above that is the provision store with seventy days' worth of food and drink, candles and soap stored in japanned lockers. The kitchen, I am already well acquainted with, and my bedroom above that.

Thereafter, we enter the *terrae incognitae* of the principal's bedroom and above his the sumptuous "*boodour*" described to me by Mr Anderson: the visiting commissioner's room. I have seen nothing of these two, both being forbidden to the junior keepers.

Above the commissioner's room is the library, and above me the light-room store with its panes in astragals, workbench and tools, so that this ark may repair itself unaided by the shore. Only thereafter does the lighthouse proper begin. Everything before this point is simply height.

In the light-room, we find the revolving mechanism, the weather instruments and, indeed, the keepers who exist to run it. Then finally the lantern's glassy crown itself. Ten chambers to support the light. Ten decks of a great barque going nowhere. *Day after day, nor breath nor motion; as idle as a painted ship upon a painted ocean.* And we three crew – three mice scuttling round the ballast.

The book in front of me on the marble table top is a history of the Commission and of lighthouses, too. I have read that the first beacons were built by the Lybians along the lower Egyptian coast and by the Cuthites, whose origins are lost amid the time of myths. Those Cuthite towers were temples devoted to Baal, whose priests knew the secrets of the constellations and engraved them on the great stone *phalloi*. Towers with names such as Caneph, Proteus, Canobus and Phanes.

It was the Cuthites who read the winds and the seasons for their secrets and built the Tower of Babel in the sun's honour, a sacred fire burning at its apex. For this hubris they were scattered without a common language and fled as colonists across the oceans.

Thus was wealthy Colchis founded, where King Aeëtes ruled and where his daughter sorceress Medea cast her spells. The Golden Fleece hung there, the Amazons rode, and fire-breathing Khalkotauroi were yoked by Jason. In distant Colchis was Prometheus cliff-chained to have his liver pecked eternally, and from Colchis Pasiphæ ventured to her encounter with Poseidon's bull.

Such is our lineage as keepers of the light: apostates of the truth, bearers of sacred and forbidden knowledge, matrices of kings, demigods and heroes. There is a too-mortal, sacrilegious impulse in the construction of these towers to the sky in mockery of both the heavens and the ocean. These vaunting pagan spires, more complex and enduring than any cathedral…

* * *

I have just awoken on the library floor with no recollection of what happened and no idea how long I may have lain there. There is a lump on my head where I must have struck the table or the floor.

Is it possible I took too much morphia? Was it a delayed fainting fit brought on the by my grisly discovery amid the seaweed? Or perhaps there exists in man some cerebral debility brought on by rapid changes in altitude. I have passed two days ascending and descending between the bird-infested upper air and sea level. No doubt, in time, a lighthouse-man may grow accustomed to such regular fluctuations.

On waking, I noted that the library seemed somewhat more disordered than when I had entered it. I returned my book to the shelf and squared the pile of newspapers which appeared skewed. In doing so, I could not help but notice the sequential dates were interrupted. Three issues were missing. I could not find them no matter where I looked.

SEVEN

That evening, I arrived in the light-room ahead of Mr Adamson, who would accompany my watch. I used my time to read the weather instruments and note their measures.

I was also particularly drawn to the watch log, which is supposed to record any notable occurrences while the lamp is lighted. What stories might it contain? What history of Ripsaw might it tell? Briefly alone in the light-room for the first time, I had the opportunity to look through the pages of this heavy, leather-bound volume.

Alas, the keeper's life is evidently as dry and as repetitive as it appears. Principle Bartholomew had made a number of observations regarding out-of-the-ordinary wind or rainfall. Mr Adamson had noted the breaking of a lantern pane by a large, long-necked bird he identified as a swan but which surely could not have been. The creature's body had been lost to the sea.

Evidently, weeks pass here with nothing extraordinary to report. Still, I was curious to find some trace of Keeper Spencer, who haunted the balcony just a few days previously, nodding in the wind as the others sat here listening to the ventilator's breathing and the ringing of the mechanism bell. Had he left something of himself except the watch-cloak he'd bequeathed to me?

I flicked the pages, looking for a different hand, until I saw a short entry from Mr Spencer:

*At approximately twenty minutes past two o'clock, I
went out on to the balcony to peer at the cowl (which
was rattling) and I thought I saw a figure standing to
my left but at the very edge of my vision. I turned to
it but saw nothing. Walking towards that place, I saw
again a dark shadow of small stature like a boy, but
again at the corner of my eye so I could see no detail.
I imagine it must be an effect of the beam, perhaps
reflecting from a bird or cloud. It was most curious.*

A note had been added by Principal Bartholomew below
the log entry: *An effect of the beam. Nothing more.* I could
find nothing more from Keeper Spencer and was ready to
read further back in time when Mr Adamson arrived panting
and irritable. He had apparently not noticed me reading the
watch log.

We went to the lantern together, where his only advice
was, "So light it." I did everything as the principal had shown
me and Mr Adamson made no comment – the height of praise
from him. Indeed, he seemed disappointed that I had done
nothing wrong.

This watch, however, was something I had been dreading
since my first encounters with him. Misanthropic as he is,
how might he react to four hours trapped in a room with me?

Rather than worry myself unduly, I reminded myself of Mr
Fowler's advice that any man may be understood if allowed
time and space and patience. Some men are prickly. Others
live within themselves. Some are angry and blame the world.
Fear drives a good proportion, and greed many more. This
was my opportunity to get to know the man.

Initially, he sat at the oaken table without speaking to or
looking at me. The bell rang constantly. The ventilator gulped
and sighed. He was clearly uncomfortable and shifted in his
seat. He went out on to the balcony after forty-five minutes
and remained there for half an hour. Evidently, conversation
is painful for him.

Nevertheless, when he returned, I decided to be bold. "May I ask what happened to Keeper Spencer?"

"He died." No expression.

"Quite. But what manner of accident befell him?"

"You even speak like a poet."

"I assure you, again, Mister Adamson, that I am not a poet."

He shifted in his seat. "Why do you want to know about Spencer? It's no concern of yours."

"Is it not? I sleep in his bed. I sit in his seat and I do his work. His death has strongly affected my life. I am here because of him. I could just as easily be at Bishop Rock or Longships."

"Well, he died in the privy." A solemn downward glance. "It was a shameful way to go."

"He was ill?"

"Nothing like that. An accident pure and simple. Spencer was a sensitive one. Like you, I expect. He liked to close the trapdoor to the water store before using the privy. Well, the stove must have had an excess of coal dust in it, or else he used coke instead of coal. Carbonic oxide in that small space… We found him when he missed breakfast next morning. His face was as red as a cherry. Stone dead."

"How horrible."

"It's common enough. He knew about the dangers from his training, but he couldn't defecate [he did not use this word] if he thought people were listening. Imagine dying only for that. For shame."

"The poor man."

"It was his own fault, Meakes. A rock lighthouse is a hazardous place. Look at your adventure today. A stray billow, a strong gust… A slip, an accident with a knife or broken glass. If you open a vein here, do you think the waves will stop for you? They will not. A wound that, on land, would not inconvenience a man can here kill him. Remember that."

"I will. What kind of man was he? Spencer, I mean?"

"I told you: sensitive."

"But was he a good keeper? Reliable? Trustworthy? Not prone to fancy or caprice?"

Mr Adamson gave me a hard stare. "He was a normal man. But sensitive."

"I don't know why I ask. I suppose I want a model. You said that the principal is a reliable man."

He seemed to hesitate before continuing. "Bartholomew is half mad, though you might not notice it. He has a mania for the weather. Have you wondered where he is all day? He's in here reading his instruments and playing with that contraption on the balcony that measures wind. Do you know he keeps a jar of leeches in his room? I've seen them. But he doesn't use them for his health. He uses them to predict the weather. Disgusting fat things. And you know what they eat, don't you, his leeches? It's not bread and butter. It's blood. *His* blood. He's feeding those slimy things with his own blood so he knows if the wind is about to change direction. He puts them on his skin, cold and slimy."

I could not think of anything to say in that moment.

"He'll tell you if you ask. He believes he can design a system that will *predict* a storm. It's all about patterns with him. If he can collect enough measurements, there will be patterns. He thinks there's going to be another storm like in 1703 when the Eddystone house was washed away. And he'll be the one to announce it. Can you imagine? Predicting the weather? Even if he could, do you think anyone would believe him?"

"Like Cassandra."

'Eh?"

"The wife of King Priam. She—"

"I'm not interested in stories. What I mean to say is: what does it matter? If it rains, it rains. You can't change it, even if you know it's coming!"

"But ships could remain in port if their captains knew—"

"Nonsense [he did not use this word]. There is always cargo to be conveyed and collected. Commerce doesn't stop for the weather. Captains are all the same. Drop sail and close-reef. That's their answer to an impending storm. Stay in port, you say? You don't know what you're talking about, Poet!"

"You were a sailor, then? Before you became a keeper?"

"I didn't say that."

"I meant no offence. It's only... I've read that many sailors become lighthouse-men."

"Some do. Some don't. What was *your* profession before coming here?"

"My father was a printer and my uncle a physician."

"I didn't ask about your family."

"I... I suppose I have been looking for a trade. Those two fields of endeavour have interested me much."

"And that's why you have decided to sit in a lighthouse listening to the wind and waves unto distraction."

"I am young. I still have time to think about my future. But may I ask you why *you* chose the life of a keeper?"

'No. You ask too much, Poet. If you want to live in a tower, you'll do well to remember that listening is better than speaking. There's already enough chatter from the reef and the birds around the lantern. If you were seeking silence for your poetry, you've come to the wrong place."

"Mister Adamson, I must insist... I don't know why you—"

He stood. "I'm going up to raise the wicks."

I know I shouldn't allow him to antagonise me so. It only encourages him when I react to his barbs. Mr Fowler taught me as much. When people seek to provoke and torment, it's because they cannot tolerate their own darkness and hope to manifest it in others. Mr Adamson is angry and wishes to see me angry. He is oppressed by Principal Bartholomew and in turn intends to exert his power over me. I understand this. It is why I am not angry.

The bell stopped.

It was only then I realised I had become accustomed to its ceaseless ringing and to the revolving mechanism's moan.

"Mister Adamson?"

The lens was no longer turning. The beam was fixed on only four points of the horizon.

"Mister Adamson?" I was standing now.

"I know, I know. I have ears, too," he said, descending from the lantern.

"What has happened?"

"I don't know. But the lens must keep on turning."

"Can you fix it?"

"Perhaps the chain... But here. You must crank it by hand."

He took a right-angled rod with a wooden sleeve for a handle and fitted it to the mechanism.

"Now look here. You see this dial? It shows you the correct velocity to turn the lever. Not too fast, not too slow. Keep your circles regular and I'll try to find the problem. You needn't go very quickly, but it may be stiff."

I beheld the crank. Old terrors coursed through me.

"Well, what are you waiting for? There are sailors out there on the sea!"

My hands would not rise to the handle. They hung heavy by my sides.

"Poet!"

"Yes. Yes."

I gripped the handle with both hands. A tide of nausea rose within. I pushed the crank away from me. The mechanism was stiff but began to turn smoothly.

"That's right, lad. Don't stop. Lives depend upon it."

I closed my eyes and turned the crank. I tried to think only of the sailors on the horizon looking for our light. Mr Adamson would soon find the fault and we would take our seats once more.

He was on his knees peering into the clockwork with a lantern.

"Can you see the problem?" I said.

"I have no idea. This has never happened before."

"Call the principal with the air-whistle. He will know."

"And wake him with our incompetence hours before his watch? Keep turning!"

I turned the crank. There was no pain as yet, but it would come. It would come if we could not find the problem.

"I am going to the lantern," said Mr Adamson. "Perhaps there's some obstruction there."

He went aloft. I watched his shadow moving through the metal mesh and saw the lens revolving at my stroke. My shoulders were starting to ache. This provoked recollections of greater pain, bone-deep pain. Exhaustion.

I waited in the dread expectation of the bucket emptied over my back. Cold water. Shirt stiff and abrading my skin. Or the strap's whip-crack lash.

These did not come. But neither did Mr Adamson. Would I really be forced to crank for three more hours? Could I?

"Mister Adamson?"

"What?"

"Can you see the problem?"

He began to descend. "Stop mithering me! I can't think with you bleating all the time."

"Is there not a latch? I recall the principal saying something about a latch."

"So you're an expert now, are you? A few hours in the house and you're lecturing me on latches? You're young and healthy, aren't you? A bit of toil is good for a man."

"Where are you going?"

"To the balcony. I need to urinate [he did not use this word]. Keep going. You're a champion."

I looked at the clock. Ten minutes later, he had not returned. Twenty. He clearly had no intention of repairing the revolving mechanism. He was waiting for Principal Bartholomew to come and solve the problem.

"Mister Adamson?"

Of course, I could have stopped at any moment and blown the whistle to call the principal. The lens would have stilled for mere seconds – not long enough to wreck a ship.

But enough time to condemn me in his eyes. A keeper on watch was responsible for just two things: the light burning and the lens moving. No excuse but death or catastrophe would be accepted.

"Mister Adamson?"

It was not the pain of turning. That pain had not yet started. I invited Mr Fowler into my mind and solicited his advice. Recall a different place, he would have said. Leave the physical realm and pass time in tranquillity of spirit.

My mind is a library. I tried to recall the book I'd been reading earlier.

Some details had struck me concerning Faraday's design for lighthouse ventilators. The problem: air and spray entering the cowl atop the cupola and blowing out the lamp. His solution: a number of inverted copper funnels joined by pins inside the upper chimney. Hot exhaust gas would rise inside and through the funnel cones towards the open air, but descending gusts would be deflected on the outer surface of the funnels into the lantern as a whole, not affecting the fragile flame. This would also help to regulate the temperature and control condensation inside the lantern…

The crank. The interminable circles. I tried not to think. My arms were becoming heavier with each turn.

'What is going on here? What is all the shouting? Where is Keeper Adamson?'

I turned to see the principal rising through the hatch into the light-room.

"Sir. The mechanism is broken. We are having to crank it by hand. Mister Adamson is on the balcony."

"Why is he on the balcony, Meakes?"

"I don't know, sir."

"Do not stop turning. I will look for the problem."

He looked inside the gear wheels and seemed to reached inside. The handle jumped in my hands and the lens began to revolve of its own accord. The bell started ringing.

"Oh! It is working, sir."

"Of course it is. Somebody had set the brake latch."

"The latch? But I asked him about the latch."

The principal opened the lee-side balcony door and called out into the night. "Mister Adamson! Come inside!"

"Oh. Mister Bartholomew," said Mr Adamson, appearing from the night. "Is it time for your shift already?"

"It is not. Can you explain why the brake latch was set and why Mister Meakes is shaking with exertion at the crank?"

"No, sir."

"You did not set the latch yourself? Mister Meakes has not been advised of its existence."

"I can only think it was an accident, sir. Perhaps one of us brushed it without noticing."

Not one of us believed that to be true. It had been Mr Adamson in the lantern when the mechanism had stopped.

The principal glared at Mr Adamson. He could prove nothing. "You know that initiations of this kind are prohibited by regulation."

"Yes, sir." I'm sure I saw a smirk.

"Well. *You* may finish your watch early, Mister Meakes. Eat something and rest well."

I walked to the hatch. Mr Adamson followed.

"Not you, Mister Adamson," said the principal. "You will share the watch with me."

"A second watch—?"

"Or I can write a report to the Commission about the events of tonight. You may choose."

Mr Adamson stared hard at me. I could not think how any of it had been my fault and yet he seemed angrier than ever at my presence in the lighthouse.

EIGHT

Sunday. The days have passed seemingly without name or number. Everything about the day is the same, except that we must wear our uniforms all day and raise the lighthouse flag at noon. Officially, the public may visit the lighthouses on Sundays to observe our work, but Ripsaw is too distant and hazardous for such casual visits. Principal Bartholomew has told me that an American gentleman came last year to investigate how a first-order house is run. Two years before that, a writer of poor-quality fiction was resident for a week in order to prepare a book, but spent the whole time painting watercolours.

Breakfast was a somewhat fractious affair, with Mr Adamson angrily banging the pots and plates while barely exchanging a word with either me or the principal. I heard him muttering to himself earlier this morning that it is absurd to wear the uniform when nobody can see it but we three.

I am inclined to agree. How would the Commission know if we obeyed the rule or not? Perhaps if one of us was on the balcony or in the lantern they might glimpse us through the telescope from the shore station. But could they discern a brass button or an epaulette from that distance? Could they tell a uniform jacket from a regular jacket? Or one man from another?

And even if they were able to identify a lack of uniform, what could they do? Apply to the Commission for an official letter of censure and hold that letter for as many weeks as were necessary for the weather to be propitious enough for the cutter to come out? Then send a vessel and crew out onto the waves where a squall may rush upon them and overturn the boat, or smash it on the reef, or wash a man overboard to his death… All for an infraction so petty as to not wear a uniform one Sunday on a rock twenty miles out to sea?

Additionally, I feel ill at ease about holding the service in the library. Perhaps it is foolish of me, but I have come to consider the library as *my* place in the lighthouse – the place where I can go for peace and solitude. The idea of sharing it with the others feels awkward.

Not only that, but sharing it with something else. With the Church's presence, which otherwise has no dominion here. This is a place of knowledge. True, there is a Bible on the shelf, but so, too, are Milton and Shakespeare, whose truths are no less eloquent and whose poetry is often more so. I like to read the Bible on occasion, but not as something more than literature.

"It's all a pantomime," said Mr Adamson as we took our seats in the library.

Principal Bartholomew deigned not to hear. "Mister Meakes – since this is your first Sunday with us at Ripsaw, I will explain. I usually read the prayer and then I invite others to read from the Bible."

"Yes, sir."

"Very well."

I cannot remember the whole of the prayer that he read. It was very long and written especially for lighthouse-men by a noted clergyman of Edinburgh or London. I remember only that, as he read it, my mind wandered to the subject of religion in general, and that I spent more time seeking the hidden motives of he who had written it.

Men are Janus-faced creatures at the best of times. We dissimulate and lie. We conceal and distort. Often, we don't understand our own thoughts or emotions. Our utterances, though they may be embroidered with the niceties of politics or gilded with the magic of poetry, are, in the end, as raw and useless as a dog's baying. They are noises we make in frustration at not knowing how to speak our purest truth. We use words. We choose words. But do they really say what we imagine? A man's truth is in how he acts towards his fellow man and his consistency of selfhood. Mr Fowler taught me all of this and more.

"Lord, thou art not confined to temples made with man's hands; the temple most acceptable to thee is the heart of the worshipper," read the principal.

And I thought: what contradictory logic! This noted clergyman in Edinburgh or London is afraid that lighthouse keepers will lose their faith and slide quickly into sin for want of a nave, a pew or altar, thus reminding us that worship is in the heart. In which case, why should any church or cathedral be constructed at colossal cost? Why should the Church itself exist when all that Christ said is in a book, and the small chamber of the human heart is sufficient to contain it?

"With shame we remember how often we have failed to study thy holy word – how often we have neglected the exercises of holy devotion – how often we have worshipped thee with our lips while our hearts were far from thee," read the principal.

And I thought: guilt. What a cheap and obvious way to manipulate an isolated man. The suggestion was clear enough: you lighthouse-men have much liberty and time. Occupy yourselves with religious study, the better to stay tranquillised and pliable and dutiful. Work daily to save your mortal soul. Stay sealed inside the jar of holy observance. Avoid fugitive thoughts and fancy. Or risk the inferno through your own lassitude.

"Save us from the temptations and the solitude which might lead us to forget our God," read the principal.

And I thought of the rhythmic creaks from Mr Adamson's bunk above me. What are these temptations but the natural impulses of animal man? What fear the Commission must have of its men returning feral from their short duty, reduced to shaggy beasts by a few weeks of distance from the civilized world!

"We pray particularly for those by whose command we are engaged in this arduous work. Bless them in their families," read the principal.

And I thought: cant! Just like those simonious lords of past times whose masses and atonement were paid for with bloodied silver, the Commission expects its captive keepers to pray for *their* souls. We, who face the wind and the ocean daily. We, who may be washed from the rock in an instant. We, who keep the light shining to preserve life. *We* must pray for *them*?

In all of this charade, they reveal their true opinions of us. We are weak. We are capricious. We are not to be trusted. We must be controlled because we are so distant. Freedom of thought and action must be curtailed at all cost lest we recognize ourselves as men with power. They fear that. They fear...

"Mister Meakes?"

"Yes? Yes, sir."

"I asked if you would like to read a passage. A verse or two. A psalm, perhaps."

"Oh. If you wish, sir."

I read Psalm 107 from memory. It seemed apt:

They that go down to the sea in ships, that do business in great waters; these see the works of the LORD, and his wonders in the deep. For he commandeth, and raiseth the stormy wind, which lifteth up the waves thereof. They mount up to the heaven, they go down again to the depths: their soul is melted because of trouble. They reel to and fro, and stagger like a drunken man, and are at their wit's end.

Mr Adamson regarded me with something between admiration and contempt.

The principal nodded. He had found the psalm in his Bible. "Very good, Mister Meakes. But you have omitted the most important part." And he read:

Then they cry unto the LORD in their trouble, and he bringeth them out of their distresses. He maketh the storm a calm, so that the waves thereof are still. Then are they glad because they be quiet; so he bringeth them unto their desired haven.

Mr Adamson snorted and tapped his fingers on the marble-top table.

"And you, Mister Adamson? Would you like to read a passage?"

"No."

"Then perhaps you would like to tell us why you sneer at Mister Meakes' choice."

"It's nothing."

"Clearly not. Out with it. What is *your* contribution this Sunday?"

"It's bad luck to talk of storms while at sea."

"A childish superstition. We are speaking of faith."

"It's a joke, that passage."

"A joke? It is scripture."

"Tell that to Winstanley at the Eddystone house. Don't you think he prayed when the storm howled about his tower? Don't you think he cried out to the Lord? But what calm did the Lord *bringeth* on that occasion? Winstanley's house was wiped from the face of the earth without a trace. Or did praying work only eighteen hundred years ago and in the Holy Land?"

"Nobody may know the will of the Lord, Mister Adamson."

"Then why bother with Him?"

Principal Bartholomew appeared vexed. "Faith is a choice we make. It is a daily practice. Perhaps Winstanley lacked faith."

"As the tempest tore his lighthouse piece by piece? I feel sure his faith was pure enough."

"Well. Enough of your insubordination. The Sunday

service is compulsory as laid down in the Commission's regulations concerning your employment. It is your job."

"Amen," muttered Mr Adamson.

"Let us pray silently for a while," said the principal. "I think we need some tranquillity."

He closed his eyes and I followed suit.

It remains a curious and novel experience to close my eyes inside the tower. One's senses compensate. The ever-present birds become louder. The reef whispers and slaps. There is an odd feeling of pressure as if the circle walls are slowly closing in. And something else: some ineffable vibration as when a note lingers silently long after a piano key has been struck. A memory of sound, perpetually resonating.

I have thought that the lighthouse is a conductor, but of what atmospheric or oceanic force I cannot say. There is some potency concentrated here, without colour or sound or smell. Something like gravity, perhaps, that we prove by experiment and equation, but which is too ubiquitous to think of.

I wondered as we prayed, if we prayed, whether those prayers congregated as they rose up through the lighthouse and out through the ventilator's Faraday funnels. Did they mingle and combine, or was each a separate wish divided into beams by the prisms in the lens? Did the cowl cough at the sudden influx of emitting prayer so much purer than the usual exhalations and emanations? Or was it simply more effluvia?

Mr Adamson was staring fixedly at me when I opened my eyes. Evidently, he had not been praying.

* * *

I stayed in the library after the other two had left, Principle Bartholomew to continue with his measurements of weather, Mr Adamson to do whatever occupied his time – perhaps reading the three newspapers he had taken from the library. I was keen to read about the ancient stylites in the volume that somebody had put into the catalogue as some manner of joke.

The first of them was Simeon, it seems: a Syrian shepherd who fled his flock for austere monasticism. That he lived beyond even this vocation was remarkable, he having attempted pious suicide numerous times. The other monks were obliged to restrain or resuscitate him.

Finally, his asceticism was not enough for him, or too much for the others. His fasting and self-castigation was extreme. He ventured to a remote hut, there to dedicate himself to starvation unto the point of revelation. He attempted to sleep standing, but often fell. This, too, was comfort beyond tolerance.

Instead, he sought a rocky mountain wilderness to make his home. But word spread of his miraculous deprivations and pilgrims came to call, requesting insight, requesting prayer, requesting benediction. He could withstand the cruellest hardships of weather and hunger, but he could not support interruption.

On the periphery of a town, he found the remnants of some Roman temple and ascended a column of nine feet in height. There he would remain in aerial penance, braving rain and sun and cold upon a tiny platform barely wide enough to support his limbs. It was not enough. His wished-for isolation was too close to the ground.

And thus he moved to higher and higher columns. Twelve feet. Twenty-two. Thirty-six. Finally, he made his home fifty feet from the ground in a space barely a yard square and surrounded by a baluster. He dressed in animal skins and bore the elements without shelter.

For another man, this might have been the highest expression of asceticism, but Simeon was no normal man. To compensate for the coddling aid of vestment, he chose to wear a heavy chain about his neck and remain standing at all times, preferably with arms out-stretched, cruciform, in constant praise. If this proved too complacent, he would bow repeatedly his head to feet. One spectator noted 1,400 consequent obeisances before ceasing to count.

Thirty-seven years in total did he spend atop one column or another, through blistering summers and chill, starry nights. Emperors, patriarchs and bishops visited him, ascending by ladder just near enough to talk. When stricken with a weeping ulcer on his thigh, he sought healing in greater piety and spent the last year of his life standing on one leg.

They say that birds used to wheel about the apex of his tower, drawn by the animal reek of his tattered clothes and unwashed body. The pilgrim hordes washed about the pedestal in waves. And he... Was not he a kind of light atop his column? Was he not a beacon for those who sought a purer truth?

Or was he, rather, like a lighthouse warning mariners to beware of perilous shallows that appeared profound?

NINE

Apart from Sundays, the other named days do not really exist in the lighthouse. It is more a question of hours. Breakfast, lunch and supper. The cleaning hours after breakfast. The raising and lowering of the signal ball between eight and ten. The partitioned hours of the watch. It seems that one is always looking at the clock.

There are innumerable small tasks requiring our attention. Baking bread and preparing meals. Bringing up provisions from the stores. Emptying ash and other waste into the sea. Checking the horizon periodically for ships. The opening and closing of windows according to the direction of the wind or rain. The lighthouse is a large machine and we must maintain it constantly with fuel and care. Or perhaps we are its fuel.

Even with such a regimen, the hours of liberty before lunch or between lunch and supper gape. It is during such periods that one regards the impassive sea and sky and recalls the epic solitude. We may be three within this house, but there is little comfort in proximity. I would like to talk to the other two, but they are rocks unto themselves, each surrounded by his own whirlpools, eddies and hidden reefs. To approach either one is to risk a wreck.

These personal hours may be anathema to some, but such men do not seek a keeper's life. The principle spends his liberty reading in his room or tinkering with his weather-measuring devices. Mr Adamson lives somewhat like a cat who roams absent for most of the day but returns for meals with nothing but a sphinx-like smile as to where he's been or what he's seen. Our paths seldom cross. He prefers the bedroom; I prefer the library.

Certainly, there is something furtive and clandestine in him. I occasionally think about the package he caught when I first landed on the rock. A bottle of whisky, perhaps, or some other contraband. I've seen no trace of it, nor smelled spirits on his breath, but there are many places to hide an item in the lighthouse.

By the by, I have wondered if he has discovered my bottle of morphia. It has not moved from its place inside a handkerchief in my drawer, but it occurred to me the other day I have not been using as much as I seem to have used. I would raise the subject with him, but I am no more permitted to have it here than he is to purloin it.

I decided to cease taking my morphia before sleeping. It provokes a deep and lasting sleep, but Mr Adamson has twice complained about my nocturnal babblings. He may not have understood anything I said, but it is wiser to remain silent. It is also more conducive to our peaceful cohabitation.

Sleeping at Ripsaw was initially difficult. I was not accustomed to the concept of being so high above the sea and so far from shore. The noises seemed interminable: wave impacts, screaming birds, the rattling chain each morning. The wheedling wind that gasps and whispers at the windows and never seems to rest, like the mind of a troubled man. The crashing reef. The ventilator's hollow moan, which fills the house whenever the lamp is lighted. And, of course, the bovine grunts of Mr Adamson above me. The creaking of his bunk. His soporific emissions. Who could have imagined that a bed so far from a city's noise could be so disturbing of a night?

Now, after a fortnight or so – is it longer? – I sleep well. Indeed, there is a deep satisfaction in lying amid darkness and listening to the circling world – more so when Mr Adamson is on his watch. I remind myself of our isolation here and see it as a privilege. I have learned to identify and appreciate the sounds to such a degree that I sometimes wake to the susurrating rain on the sea's surface and it calms me to know I am warm and dry in this tower. I hear the beguiling wind around the windows and hear it swing from east to south, from north to west.

Sometimes, on a still night, on a warmer night, with the windows open, I fancy it is possible to hear the shore. A belltower's chime. An angry dog. The sounds cross the water as trembling echoes, skipping like a pebble to greater distances than they may on land. It may be my imagination.

One knows one is settled in a place when every sound has its source and explanation. The kitchen stove's clang. Footsteps on the metal staircase to the lens. The flat slap of a trapdoor closing between levels. I can even differentiate the footfalls of the other two upon the stairs: the principal's measured pace and Mr Adamson's clumsy gait.

It is the same with smells, of course. I have become a perfumer of this place, able to identify and catalogue its various aromas as a Florentine master may discern his civet, his calamus, his ambergris or cypress. There is the rank seaweed iodine, the north wind's heady ozone, the fishy fetor of the herring gulls. The ladder's ferric sapor. I can often tell which man is ascending to the lantern if I'm aloft. One might not think this granite eminence could harbour so much scent, but our senses become more sophisticated when surrounded by the void.

* * *

I am now permitted to observe my watches alone in the light-room, Principal Bartholomew having said that he is well pleased with my diligence and attention. It is a great blessing because my watches with the other two were usually uncomfortable.

The principal would sit there like a portrait with his book

and ignore my presence totally. There was no ill intention, I believe, in his silences. In his mind, he was alone. This was preferable to the nights with Mr Adamson, whose inconsistencies unnerved me greatly. Some nights, he would spend his time out on the balcony or pacing in the lantern. Other nights, he would remind me of his double watch and how it was my fault, or complain about the smallest flaws he could find in my endeavours as a keeper. My bread was under-baked. I moved too frequently while sleeping. I spent too long polishing the lens.

Other times, I simply could not discern his motives. One night, after I had completed my watch with the principal and was just going off to sleep, Mr Adamson called me to the light-room with the whistle. I could not think of refusing the call. I dressed quickly and ascended.

"Meakes," he said. "I need you to go out on the balcony and check something."

"I can wait in the light-room if you need to go out."

"No. I need *you* to go outside."

"Why? What for?"

"Just go out and walk a few circuits. Tell me if you see or hear anything odd."

"What do you mean by *odd*?"

"Darn it, lad! [He did not use these words.] Just go out and have a look."

I did not trust him after the incident with the crank. Still, to refuse his order could be classed as insubordination and result in my immediate dismissal. He knew this, as he has always known it.

It was a zesty night. The wind was blowing from the west and the rain was intermittent but determined. I chose the lee door and emerged into a mischievous gust that whipped my cloak about me. The revolving beam picked out vaporous precipitation. The sea writhed ecstatically upon the reef. I kept close to the masonry wall lest a sudden gust unfoot me at the rail.

Something odd, he'd said. I recalled Spencer's log entry about the figure of a boy at the periphery of his vision. But there was nothing to see. Only the dripping rail and the scudding sky. Only feathered corpses and the whirring silvered cups of Principal Bartholomew's wind apparatus. I walked two perimeters, my shoulder close the wall. On the weather side, the wind pushed and jostled. The raindrops pinned my face. Finally, I returned to the door, which Mr Adamson had bolted open in one of the floor holes. I knocked and he appeared at the crack, perspiring – or so it seemed to me.

"What have you seen?" he said.

"Nothing out of the ordinary."

"What have you heard?"

"Only the wind and the sea."

"Nothing odd?"

"Mister Adamson – the weather is very inclement and I have done my watch."

"Aye, and I'm doing two watches thanks to you."

"There is nothing out here but the elements. Is this about Keeper Spencer's log entry?"

"What log entry?"

"The watch log. He said he saw—"

"I don't care a fig for what Spencer wrote or didn't write."

"Will you open the door?"

His face disappeared but the door didn't open. I waited. It seemed quite credible that he would leave me outside until the morning and claim it as an accident.

But I saw his hand unlock the bolt and I entered with a bawdy gust. He seemed distracted.

"Is everything all right, Mister Adamson?"

"Go to bed, lad. Go to bed. It's nothing. I am tired. So are you. Go to bed."

I still have no explanation for his behaviour.

* * *

I have looked again at the place in the water store where I saw the message scratched on the wall. Nothing remains and I wonder now if I really saw it. I had but recently arrived and wasn't accustomed to the place. Still, the words remain clear in my mind – *Lord, deliver me from this windowless pit* – and their specificity suggests I could not have imagined them.

Still, there are moments when things may pass that we feel have passed before. A gesture. A snatch of conversation. Often, all of these things in combination. Other times, we cannot differentiate what is memory and what was dream. The two seem quite interchangeable. The mind is unreliable.

Mr Fowler always used to say that every man is but a mere conglomeration of temporary states. Catch him in any one of these states – anger, contemplation, grief, drunkenness, confusion – and you see just a fragment of who he is. It's necessary to see the whole: the white light rather than the prismatic spectrum. No man is red or blue alone. Or violet.

Perhaps I saw the writing when in a distracted state. The body on the reef, however, was unequivocal. Mr Adamson saw it, too. I have not seen it since, but things do not linger on the rocks. They pause here only on longer journeys.

* * *

This morning on the balcony after cleaning, I observed Principal Bartholomew making adjustments to his wind machine. He seemed perturbed and so I enquired about his efforts.

He explained that the machine is an anemometer to measure wind velocity. It has four hemispherical tin cups mounted at the four ends of a horizontal cross. These rotate when impelled by the wind and the number of their revolutions denotes wind speed. The principle is simple enough, but the practice is somewhat more complicated.

How, for example, does one translate the number of revolutions into a wind speed? Some have mounted the instrument upon a locomotive and calibrated it according to a known land speed. Alas, the wind is hardly ever constant on land and even less so at sea. Nor does it blow in a straight line. It gusts and pauses constantly, switching direction, and cheekily avoiding all measurement.

Then there is the question of humidity and temperature, which affect the density of air and thus its pressure on the cups. There are light winds and heavy winds. Often, the air is loaded with spray or rain, to further confuse the instrument.

As if these problems weren't enough, there's the matter of turbulence as air eddies and deflects from surrounding structures. Thus the machine may influence and warp its own readings. The lighthouse, too, is an enormous vane that twists and bends the air around it. One experimental answer to this problem, it seems, has been for the principal to attach a kite or a small parachute to a cord, the other end of which is connected to a spring mechanism that measures the resistance exerted by the wind. This might work if attached to the very peak of the lighthouse, at the very cowl, but every pause in wind velocity would cause the airborne device to drop, the cord to sag and the whole apparatus to either wind itself around the lantern or be dashed against the tower. The principal's frustration seems entirely justified.

Science aside, the notion of measuring the wind here at Ripsaw appears to me to have a profounder connotation. The root of *anemometry* is the Greek word άνεμος for *wind*. The Latins took it to form their word *anima*, meaning *soul* or essence of life. And are we not consequently reminded of the biblical Genesis in which God takes his terrene creation Man and breathes the breath of life into his nostrils? The Hebrew word used in that ancient record, *ruah*, also signifies *wind*.

What the principal seeks to measure on the balcony with his flawed and clumsy instruments is nothing less than an eternal force. It *is* nature. It mocks measurement. We may observe and annotate it, but in the end we can only marvel at its erratic will and brace ourselves in awe to face its fury, its cajoling, eccentric whims.

He teased the scalloped edge of fragile tip cup between thumb and forefinger to improve its appetite for wind. "A commissioner will soon be visiting the lighthouse. One comes every year to inspect the facilities, interview the keepers and collect the previous season's logbooks. Our standards of cleanliness and order have to be exemplary until the boat arrives."

I watched him mould the dull grey metal as he had been moulding me. "Yes, sir."

"They signalled from shore." He did not look up. "It seems there has been some trouble with your character reference from Mister Fowler."

"Trouble, sir?"

He stood and looked upon his work. Then upon me. "The commissioner will make everything clear, I am sure."

* * *

I have spent much time reading in the library today. Shakespeare. Milton. Coleridge. There are different worlds among the books, and different ages. Here, beneath the stucco mouldings and with a blank horizon beyond the windows, I could be anywhere and anytime. In Florence or Venice. In Xanadu or in the very depths of Hades. Travel is limitless within the mind.

I have been thinking much about distance. We are just twenty miles from the shore but more inaccessible than a mountain peak or an oasis in a desert. With time, resources and determination, one may reach such places. Here, the sea and reef prevent access almost all year round.

Marco Polo may have voyaged to such unimagined and unmapped regions as Bukhara, Zaitun and Hormuz, but he could not have entered the door of our lighthouse, not with all his camel caravans and convoys. The sea would have tossed him back at shore.

It is a distance that taunts with apparent proximity – real

through the telescope but quite beyond reach. We are living on the moon! Fewer men have set the lens in motion at Ripsaw Reef than have circumnavigated the globe.

* * *

I have been looking through Mr Adamson's possessions when he is on his watch. Four hours allow me sufficient tranquillity to take my time in the bedroom.

In truth, there is not much to find. There is a cache of some few, small items that evidently mean something to him: a pocketknife, an ink pen, a leather bag of coins that are quite useless here in the lighthouse. Indeed, a hoard of gold and jewels would be equally useless. We are simultaneously kings and serfs.

I have found no alcohol, nor anything illicit. I have, however, discovered the missing newspapers – those printed in the weeks during which he was onshore prior to his latest duty at Ripsaw (as near as I can calculate). He keeps these three local publications hidden under the foot of his mattress. What secret lies within these pages? I have given it much thought.

There must be some information with especial significance to him. The fact that there are three consecutive issues suggests a story that continues and develops. My first thought: a crime he has committed just prior to leaving shore and whose investigation he is anxious to follow. Yet I have been unable to find his name in any of the police columns. Nor have I seen a story continuing for three days that seems in any way connected with him.

My next thought: somebody sought to communicate with him through the public notices. A clever man would have worked out a code whereby three raincoats or half a ton of coal for sale could be read as a concealed message. But I have not noticed any curious patterns in these notices, which, for the most part, are repeated for a week or so.

Could it be that there is a story that concerns a family member? Or perhaps he simply has an urgent interest in that artic expedition, that terrible fire in Bristol, the trading price of wool or hessian. Was he interested in the sailing of some important vessel? The possibilities are endless.

I know I shouldn't read so. But a minim of morphia calms my mind and I can apply all of my faculties to the task at hand. Patterns will eventually emerge from the sea of words. These are my Cuthite constellation maps. I read. I seek a line through the labyrinth.

A hint to the soporific... Paragon, Temiscounta, Chrysolite, Luna... Robert Tait, a youth whose countenance betrayed a mixture of guilt and fatuity.

Rotation of the earth made visible... The frontals are of rich silk of the ecclesiastical colours... Man boiled to death in vapour bath at Bains de la Samaritaine... Six Ojibeway Indians sang war songs.

The infuriated ox created no small consternation... Sailed 27th: Phoenician Sproat, Anemone, Ariel, Gitana, Sultana... The vegetarians congregated to assist in the almost mystic rites of their soiree... Aeronaut Madame Palmyre Garneron took her disastrous flight.

The aggregate number of eggs from hens, ducks and other poultry cannot be less than 1,500,000,000. Sudden death from excitement...

I have four hours of absolute security each night in which to discern the secret truth of Mr Adamson. An answer lies somewhere in those three papers...

TEN

The principal was first to see the cutter coming out today and has been a tyrant over the cleaning of the lantern. Mr Adamson and I have been hard at work this morning while the principal sat in the light-room feverishly reading over provision book and ship log, watch notes and weather charts.

The commissioner is to spend one night only in the lighthouse and conclude his business during the first afternoon. That will mean each of us sitting with him for an hour or so in his room and discussing all matters related to our work. Thereafter, he will apply himself to the records and compare them with notes he made on last year's season. Has Ripsaw used more butter than it should? Is the lantern burning too much oil? How many pints of small beer have been consumed against the national average?

The principal has been especially careful with the oil measures. I watched him briefly in the oil store applying graduated gauging rods to each cistern and corroborating numbers with his log. He checked every measure – one gallon, half gallon, quarter gallon, pint and half pint – and even the drip-pan where they hang, ensuring that not a single drop has gone to waste. I thought of Mr Fowler measuring medicines by the drachm and grain and minim.

Mr Adamson joked, as we cleaned the brass, copper and glass, that the commissioner was visiting us solely to recall the principal to a shore posting. But for all his joking he, too, seems worried. We are in uniform and he has not complained once.

* * *

The commissioner is a corpulent gentleman with a bloated red face, an effusion of curly blond hair, and the gout. He limps and grunts as he limps. He arrived in a black humour because the sea had washed his lower trousers on landing and he had been nauseous for the whole trip. Climbing the steep steps between each floor caused him to breathe laboriously and pant "Lord. Oh, Lord!" at every trapdoor.

We had prepared a breakfast for the commissioner but his stomach would not permit him even to drink some tea. Instead, he retired with the principal to the commissioner's room, there to discuss the order of business for the afternoon.

Mr Adamson continued nervous. For him, as for many lighthouse-men, the whole of worldly existence is a bipartite thing: tower and shore. The commissioner's arrival had thrown that certainty into confusion and doubt. The shore had come to the tower. We may be under constant observation through the telescope's glassy eye, but we can close the window shutters, avoid the lantern and burrow deeper out of sight. Not now. Now our covering rock is raised and we blink up at the deity that controls our fate.

The commissioner had been with the principal for perhaps half an hour when I decided to ascend to the library from the kitchen. It was on the stairway between bedrooms that I encountered Mr Adamson eavesdropping on the conversation.

"What are you doing?" I whispered.

He fixed me with a lethal glare and held a finger to his lips. I continued past him to the library.

I was not planning to read. It seemed to me that a better place to listen to the secret conversation might be the cupboard by the window in the library – a false cupboard that is in fact merely a door covering the space where a metal chimney passes up from the kitchen stove to the cupola. More importantly, the gap around this chimney passes through all bedrooms and the commissioner's is directly below the library.

I opened the wainscot door and stood close by the chimney pipe. The voices were distorted but audible:

"And Assistant Keeper Adamson – he remains sober?"

"Yes, Commissioner. He is always very keen with his beer at supper, but there has been nothing of what occurred previously."

"And his comportment, generally?"

"He can be difficult. Petulant. Childish. Antagonistic. Prior to the arrival of Mister Meakes, he did not speak to me for nearly two weeks. He is recalcitrant at every Sunday service. There was also an incident where he obliged Meakes to crank the lens for almost a whole watch – I suppose as some form of childish initiation. I have written reports on all of these situations."

"Then this punitive posting has done little to calm him."

"I fear not. It may have made him worse."

"I see. I see. Well, I will talk to him now. Will you fetch him?"

I closed the cupboard door and went quickly to the marble-top table lest the principal appear at the door. I imagined Mr Adamson similarly dissimulating innocence.

I heard voices and the commissioner's door closing. The principal descended to his room and I heard the distinctive creak of his partition. Still, I waited a few minutes before approaching the cupboard once again to listen.

"… Why you did not speak to Principal Bartholomew for two weeks?"

"He said two weeks? It may have been a day or two."

"There is no difference, Mister Adamson. The keepers are required to communicate at all times. You know the regulations."

"He's a martinet."

"He is your superior… But I see from your smirk that you think otherwise."

"Is it not time for *him* to go ashore? He's old."

"That is not your decision. Rather, it is *you* who should be on shore. You are clearly unfitted for the work. Now that Mister Meakes is able to do his watches alone, you will return to shore with me tomorrow and a replacement will come out the same day."

"Wait. Wait. I can't go back to shore—"

"You can and you will."

"You don't understand…"

The creak of the principal's partition signalled his approach and I was obliged to sit at the table once again. Somebody had left a volume there: the book of weather predictors. It was open at the chapter on cloud formations and four sooty etchings showed on-coming storms. There was an inky smudge on the left-hand exterior margin. A smudge, or an illustrated figure? A lurking, diminutive figure in silhouette.

"Mister Meakes? The commissioner will see you now."

"Yes, sir."

"I see you are studying cloud forms. Very good. Perhaps you have discerned that fog may be coming. A certain diffusion in the air. Let us hope not, for the commissioner's sake."

"Sir. The book was already open and…"

But he had turned and was descending. I followed him down to the commissioner's room.

It was almost exactly as Mr Adamson had described: a bourgeois parlour or the reading room of a gentleman's club (I imagine). There was indeed carpet on the floor and plaster mouldings in the vaulted roof. An oil painting of the lighthouse amid an angry sea hung over a bed with a carved headboard. And, yes, heavy damask curtains with lace trim framed each window. The air was blue with pipe smoke – something the principal normally forbade.

The man himself seemed larger when seated, his head resting on a ring of pale fat around his neck. His nose was bulbous, red and veiny, like something that might cling to the rock below us. He gestured to the other seat at his table and I sat.

"Mister Meakes. I have heard commendable things about your apprenticeship so far at Ripsaw. You are a quick study and reliable. These are qualities to be prized in the lighthouse service."

"Thank you, sir."

He turned and took a sheaf of papers from a leather case on the bed, grunting as he did so. He put on a pair of half-moon glasses and squinted at a page, more for theatrical effect, I thought, than to remind himself of anything.

"Nevertheless, there a couple of irregularities in your application that we need to address."

"Irregularities, sir?"

"Indeed. They primarily concern your recommender: Mister Fowler. Your paternal uncle, I understand."

"That's right, sir."

"Are you aware of the recent unfortunate circumstances concerning Mister Fowler?"

"No, sir… May I ask what circumstances?"

"Then, forgive me. I'm afraid I must be the bearer of grievous news. Mister Fowler has been found dead."

His expression was one of sympathy, but he was also watching me quite carefully.

"Oh! Dead? But *how*? He was the healthiest man I knew!"

"Apparently, he was murdered: bludgeoned about the head, partially dismembered and bundled into a seaman's chest that was found half-submerged in the river less than half a mile from his home."

"Oh! Oh! It is horrible…"

"One of his patients is suspected. I understand that some of them are prone to violent outbursts. A man called Tibbotson was found to have a bloodied cudgel concealed in his bed."

"Oh! Mister Fowler…" I could barely speak for weeping.

The commissioner seemed caught between his impulse to console and the matter at hand. The latter was victorious.

"It's just that... Well, the letter he sent in reply to our questions about your character seems to be dated *after* he must have died. Our investigator has discerned that Mister Fowler had been missing for some days before the discovery of his body. Can you explain how that might have happened?"

"I'm afraid I can't, sir. It is difficult to think... This news is... Might not he have written the wrong date in error? It is easily done. A busy man as he was... Constantly pulled away from his desk for some emergency or other..."

"It is possible, of course. But you understand: these are important documents. The Commission does not permit just any fellow to enter the service."

"I understand it, sir. And I am grateful to have been chosen. I hope my work here shows my suitability for the position."

He was no fool, the commissioner. He continued to watch me carefully.

"Your uncle was a physician. Is that right?"

"Yes, sir, and very well respected... Forgive me my emotional state. He wrote a book."

"And he kept a house for the insane."

"No sir. His was a house for gentlemen with nervous complaints."

He steepled his fingers. "I fear I cannot see a difference."

"Well, sir, a gentleman with a nervous complaint retains the power to manage himself personally, professionally and domestically. He may have problems, but he can usually control how he appears or behaves. He may seem odd sometimes, but on the whole is not a danger to others. The insane, however, can make no such choice. They are victims of their own erratic, uncontrollable and usually unwitting behaviour. A mental illness is properly an illness of the mind, but insanity is an infirmity of the brain. The former may be cured, the latter rarely so."

He smiled then, as if he had caught me in a lie.

"You seem to know a lot about it, Mister Meakes."

"I was very close to my uncle."

"Indeed, you lived with him – in this house for eccentrics?"

"After the death of my parents. Yes, sir. But adjacent to the house. Not *with* his gentlemen patients."

"It is interesting." He leaned back. "Your distinction between the eccentric and the mad is a fine one. By your definition, many men among us could be said to have nervous complaints."

"That is true, sir. Sufferers are often the students of language or science. They are the imaginative, the speculative, the extravagant. They are the amative, the unoccupied, the deserted, the onanistic and the oppressed. The nervous man typically has a high degree of mental capability, though he is easily excited or distracted."

"And how does one treat such a fellow, to cure him?"

"There are many ways, sir – some of them barbaric. Restraints, cold showers, beatings. Solitary incarceration. But these are not the work of the modern physician. Mister Fowler sought to diminish excitability and irritability   to avoid extravagant ecstasies such as music or theatrical performances. His answer lay in seclusion, tranquillity, muscular exertion and habitual activity. If the mind is prone to excessive activity, we must distract or disperse that activity by other means. A man must be occupied whenever possible – not allowed to spend too much time inside his own thoughts, nor overstimulated by things around him."

"And would you say that a lighthouse-man's duties might fulfil these requirements for seclusion, habitual activity or occupation?"

"It rather depends on the individual case. I suppose it might. But the physician would have to know the man and approve."

"As your uncle approved you?"

"Indeed, he approved me for this position, sir. But I was never a patient in my uncle's house."

He looked at me over the top of his half-moon spectacles. "I don't believe I have suggested as much. Tell me about your muriate of morphia."

"Excuse me, sir?"

"You have a bottle of such medicine here with you in the lighthouse. Why?"

Mr Adamson. The snake. The Judas. So he *had* been stealing my morphia! He must have tried to bargain for his own position with this illicit knowledge.

"It helps me sleep, sir."

"Are you aware that Commission regulations forbid possession of all intoxicants and soporifics?"

"I know that spirits are prohibited, sir."

"Was this substance given to you by your uncle?"

"He suggested it, sir."

"As a treatment?"

"No, sir. As an aid to sleep."

"Sleep is not your purpose here, Mister Meakes. We need you to be alert and observant during the watch."

"Yes, sir."

"I will take that bottle of morphia. Do you have it with you now, or will you fetch it from your room?"

"I have it, sir." I handed him the bottle.

He looked at it, opened it, sniffed it, and put it on the table between us: my guilt exemplified.

I thought about telling the commissioner how Mr Adamson had also been taking the morphia and was thus as culpable as I. But he would soon be leaving the lighthouse. Would the same fate now be mine?

"You have the makings of a fine keeper, Mister Meakes."

"I think so, sir."

"But I must tell you that our investigations will continue. The date on Mister Fowler's letter casts everything in doubt. Our investigator will go over all of the details of your application with a fine comb. Do you understand?"

"Yes, sir."

"If there is anything you would like to tell me now, it would be better for you later, should any further irregularities come to light."

"I can think of no irregularities, sir. Nor do I understand the confusion with the date. I believe I was not with my uncle when he received the letter. I stayed in London after my meeting at the Commission."

He nodded. "We will talk again. It may be before your next posting at a catoptric house, or when you return to shore. I do not anticipate visiting Ripsaw again until the summer."

"Yes, sir. And my apologies, sir, about the morphia."

Another nod. He stood with a grunt. "And now I must make my tour of the house with Principal Bartholomew. I leave you to your liberty."

I stood also. For a moment I considered whether this was my opportunity to tell him about the words on the privy wall, or Mr Adamson's secret cache of newspapers, or Mr Spencer's curious log entry, but such things suddenly had a dubious ring to them. But my impulse was to keep my counsel and to continue with my work. That was the best way to proceed. That's what Mr Fowler would have suggested, God rest his soul.

ELEVEN

The commissioner may be with us for longer because the fog now envelops Ripsaw quite completely. The principal was right. I watched its approach through the library windows, creeping slowly from the open sea – a colossal wave of milky vapour. We are now *imbosomed without firmament; uncertain which, in ocean or in air.*

It is a curious sensation to look out and see nothing but white wraiths swirling and inveigling about the column. We perceive nothing and cannot be perceived, neither from shore nor from the sea. Two hours remain before dusk but the principal has set the fog bells going and their periodic toll is a timid, tinny noise amid the muffling fog. We will soon light the lamp, though its beam will be reflected and baffled by the fog – no more effective than a knife cutting smoke.

I have been reading the book by Mr Allan Poe, a strange, dark tale on which I have not been able to concentrate fully. I think about the absence of my morphia. Mr Fowler did tell me it was a temporary solution: a means of transition. He said it was not strictly necessary – merely an aid. With a clear mind and an avoidance of agitation, I should be able to sleep perfectly well without it.

I think, too, about Mr Adamson's betrayal. His removal from the lighthouse ought to satisfy me, but it seems he will not be leaving quite yet. Principal Bartholomew believes the fog will continue into tomorrow, meaning the cutter can't come out. We are thus in a condition of hiatus here. The usual patterns have been disturbed. The commissioner's presence has created an imbalance and the mood inside the house is altered.

The principal, too, seems preoccupied. I wonder if the Commission has requested that he finally returns to shore as Mr Adamson had suggested to me that first morning – away from his weather charts, his storm-tube, his leeches and his anemometer. He has spent years accumulating data in this place that, for him, is one great instrument. He knows the earth beneath his feet will be his undoing.

* * *

The first watch was mine and the vista from the lantern was phantasmic. What is usually a crystal frame of sky and sea had been transformed into a case of pale light – white in every aspect, pressing, breathing, against the panes. There was no sense of height or space or distance. The house seemed weightless, airborne. Meanwhile, the suffocating vapour acted on the atmosphere in such a way that the reef was sometimes silent, sometimes echoing spectrally about the tower like someone calling from inaudible distance. The perpetual birds had abandoned us entirely.

The effect inside the lens was yet more disorienting. White magnified. White distilled. White refracted. One had to circle the lamp apparatus only once to lose all sense of compass points.

It was inside the lens, lighting the lamp, that I first became aware of the shadow. Initially, I took it merely for the distortion of the astragals amid concentric rings of glass. But then I noted it was moving even if I was not, always at the periphery of my vision. I turned and it was gone. I focused on the wicks and it flitted darkly about the lantern.

I remembered Mr Spencer's log entry. He had seen something like a figure, but on the balcony rather than in the lantern.

And there it was again. And again.

Whenever I turned to see it, it was gone.

I entered the lantern space around the lens and waited. Nothing. Nothing but the moving disc of light illuminating galactic dusk.

"Oh!"

I started as the shadow erupted from the fog before my very face. It was a great tawny owl, its wings spread wide, its talons open. It gripped the pane's exterior and perched there uneasily, settling itself, its beak tapping gently at the glass. Evidently, it had been caught amid the fog and lost its bearings.

It gazed upon me with its jet-black eyes. A large face. An old man's face. It seemed to want to communicate with me, if only I could interpret the fixity of its stare. It had some urgent message for me. But what should I make of this fabled animal's many contradictions? Presager of death. Protector. Archetype of wisdom and foresight. There was something in its manner... A memory of a man I'd known...

"Mister Meakes? Are you aloft?"

The commissioner.

"Yes, sir. In the lantern. I will come down."

He was panting in the light-room, leaning against the table.

"Is everything all right, sir?"

"Yes, yes. Though it seems I may not be leaving tomorrow if this fog persists."

"Yes, sir."

"I thought I would go out on the balcony. My doctor tells me I should walk to alleviate my gout. I'm not sure I believe him, but..."

"Very well, sir. I will be here in the light-room for another three hours."

He took out his pipe and went to the balcony door, leaving it ajar. There was no wind at all so I did not bolt it in place. Moments later, I smelled his tobacco.

I went back to the lantern but the owl was gone. I waited

for the light to beckon it again, but there was nothing – only the occasional shadow flitting through the fog. Perhaps it would return. I leaned against the panes and took out my book: The Collected Shakespeare. *Macbeth*.

> *It was the owl that shrieked, that fatal bellman*, I read,
> *Which gives the stern'st good-night. The obscure bird*
> */ clamoured the livelong night. / Some say, the earth*
> *was feverous and did shake.*

Regicide. Good King Duncan visits Macbeth's castle as a guest, bestowing gifts and garlands, and is slain without pity in his bedchamber. Macbeth's wife admonishes his horror: *The sleeping and the dead / Are but as pictures; 'tis the eye of childhood / That fears a painted devil.*

I must have read the whole play by the time Mr Adamson came to relieve me. He was his jovial self.

"Meakes? Where are you?"

"Above. In the lantern."

"Well, come down. I don't know why I bother if they're going to take me back to shore. I might as well stay in bed."

"I suppose so."

"You're happy, aren't you? Admit it."

"I should tell you, perhaps, that the commissioner is on the balcony. He went out to smoke and to move his foot, he said."

"He's out there now?"

I nodded.

"Well, I am here. You are relieved. Go to bed or whatever you do with yourself."

I returned my book to the library and went to the bedroom, grateful that it was a quiet night without waves or birds to prevent my rest. It was also an opportunity to continue studying the hidden newspapers for whatever clue they held.

So much information! If a savage from some mid-Pacific isle should find himself in possession of *The Times* or *The Penny Illustrated News*, what must he think of a culture that produced so many words each day? A newspaper is like a net that catches everything with indiscriminate greed, from the cost of coffee to the latest accident. There is enough to send a rational man insane if he were to consider every piece of information significant.

Stout doeskin trousers. Beaver paletots. Rich Genoa vest. Inn to let, Whitsunday next. Very fine Westphalian hams, superior to those shipped at Rotterdam. Rostok, 24th – Tallow dull and low.

Peas, white. Flour, best. Ditto, feed. Messrs Lumsden, Gildawie and Urquhart.

Some wretch with a diabolical intention placed a trunk of workmen's tools on the railway lines. Havre, 5th – cotton brisk...

* * *

I must have fallen asleep, for I awoke on the floor to the light-room whistle. It was blowing in my room and then in the principal's room. Some emergency must have occurred. I took my watch-cloak from its hook and ascended. The principal was already ahead of me on the stairs.

"He's gone," said Mr Adamson. "The commissioner has vanished."

He appeared nervous and was perspiring, though the light-room was always somewhat chill from the open windows.

"Explain," said Principal Bartholomew.

"Meakes said he was out on the balcony smoking, but when I went out there for a... To take a stroll, there was no sign of him."

"Are you sure you didn't miss him in the fog?" said the principal. "It is as dense as I've ever seen it."

Mr Adamson scowled. "Not so dense I'd miss a man of his size in so small a perimeter."

"And he did not come in from the balcony at any time?"

"That's what I'm saying. Unless Meakes is lying..."

"He came up on my watch and went out to smoke," I said. "He was still outside when Mister Adamson relieved me."

"Very well. Very well. We will go out on the balcony. I will take the weather side, you the lee side, Mister Meakes. We will circle to enter the same door we exited. You remain right here, Mister Adamson."

The fog was indeed exceptionally thick, curling lazily and cold on the skin. One could barely see the railing for the milky opacity of it. I walked slowly with my arms outstretched, shuffling my feet over the hob-nailed surface. The fog embraced me and passed through my open fingers. But there was no sign of the commissioner.

"Is it possible," said the principal, "that he returned from the balcony and you simply didn't notice? Perhaps you were reading, Mister Meakes. Perhaps you were sleeping, Mister Adamson."

"I resent that implication," said Adamson.

"I am sure not," I said. "The commissioner tended to pant and grunt. I would have noticed."

"Then there is nothing to do but search the house," said the principal. "I feel sure he is here somewhere."

We descended together. The library was empty. The commissioner's bedroom also was empty, though the door was open. A lamp was lighted within and all appeared normal.

The principal entered his bedroom alone and returned within a moment to say that it was empty. The same was true of mine and Mr Adamson's.

I thought the kitchen was a likely contender, but it, too, held nobody and no sign. The provision store: empty. The coal and oil store: empty.

We three stood finally in the cold dungeon of the water store. It could not be clearer: the commissioner was not inside Ripsaw lighthouse. The principal was paler than usual.

"The main door?" said Mr Adamson. "Maybe he wanted to… I don't know, look at the sea?"

We opened the first door and passed into the vestibule.

We unbolted the great exterior door and beheld a wall of shifting fog.

"Commissioner!" called Mr Adamson.

"Commissioner!" called Principal Bartholomew.

There was a moan: a low and mournful thing, as if a man was lying broken on the reef. There was a groan: half sigh, half expression of pure hopelessness. There was a bubbling snuffle: the last throes of a man slowly drowning face-down in a rock pool.

The sounds seemed to come from the air rather than the sea – spirits caught and lost in aether. After reading *Macbeth*, I felt the black chill of witchcraft breathing at my neck. Would the gore-dripping commissioner's head appear bobbing at our feet?

"That sound. It is his ghost!" I said, unwittingly.

"No, Meakes," said the principal. "That is the seals' call."

"But where is the commissioner?"

"We must assume he has fallen from the balcony," said the principal. "The boat will come tomorrow morning to collect him. I will have to write a report."

He appeared as horror-stricken as the Thane of Glamis (now of Cawdor). In the fog's pallid luminescence, we three might have been a coven casting spells. The great lighthouse tower was a massive shadow rearing upwards, we at its darkest extremity.

TWELVE

I have slept hardly a wink for thinking about the commissioner's disappearance. There is a tense and brittle atmosphere within the house. Principal Bartholomew keeps saying, "There will be dire consequences. There will be dire consequences."

The search did not end last night. Like a confused old relative who pats his pockets again and again for a tobacco pouch that is not there, we went up and down the lighthouse in the futile hope of finding that corpulent man. When one has looked in all of the places something should be, one has no choice but to look where it should not be. Sherlock Holmes said something along those lines. This morning, I caught Mr Adamson peering into a kitchen cupboard and we both recognised the absurdity.

We agreed that as soon as the light permitted, and if the fog had lifted, we would scan the reef with telescopes for any sign of the commissioner. Such a thought was ridiculous, of course. The scouring tides would not permit even his weight to remain atop the rocks.

Well, the fog has indeed cleared and the sea is a field of lead. The three of us have been circling the balcony in vain. Principle Bartholomew has not raised the signal ball, indicating that all is not well at the house. It was unnecessary. The cutter is coming out regardless to collect the commissioner. We watch it approach even now. Principal Bartholomew knows he will have to tell them what has happened.

* * *

Mr Adamson and I descended the ladder to secure the cutter's ropes.

"Where is the commissioner?" called the skipper from the foredeck.

"He is not here," said the principal at the door.

"What do you mean?"

"He has vanished. We... We cannot find him in the lighthouse."

"Vanished? Did you say *vanished*?"

"He has gone. Perhaps he fell..."

The skipper turned and spoke to one of his crew. It seemed as if he was corroborating what he thought he had heard.

"The commissioner is dead?" he called, finally.

"I cannot say... We cannot find him. We must assume..."

Glances were exchanged. The first mate approached the skipper and said something we couldn't hear. The skipper nodded.

"The commissioner's documents," he called. "A leather case. Can you fetch it?"

"I will go!"

We waited, Mr Adamson and I, as the principal ascended to the commissioner's room. The boat rocked. The reef hissed and gurgled. The straining ropes dripped. We felt the accusing stares of the crew upon us – we who had accepted the esteemed guest into our house and carelessly lost him to the void.

At the same time, we knew what details were in that leather case: my muriate of morphia; Mr Adamson's return to land; whatever it was that had made the principal so worried. Even if the commissioner did not return, his verdicts would. Then another cutter would come at the first opportunity with replacements and retribution.

I am sure we thought the same: a keeper may be lost like a handkerchief or an umbrella. A slip from the rocks. A gust from the balcony. Asphyxiation in the privy. Such things happen in the lighthouse service. But a commissioner? That cannot happen. That must entail an investigation and penalties.

The principal appeared at the door. There was a hectic cast to his face. His white hair was stuck to his forehead with perspiration.

"The case?" called the skipper.

"I can't find it. It's not in his room. It is not anywhere. Perhaps he had it with him when…"

The skipper shrugged. He had done his job. Now the Commission would take up the matter. The headquarters in London and Edinburgh would become involved. Our names would be discussed in chambers.

But the light had to keep burning. That was the first rule. We would have to stay at the house until a solution was found. The light was our sanctuary. It needed us and, for the time being, we needed it.

* * *

"Where is that case?" said the principal.

We were in the library. The cutter was still visible between the lighthouse and the shore.

"He must have had it with him," said Mr Adamson.

"Mister Meakes?" said the principal.

"Yes, sir."

"Did the commissioner have his case with him when he arrived in the light-room last night?"

"No, sir. I am sure he would not have been able to climb the stairs with it. I believe Mister Adamson carried it when the Commissioner first arrived at the house."

"That's true. I did."

"Very well. Then there is but a single conclusion: one of you two took it."

"What?" said Mr Adamson.

"Sir… I can assure you—"

"Mister Meakes – you had an opportunity to enter the

commissioner's room after your watch. He left his door unlocked. Mister Adamson – you had an opportunity to take the case when I was on my watch."

"And *you*?" said Mr Adamson. "What were *you* doing while we two were on our watches?"

"I am the principal of this house—"

"Where were *you*?"

"—and I will not have my integrity questioned by you, Mister Adamson."

"Then let us consider motive if integrity is not the question. Perhaps the commissioner wanted you to return to shore—"

"I will not discuss the private matter of my meeting with him."

"And you don't want to return to shore duty. Or to retire."

"So… So what do you suggest happened, Mister Adamson? That I took his case and tossed it out of the window? Why? He could simply have rewritten his notes. I had no clue that he had gone missing. *That* happened on your watches. Hence, there was no advantage in my taking the case."

"Who says it was taken while the commissioner was aloft?" said Mr Adamson.

"I beg your pardon?"

"Who's to say that you didn't take the case after his disappearance was discovered? We were looking for his body when we searched the house – not for his case. In the confusion, you had many opportunities to dispose of his notes. Or perhaps it occurred to you to hide them when you went up to get them for the skipper."

"And you, Mister Adamson? What did those notes say about *your* situation?"

"That's a confidential matter."

"No, it is not. As Principal of this lighthouse, I had to countersign the commissioner's recommendation that *you* be taken to shore as soon as a replacement could come and that you be released from the lighthouse service as someone entirely unfitted for the responsibility."

"What about *him*?" said Mr Adamson, jerking a thumb at me. "He's very quiet all of a sudden. What did the commissioner write about *him*?"

"He… Well, he said he was pleased with my work," I said.

"He was asking questions about your family. He had his suspicions."

"You were listening at the door?" I said.

Principal Bartholomew turned fully to Mr Adamson. "Or you read about it in the notes. Either way, you have now incriminated yourself."

"He had illicit morphia," said Mr Adamson. "I discovered it and told the commissioner. I didn't read about *that* in any notes. I know it for a fact."

We stood staring at each other. The cutter was now a mere dot on the sea. The herring gulls laughed their manic, staccato laugh.

"The morphia," I said. "Perhaps that is the solution to this mystery."

"Explain yourself," said the principal.

"I gave the bottle to the commissioner. What if… What if he took it with him to the balcony? What if he, not knowing the dosage, took too much and… I don't know, toppled from the railing?"

"A man of his size?" scoffed Mr Adamson. "He would have to climb over it. He could barely climb the stairs!"

"Wait one moment," said the principal. "Mister Meakes may have something here."

"You mean an alibi?" said Mr Adamson.

"How long was the commissioner on the balcony, Mister Meakes?"

"I couldn't say for sure, sir. I lose track of time when I am reading."

"Convenient," said Mr Adamson.

"But he did not return for the whole of your watch," said the principal.

"That's right, sir."

"Then he could have been outside for almost four hours. Perhaps even longer because he did not return during Mister Adamson's watch."

"Or he fell from the railing within minutes of venturing out," I said. "It would have been easy to become disoriented in the fog."

"My question," said Mr Adamson, "is why Meakes wasn't at all concerned when the commissioner went out but didn't return for four hours. That strikes me as very suspicious."

"One could say the same of you," said the principal. "How long did *you* wait before going on to the balcony? Did it not strike *you* as odd that the commissioner had been out there for so long?"

"Meakes was the last to see him alive," said Adamson, folding his arms.

"Or so we assume," said the principal. "The fact that Meakes was the last person to see the commissioner appears to inculpate him, but how do we know that you didn't converse with him out on the balcony? Perhaps an altercation took place..."

"You're determined to see me hang for this, Bartholomew!"

"Why did you go out on the balcony? And don't tell me you were looking for ships. There was nothing to see last night."

"I went out to relieve myself, all right? I know you frown on that, but what are we supposed to do if we can't leave the light-room?"

"You should visit the privy before your watch. I have been quite clear on—"

"Can't you accept that accidents happen? How many men have died here just this year? In fact... In fact, let us consider *that* for a moment! Who has been the constant presence at Ripsaw while all those other keepers died? Losing one keeper might be an accident. Two an unfortunate occurrence. But three? Perhaps more that we don't know about. And now the commissioner? If there's a pattern to be found, if there's one common factor in all of these deaths, it stands before us now!"

"That is quite ridiculous. You are demonstrating exactly the kind of histrionics that unfit you for this work."

I thought Mr Adamson would strike the principal. His arms were raised and tense. His face was flushed a terrible scarlet. He could be a violent man. Prone to outbursts.

If the principal was afraid, he did not show it. More than a decade at Ripsaw had made him regent here. He did not yield to the battering elements and he did not yield to the storms of Mr Adamson.

"I have a suggestion," he said. "Let us search for this bottle of morphia. If it is not to be found in the commissioner's room, or between his room and the balcony, then we may entertain Mister Meakes' version of events. I must write a report. We must have all the facts to hand."

"And the missing notes?" said Mr Adamson. "That fact points to the guilt of someone in this house. How can we know if that same person hasn't also concealed the bottle of morphia?"

He was looking at me as he said it.

"There are a few certainties," said the principal. "I would not like to think that one of us here is guilty, but there are unanswered questions, which will be answered sooner or later. None of us is leaving the house. We are all detained here as the Commission makes its deliberations on shore. When they are ready, they will come with more questions, and whoever is not telling the truth will be found out. I leave you both to think about that."

"As should you," said Mr Adamson.

* * *

Of course, we looked for the bottle of morphia. Of course, we did not find it. It had disappeared as certainly as had the leather note-case and the commissioner himself.

The plan devised by the principal was that we would search the lighthouse chamber by chamber – one man looking and the other two observing him to ensure that he did not covertly discover, or attempt to discard, the bottle.

I was allocated the kitchen: an onerous task due to the quantity and variety of things within it. I dirtied my hands looking in the coal depot and inside the warm ash bucket. I diligently removed the contents of the cupboards and laid them on the table so that we could all witness the empty space within.

And as I laboured at this futile task, I found my mind working at the puzzles of the crockery and cutlery. Why twenty-one flat plates but only four cups? Were plates more likely to break than cups? And why so many plates? Even if a ship was wrecked and we had to take in a crew of dripping mariners, the lighthouse could barely support eighteen of them. They would have to share their cups.

Why eleven knives? Did the Commission assume that so many would be lost or go blunt? We also have twelve wine glasses and two carafes, but I have never seen a bottle of wine at Ripsaw. I could, and can, see no logic behind these provisions. It is as if the Commission has dressed a theatrical set – an imaginary scene – based on lists of perceived necessities. The house, for them, is a mere concept, a distant El Dorado. The realm of Prester John. It exists only on a sea chart and in the columns of financial accounts. Its physical reality to those on shore is notional and the souls within it mere names upon a list. We are the *dramatis personae* and this tower the Battlements of Elsinore.

I was on my knees with dusty cuffs, retrieving five cast-iron goblets (for medieval banqueting?) when I saw the writing at the back of the cupboard. It was the same hand as the message in the privy, but scribbled apparently in charcoal on the bare stone blocks. Whoever had written it must have been crouching half inside the cupboard as I was at that moment. *Lord, deliver me from this dark knowledge.* I must have paused or jerked.

"Do you see something?" said the principal.

"No, sir. Just a shadow. The cupboard is quite empty."

"Then let us continue."

We continued. I wondered if perhaps the other two were also seeing similar messages but saying nothing.

* * *

I sit now in the library, which has become my habitual sanctuary. It is light and dissimulates the comforts of home, though perhaps not as convincingly as the commissioner's room. At night, before or after my watch, I find the gentle hum of the revolving mechanism quite soothing.

The books, too, are a place to visit. I have been reading *Robinson Crusoe* again. It is one of those stories that seems to change between readings, as if Defoe has been redrafting and inserting passages in my absence. Each page has something to make one pause and cogitate on its truth, fantasy though the whole thing must surely be:

The fear of danger is ten thousand times more terrifying than danger itself, when apparent to the eyes; and we find the burden of anxiety greater by much than the evil which we are anxious about...

It is never quite the way I remember it.

THIRTEEN

The cutter has not come out again. We live in a limbo of expectation and mutual distrust. One of us is guilty – at the very least of theft and dishonesty. At worst, of murder. There is little doubt in my mind that Mr Adamson is the culprit. He has the most to lose. He is the character most prone to crime. The principal clearly agrees with me.

Still, not one of us awaits the cutter with enthusiasm. I have become accustomed to my fellow keepers and would prefer not to have to acquaint myself with two new men, both of them superior in rank and experience. Thus, there exists an unsteady equilibrium at Ripsaw, in which we wait and wait for judgement.

It would be mostly bearable but for the mealtimes, which can be awkward. Principal Bartholomew has insisted that we adhere to the regulations as if nothing had happened and nothing is about to happen. That means cleaning the lens and lamp every morning. It means emptying the ash and following the cooking rota. It means wearing the uniform on Sundays and participating in the service charade. And it means eating together even if barely a word is shared.

The situation is altogether absurd, but I understand the method in the principal's madness. We could so easily slide into chaos and confrontation. The house's rules and rituals provide a sort of order, no matter how flimsy and ephemeral it may seem. The lamp is lighted every evening and extinguished at first light. Each drop of oil is recorded, each degree of temperature logged. That is our function and we fulfil it. How long may we prolong retribution if we continue with this fealty?

I spoke with the principal amid the dull acoustics and glistening aromas of the coal store.

"I am certain," he said, slowly sweeping stone, "that the matter is being taken very seriously at the Commission."

"Has such a thing happened before, sir?"

"I can recall only one previous instance of a commissioner dying at a lighthouse." The broom paused. "On that occasion, the intemperate fellow had demanded a boat come to collect him rather than spend another night in the tower. The waves were too high to go aboard and so he was winched there by the lighthouse crane. It is a common enough procedure, but a rope snapped or the tackle buckled. He fell into the surf, there to be smashed against the rocks and drowned."

"How terrible. But I suppose... I suppose it had been the commissioner's fault."

"The ensuing investigation absolved all keepers and crew of blame. As you suggest, the commissioner had insisted – despite warnings from those concerned."

"Quite so."

"That is patently not the case here. There will be convocations and deliberations in the Commission's panelled rooms. Explanations must be given. Examples must be made. Names must be written."

And so we wait.

The weather has worsened somewhat. It could be the moon's waxing or the oncoming winter, but the waves are spirited and a strong wind has been blowing from the south east. Billows strike the lighthouse and rattle the cutlery. The shore is often lost in spray. This also means we cannot get out on to the rock to fish, and that the majority of birds remain on shore. My bowels are becoming blocked with a diet of salt beef and sprouting potatoes.

I was in the library this afternoon, ostensibly reading but in reality daydreaming. Something – the reef's interminable gossip? The herring gull's manic cry that so resembles both laughter and sobbing? – set me thinking about Mr Fowler's house and the gentlemen who lived there. I had known them all.

There was small, grey Parkinson and his fear of open spaces. Even a room was too great an expanse for him to bear. He slept in a converted wardrobe and passed his afternoons in the garden whittling or carving in a private enclosure, surrounded by a hedge. Curiously enough, the great vault of the sky caused him no discomfort, only the peopled world.

There was the demi-giant Mayhew, who sought constantly to tear his skin with teeth or nails or by abrasion. He could easily be distracted with a game of chess or an afternoon of watercolours, but, if idle, would not be happy until he bled. Mr Fowler had a quilted suit made for Mayhew, with a high collar and with elegant gloves to match.

Cuthbert was afraid of poisoning and insisted that every meal was tasted before he ate. Even then, he was quite often racked with vomiting, convinced the fatal venom had passed into his blood. Poor Cuthbert. He was a pale frame of bones and sorry eyes.

And Tibbotson, of course: tiny, quaking Tibbotson who could be roused to fury at the merest provocation. A tinkling teaspoon in a cup. A repetitive cough. Bread cut in irregular slices.

Some heard voices as real as the ones around them. One ate his own faeces. All were fugitives from shame, all alienated, all cast out.

Mr Fowler welcomed them. Not for him cold showers, beatings and restraints. Not for him bloodletting and trepanning. He set his gentlemen to work according to their infirmity. Growing vegetables. Carpentry. Embroidery. If a man had aggression to spare, he could be put to work with a hammer or saw and pour his anger into construction. If a man was stricken by voluntary muteness, he could master the piano. For every man, a distraction that might cure. For every man, a reason to avoid the reefs and sandbanks of his mind.

There was a gentleman, indeed, very like the commissioner. He, too, was corpulent and red-faced with tight blond curls. Trelawny was his name, or Trevithick. He was prone to eat all sorts of things, none of which were alimentary. Coal. Soil. A broken terracotta plant pot. Unfortunate Trevithick (or Trelawny) fell to his death from an upper storey, for what reason nobody was able to discern. His body, so large in life, turned slowly and seemed smaller as it fell, his hands grasping at the air as if he might get hold of it. He didn't scream, perhaps through terror. Nor did his body make any audible impact, muffled as it was by suffocating fog.

Mr Fowler used to say that the great majority of men harbour their eccentricities, large or small. Only circumstance decides whether they wax or wane. Adversity, sorrow, grief – anything may provoke the change. Or a man may live his whole life and never know the quirk that resides inside him.

* * *

I went into the principal's room tonight while he was on his watch. Mr Adamson was sleeping after his watch. It is exciting to explore a previously unmapped chamber of the house. It reminds me of the dream I often had as a child that there existed a room in the house – an attic or a cellar – that contained all the things I dreamed of. A rocking horse. Building blocks. All the books I could possibly read. But the location of this room was only clear in dreams, and even then subject to the strange oneiric geography in which walls move and doors just opened cease to exist in the next moment.

There are many books in the principal's room, most of them about weather. I was delighted to find that he, too, keeps a journal, in which he notes the progress with his grand scheme to devise a storm prognostication system. Not only this, apparently, but he also intends to improve the way that storms are categorised.

There are systems already in existence, it seems, but these are flawed or subject to many variables. Denham calls 49–69 miles per hour a Great Storm, while for Lind a violent hurricane is precisely 109 miles per hour. Rouse claims that a wind of 110 miles per hour will throw down buildings. The Beaufort scale, meanwhile, measures storms according to the maritime world. Thus, a moderate wind is that which permits a vessel to set all sails without peril, while a strong gale requires triple-reefed topsails.

But this (the principal notes) depends much on the kind of vessel in question – how much sail it can carry, how fast it is going and in which direction. How does one measure wind if the instrument itself is moving? For this reason, Principal Bartholomew insists that a fixed object at sea – a lighthouse – is the only way to adequately measure wind speed and force.

He has volumes and volumes of weather recordings: wind, temperature, pressure, rainfall, cloud patterns, lunar movements, stellar observations. Ten years of figures are listed here, and not only for Ripsaw. There are annual rainfall figures from lighthouses and shore stations around the country: Caithness (33 inches), Orkney (45 inches), Lewis (70 inches and 237 days of rain). The pages are rain themselves – pouring numeric columns, puddling totals, swirling calculations and equation cloudbursts wherein mere water seeks impossible form.

I wonder what Mr Fowler would have prescribed in this case? Long walks on the moor, perhaps. No pen or paper permitted.

There is also among these papers the principal's own notes from his conversation with the commissioner: discussions they had about the lighthouse and the keepers. Here, I read that the Commission is especially preoccupied about the number of accidents at Ripsaw – more than at any other house in the past ten years.

It is common for such things to be reported in the local press and soon forgotten, but it seems that one or two of the national sheets have seen a pattern and begun to question the Commission's intent in imperilling the lives of men in such a way. It is mere cant, of course; the lighthouse saves more lives than it costs. Still, some editors are calling it the Fatal Tower and writing sensational pieces accompanied by dark and brooding etchings. (I must check the library.)

I read also that Mr Adamson has a history of drinking on duty and that he attempted to strike a principal during a previous posting onshore. He has also been known to bully fellow keepers. How he has remained in the service is a mystery.

I admit that I quite lost account of the time, so absorbed was I by all of this new material. I was, therefore, unpleasantly surprised when a shadow appeared in the doorway. Mr Adamson.

"Meakes? What in [the Lord's name] are you doing in here?"

"I… Was looking for the principal."

"In his drawers? In his books? Liar. You know he's on watch."

"I accidentally knocked something to the floor. I was picking it up."

"You're sitting! What is that you're reading?"

"Nothing… Just some notes…"

"Let me see… Give it to me."

"No…"

He snatched the paper and stared at it. He saw his own name. "Reading about me, are you?"

"Purely accidentally. I—"

"Have you been looking in *my* drawers as well?"

"Of course not!"

"I knew there was something odd about you, Meakes. I knew it from the start. You're furtive. Evasive. You were in gaol – admit it."

"I was not."

"You were. I've seen the scars on your wrist and your back. From the restraints. From the beatings. You were in irons. Admit it. And that business with the hand-crank – that is my proof. I saw your reaction well enough. You've been in a solitary cell condemned to hard punishment. Admit it."

"I have not."

"It was you: the commissioner's disappearance, his notes. The morphia. It was all you. I'm going to Bartholomew right now."

"You can't... You shouldn't disturb him on his watch."

"He'll want to hear this."

"Then maybe he will want to hear about the newspapers under your mattress."

His mouth was quite agape. "What newspapers?"

"The three newspapers you took from the library. I know they contain your secret."

"What are you talking about, Meakes? What secret?"

"Something you did on shore in August."

"And what did I do in August, Meakes, that is written in the newspapers?"

"*You* know what."

"I am going to the principal."

"No!"

"Let go of me, Meakes. I will knock you senseless, I swear!"

"Yes, yes... That's your way, isn't it? You bully!"

It was futile to struggle with him. He is a much stronger man. But I found some reserve of strength and I would not release his wrist though he tossed me about like a handkerchief.

"*WHAT* is going on here?"

Principal Bartholomew was standing in the doorway. His face was a squall about to break.

"He was in your room," said Mr Adamson. "Looking through your things."

"Do you realise I have had to abandon my watch to intervene in your childish conflict?"

"But, sir—" attempted Mr Adamson.

"*You* go to your room and stay there until your next watch. *You*, Mister Meakes, will go to the library. You will sleep there until the cutter next comes out. It seems you two cannot live together. Out. Out of my room."

Out, damned spot! Out, I say! Hell is murky!

"But don't you see, sir?" attempted Mr Adamson.

"Go. Both of you. I will not leave the lamp another moment for this nonsense."

Mr Adamson dropped the principal's notes on the table and passed me with a brutal shoulder shove. "Wait until tomorrow," he muttered.

Tomorrow, and tomorrow, and tomorrow.

I went shame-faced to the library, knowing that Mr Adamson would soon be looking through my private things in retribution.

* * *

I now sit in the light-room on my watch. It is dark and the beam casts its light to the horizon. The wind moans about the column and the waves thump for our attention. It has become colder.

I feel somehow more at ease within the influence of lamp and lens. Its coursing prismatic sparks and blue-green reflections are not quite of this earthly world. They are Genesiac sprites caught in glass. And yet there remains a ball of agitation in my breast. This apprenticeship at Ripsaw has not proceeded at all as I'd hoped for. Where is the peace? Where is the comfort of routine?

I do not want to succumb to self-pity. That is a terrible hole to fall into. Therein, one sees the world as from the bottom of a well: a tiny circle of light through which all is miniature and indistinct. Shadows only. *That* is undoubtedly a prison, that column of darkness in whose depths one thrashes to stay afloat.

I wish that Mr Fowler were here. He would talk to me in calm and rational tones. He would go through his usual catechism.

What is it you fear?
Why do you fear it so?
What should you avoid?
How should you behave?
What effect will this produce?
Will you be better then?
I fear him.
Because I do not understand him.
Hectic thoughts and overstimulation.
With tranquillity, honesty and reason.
Calmness and clarity of vision.
Experience tells me so. I believe so. I hope so.

FOURTEEN

Today, I woke for the first time in the library and for the briefest of moments I thought myself at home. The real bed, the carpet and the stucco ceiling persuaded me so. The books on the shelves. The heavy wooden chairs. I lay there and I thought: *this* is the secret room I dreamed of as a child – the room that exists just for me.

It was preternaturally quiet. No birds. No reef. No wind. The windows were thick with condensation and showed only rectangles of white. I deduced more fog. We were hidden again. Enwraithed. Invisible to the Commission and to the world.

On rising, however, I saw I had been mistaken. It was snowing: a steady fall of fat, feathery flakes as dense as any fog but far more soothing. I must have stood at the open window for minutes watching the icy down descending to the slate-grey sea. My legs became quite chilled as I followed individual flakes from sooty silhouette to salty inundation. This was another day that the boat could not come out to Ripsaw – another day that we would wait unknowing, anticipating.

And I wondered: is there not something of religion in our suspended state of being? We answer to a higher power that exists in a place we cannot know or see. We obediently follow its rules and regulations and hope to avoid its wrathful retribution. It controls us through our observance of its rituals and we live in expectation of some sign, some indication that our observance has been noted. But we are so far, so terribly far away. We are the sole arbiters of our own actions and decisions. In truth, is not the real world here at Ripsaw and everything beyond it mere imagination?

* * *

Principal Bartholomew is very angry after yesterday's argument. He said at breakfast that he will not hear our versions of events because that would only stir more resentment. I agree with him. He says that we are both equally responsible. He has also fitted a hasp and padlock to his door.

I spent the morning with him cleaning the lamp and the lens – work we did almost totally in silence. The lantern was quite magical with the snow swirling all about outside. We might have been travelling through the clouds many miles above the earth. Inside the lens, it appeared that the very sky was disintegrating into shards of light.

"Did you enter my room as Mister Adamson accuses?" said the principal. Clearly, he *did* want to hear my version.

"I did, sir… But with no dishonest intent. The door was open – I don't know why – and I saw your leeches in their jar. I suppose I was intrigued."

He did not look at me. He continued wordlessly polishing the glass.

"And I saw all of your books on weather measurement and… Well, my grandfather was something of a weather enthusiast. He knew many traditional sayings and predictors."

Still he polished with great intent, but he was listening.

"He kept leeches also. I recall that he changed the water every few days."

"Rainwater?"

"Of course, sir. He measured rainfall, too."

"Do you remember any of his proverbs?"

"Let me see… *When rise begins after low, squalls expect and clear blow.* He was one of the first men to take an interest in the barometer."

The principal smiled.

I said: "*When rain comes before wind, halyard sheets and braces mind*. That was another one of his."

He stopped his polishing. "I have another one for you: *Long foretold, long last; short notice, soon past*."

"Have you found a pattern, sir? Have you seen what will come?"

"It is almost more art than science, Meakes. The numbers tell their story, but a man must observe the elements themselves. They speak to us more eloquently."

"Have you seen something?"

"The clouds. They are ephemeral, but their forms may be read in conjunction with the moon, with the tides, with the barometer's fluctuations."

"And this is why you cannot leave Ripsaw – because you work is not completed… Because you cannot complete it on land…"

"Who told you I am leaving Ripsaw?"

"Nobody. I mean… Mister Adamson intimated to me that you might be leaving."

"I have no plans to leave, Mister Meakes. Keeper Adamson speaks from his own desires."

"No, sir. I didn't mean to… This snow is rather unseasonable, no?"

"It comes early this year, yes."

"Is it a sign?"

"It may be. We will see."

There was something sphinx-like in the set of his mouth that said he knew more than he would say.

"Principal… Do you think that London and Edinburgh knew about the commissioner's recommendations? And about the subjects of his interviews?"

"In my experience, they know everything. They know how many hairs are on your head. There is no escaping their attention."

I smiled and quoted: "*But even the very hairs of your head are all numbered. Fear not therefore: ye are of more value than many sparrows.*"

He paused his polishing once more. "You have a facility for feats of memory. I wonder why we find you here, rubbing brass and copper with a linen rag."

"It is an accidental talent, sir. It costs me no effort. Indeed, I sometimes regret the noise it creates inside my mind."

"You have an unsettled mind, Mister Meakes?"

"No, sir. I have not explained myself. It's just that, well, I am drawn to words and tend to remember them whether I wish to or not. Sometimes... And you, sir? Do you like to read?"

"I like to learn. I would rather read an encyclopaedia than a novel. Much time may be wasted on stories. They unfit the mind and dull our purpose. They make us daydreamers." He applied more pressure to a spot, rubbing away imagination.

"I suppose you are right, sir."

"You have the makings of a good keeper, Mister Meakes."

"Thank you, sir."

"You might even be a principal one day."

I am thane of Glamis; but how of Cawdor? And to be king stands not within the prospect of belief.

"Perhaps, sir. Perhaps so."

He stopped polishing and looked at me. "Do not attempt to enter my room again."

"No, sir."

* * *

Something remarkable has just occurred. I was down at the main door emptying the ash bucket when I heard the clink of glass. There was a bottle bobbing in a rock pool below and I was amazed to see that there appeared to be a piece of paper inside it.

The air was frigid. My breath was vaporous about my face. The exposed parts of the reef were dusted with snow. I laid the ash bucket to one side and looked at the ladder, whose every rung was sheathed in filmy ice. But my curiosity outweighed my common sense. I descended to the rock.

The sea was only beginning to recede and the surface was still awash with writhing weeds that coiled serpent-like about my boots. I knew the danger of my actions. A slip, an errant wave, and I would be the next Ripsaw keeper added to the list of the missing.

The pale-green bottle was square with a stubby neck and a half-inserted cork. It was tapping gently at the perimeter of its pool but could be washed away at any moment by the ebbing tide. I knelt in miry slime and felt the freezing water soak my trousers, my jacket cuffs. The bottle spun on its horizontal axis, mischievously evading my grasp. There was certainly a roll of paper within it.

I snatched at the neck and pulled it dripping from the pool. It appeared to be one of the self-same bottles I had seen in the provision store containing vinegar. I thrust it inside my jacket and returned to the ladder before anyone could note my tardiness in returning.

Naturally, the urge to open the bottle message and read it was almost irresistible, but two other souls inhabit this place. I knew that my only assurance of privacy, without observation or interruption, would be my watch. I would have to wait the whole day before opening my prize!

I bolted the main door. I closed the inner vestibule door. I ascended the stone staircase to the oil store. Where? Where might I hide the bottle?

Following our search for the commissioner's notes and the missing morphia, the lighthouse seemed to have very few hiding places. We all knew where a thing might be secreted. We had uncovered every possible hiding place. But something novel occurred to me as I passed the provision store.

Why not simply put the message bottle alongside the others of its ilk: behind the others but of the group. Nobody would be using vinegar today. Even if someone did take a bottle, they would take the first available one. Accordingly,

I rearranged the bottles and placed mine at the back. Its cork stood a little higher than the others so I used my pocketknife to trim it flush against the neck. Then to wait…

I can barely tolerate the anticipation. Twice, I have been back to the provision store on some imagined errand to check the bottle. I have even thought about moving it to somewhere more concealed. Inside an oil cistern? But one never knows when the principle will do his rounds with the measuring rod.

And I wonder feverishly who tossed the bottle to the waves. Keeper Spencer before his carbonic oxide asphyxiation? The commissioner as he circled the fog-bound balcony? Those other, nameless, men who toppled from the pediment? Which one kept a secret so momentous that he could share it only with the wayward sea?

Or perhaps the bottle is nothing more than an experiment of the principal's to measure tides and currents round the reef. Captains and hydrographers have also been known to cast a bottle to the ocean to see where ludic Zephyrus or Boreas will blow it. I must prepare myself for the disappointment that the slip of paper contains nothing more than time, date and co-ordinates.

Meanwhile, the snow continues heavy and relentless. On shore, it will be accumulating on walls and lawns and hedges, transforming the landscape into gentle curves. Naked trees will rake the sky. Bushes will bow and sag beneath the weight. But here nothing settles. The sea swallows all. The heavens may empty a blizzard upon us and the only sign is on the balcony or perhaps a windowsill. The lighthouse weathers all, mocking the winds, impervious to rain, slaked with clotted spume – pristine in its triumph.

* * *

I write this only after drinking two large mugs of tea, my fingers wrapped about the mug to quiet my stiff and shaking hands. It started when Principal Bartholomew asked me to sweep the balcony for some reason known only to himself. Dusk was approaching and the snow was falling without pause. It would have made much more sense to wait until morning.

I dutifully put on my watch-cloak and took the broom out to face four inches of heavy, wet snow that adhered to the balcony as if it were afraid to be swept into the void. All the time I laboured, more snow fell: wetting my cheeks, blighting my eyes and dampening my shoulders even through the thick wool. Here was the labour of Sisyphus made real as I circled and circled the lighthouse.

The light of day was almost gone when I saw a shadow at the periphery of my vision. I turned but it was gone. I leaned the brush against the wall and walked to where I'd seen it. This time, the blur occurred in just the spot I'd left the brush: a formless silhouette perhaps half a grown man's height.

"Mister Adamson? Is that you?"

I knew that he was on first watch and would be in the light-room at that very moment. It would not be at all surprising if he wanted to alarm or irritate me. If he had seen Mr Spencer's watch-log entry…

"Did you call for me, Meakes?" He was standing at the door.

"No… I thought I saw something."

"Saw what?"

"Nothing. You. I don't know…"

He looked at me, his lips pursed in disgust. "Anyway. I need you to do something. Bring your broom."

I shook the snow from my cloak, stamped my boots clear of it and went inside.

"Come with me," he said. "No – bring the broom."

"But…"

I followed him up into the lantern, in which the map had been lit and the lens was slowly revolving.

"Look at that," he said, pointing to the accumulation of snow on the weather-side panes. "You'll need to go out on the parapet and clear the snow. If not, it will block the beam."

"Out there?" I looked at the parapet: barely a foot of metal mesh around the lantern, above the balcony.

"Well, you can't reach it from below."

"But… It's *your* watch, not mine. Why don't *you* go out?"

His chest went out. "Are you disobeying an order from your direct superior, Meakes?"

"It's dark and the metal is slippery with ice."

"Have you forgotten the purpose of our work here? If the panes are thick with snow, the light will simply reflect back into the lantern. What if there is a ship at that precise point on the horizon?"

I looked again at the parapet. Each external astragal node had a hand-ring support. I had already seen the principal using them.

"Well?" said Mr Adamson.

I felt hot the tears of fear and blinked them away. I tried to recall the words of Mr Fowler. Face your fears; they are worse in anticipation than in reality. Had I not also read something similar in Defoe? Mr Adamson *expected* me to fail. This was my duty and I followed my duty more faithfully than he did.

"Very well," I said.

A section of triangular panes opened inwards to allow access to the parapet. The glass was quite thick with snow. I unbolted it and crouched to go out. Snow entered on the freezing wind.

"Quick!" said Mr Adamson. "We don't want moisture inside."

The night's ice-speckled emptiness and the sea yawned before me. A fall of two hundred feet would kill me as surely as it had killed the commissioner. I was dizzy at the thought of it.

"Meakes! The snow."

I stepped out on to the parapet and groped blindly for the nearest ring. My back faced the void. I felt it pulling at me, willing me to slip, to topple, to plummet. Too afraid to scream.

Rigid with shock and surprise as the sea rushed suddenly to smash me.

My breath steamed the pane before my face and billowed all about me, but I could see Mr Adamson miming that I should clear the snow. He had closed the section. Was this his plan? That I would lose feeling in my hands... Then my balance?

I gripped the ring with one hand and held myself almost fully against the lantern. Without looking down, I swiped clumsily with the broom, not even looking to see if the snow was coming off. The beam of light swept slowly past me and illuminated flocculent air: a million floating pieces caught startled in a dark solution. And at each pass of the lens, Mr Adamson became a darkened statue watching me.

Perhaps one third of the lower lantern was clogged with snow. I cleared the first section and looked for the next hand ring. Though less than two feet distant, it seemed two yards. I would have to release my hold on one and reach for the next, momentarily unsupported.

The night gaped. All was air and gravity. I removed my hand from the ring, barely uncurling chilled fingers, and reached slowly in front of myself –away from the glass, towards the drop! – to grasp the other ring. I shuffled my feet, dislodging snow.

Inside the lantern, Mr Adamson watched.

The cold had now quite soaked through my clothes and into my bones. I felt heavy. Weary. The bristles squeaked at the panes. My knees were locked rigid at a half-bend. It would have been so easy to just drop the broom, let go release the ring and fall. The air would embrace me. The snow's soft down would cushion me and permit me no harm.

I looked through the misted glass and saw the dark figure of Mr Adamson. But there was now a *second*, smaller figure standing behind him. All was indistinct. I didn't have a free hand to wipe the glass.

The smaller figure seemed to raise an arm as if to strike. There was some instrument in his hand. A hammer? A knife?

I banged on the pane with the broom handle.

"Mister Adamson! Behind you!"

I slipped. My fingers were too numb to hold on to the ring. I saw the parapet rushing towards my face…

"Meakes! Meakes! What are you doing?"

Mr Adamson was leaning half out of the lantern and tugging at my arm. Cold metal was hard against my cheek. I tasted copper. I realised with a nauseating rush that I was lying on the parapet, one leg swinging into nothingness.

"Come closer to the door! Meakes! Can you hear me?"

"What… What happened?"

"You fell. Here – take my hand. Drop the broom. Drop it!"

I heard it clatter on the balcony. I crawled along the parapet towards him, the mesh biting into my knees. Snow flecked my eyes.

"Careful… That's right, Meakes… Almost there."

He gave a tremendous tug and I was dragged into the lantern. I heard but did not see the door close.

"What's wrong with you, Meakes? You can't be jumping around on the parapet like that."

"I thought I saw…"

"Saw what, lad? You're quite chilled to the bone. And it looks like you've bitten your tongue. You need to get yourself down to the kitchen and drink a good hot cup of tea with plenty of sugar. Can you walk?"

"I think so."

"Well. Off with you. Your watch starts in three hours."

Thus, I sit in the library having drunk my two mugs of hot tea. My tongue stings doubly for having bitten it in my fall and having burned it with the tea. I have changed my clothes and heat is returning to my body.

I am struck by the fact of Mr Adamson saving my life. He could have left me to freeze to death on the parapet, or waited for me to roll into the sea. I have seen almost no sign of kindness from him in all my time at Ripsaw and yet he pulled me into warmth and light from darkness.

In a matter of thirty minutes, I will reclaim the bottle message from the provision store and take it with me to my watch. There, I will have the time and privacy to read its contents.

* * *

I put more coal in the light-room stove – an essential task since the windows were to remain open for ventilation – and I waited a further thirty minutes before taking the bottle out of my greatcoat pocket. Only after that period could I feel more certain that the others were engaged in whatever they were doing.

The cork was difficult to extract, having been cut off in the middle. I ended up pushing it into the bottle before inserting my index finger to pull out the curled sheet. It would have been easier to simply break the glass, but I wanted to avoid noise. Besides, I felt sure that Principal Bartholomew would find even the smallest shard and ask questions.

The process had something of ritual to it. I did not want to rush. If this message had come from the lighthouse as I expected, its contents must surely have some significance. I unrolled the paper on the table and saw a mass of fine writing that quite filled the sheet. There were no paragraphs. I have read in *Bottle Messages: Their History and Some Remarkable Accounts* that this is a common feature of such texts. Space is limited and often so is time. A message must be scribbled in haste and tossed to the waves as a ship goes down or as the tide awaits.

Nothing was common about the contents of this bottle, however. I copy the text verbatim:

Dear James

You live in a lighthouse, but you are already dangerously close to the reef that could send you to the depths. Why are you sleeping in the library? You know it is a perilous environment. I wonder – have you seen Jimmy? Seclusion is beneficial, but remember to diminish excitement, reduce increased sensibility and allay irritability. Avoid feats of imagination or creation. Limit yourself to only the most repetitive and predictable tasks. Are you reading, James? You know you shouldn't be reading. I advise you to have your hair shorn if you are experiencing any overheating of the cerebrum. I must also warn you about your fellow keeper Mr Adamson. You have discerned that he has a secret. It is this: he is a criminal. When last on shore, he drunkenly killed a man but fled before anyone could identify or restrain him. He is a fugitive at Ripsaw. The deceased keeper, Mr Spencer, discovered this secret and confronted Mr Adamson with it, whereupon the latter filled the water-store stove with coke. He knew that Mr Spencer always closed the hatch. You are in danger, James. There are many ways to die in a rock-bound lighthouse – many ways for a body to simply vanish and appear an accident. You are also a danger to yourself. Take care. Remember what you have learned. Take care, James.

My hand shook as I read and re-read the letter. It shook with outrage that somebody was playing with my sensibility. It is shaking now. Who had thrown this note into the sea? And when?

Whoever did so clearly knew more about me than I have told to anyone. Somebody must have spoken to Mr Fowler before his unfortunate death... or has seen notes about his work. My first thought on reading the message: Mr Adamson. He must have gone into the commissioner's room while the man was up on the balcony and read through whatever notes he had on me. But Mr Adamson is himself incriminated in the letter! And just today he has saved my life!

Principal Bartholomew? Is it possible that he saw some notes made by the commissioner? Perhaps he wanted to tell me the facts about Mr Adamson but was afraid to do so verbally lest he be overheard. But the idea of his putting such information into a bottle and tossing it into the sea was quite ludicrous. The chances of me seeing it or being able to recover it are infinitesimal. He could just have easily written it on a slip of paper and handed it to me!

My brain is quite hot thinking about it. Could the commissioner himself have sent me this message? If he had seen something ominous in the atmosphere of the lighthouse... If he had learned the true facts of Mr Adamson's crimes... If he had learned something of Mr Fowler's methods and wished to advise me... He fears for my safety. He comes up to the light-room to confide in me, but he knows my nemesis is always waiting, listening. He thus goes out to the balcony, waiting for me to come out. But when I stay inside, he knows he cannot face the dangerous Mr Adamson in the light-room and so writes his warnings in a bottle message that he flings to the foggy night. It is just as well, because he is soon thrown from the balcony himself.

I am feverishly surmising stories. My mind is racing.

What fantastical combination of chance conspired that I alone would be the one to receive this message intended for me? That the bottle would not break. That the bottle would not drift to the Isles of Scilly or to the Faroes, to Dublin or New York, there to be found by a complete stranger for whom the note would have no significance. That the waves would nudge it gently to my very feet at the precise moment when I was standing at the door – delivered to this solitary column amid a wilderness where bodies disappear and cannonballs float.

This was not only a message from a man. It was a message from a colluding world. The winds, the waters, gravity and time had together intrigued to put this paper in my hands.

I knew I must hide it. Again, I thought of all the places I could conceal it and all the places it could be found. I had an idea: there is a japanned metal locker in the provision store. It contains a mass of hard-tack to be eaten if all else is consumed. Nobody eats it. There is a lining of old newspaper under the biscuits and I could secrete my note beneath it with almost total security that nobody would think to look there.

I went directly to the store after my watch and put the note inside the locker. Nobody saw me. But I encountered Mr Adamson coming down the stairs from the kitchen as I went up. I had to stand to one side for him pass.

"What are you doing, Meakes?"

"I was checking the oil store. If the temperature falls any further, we will have to cover the cisterns with blankets."

"You're becoming quite at home here, aren't you?"

"I like to be diligent. Is it still snowing?"

"Aye. Without pause. Well… I must relieve myself."

He continued towards the privy and I went to the library. I moved one of the heavy wooden chairs beside the stove and tried to read for a while by lamplight. I could not concentrate.

Instead, I stood at the window and watched snow caught in the circling beam. How wondrous a sight it is. How rare in nature. Precipitously descending rain prevents one from appreciating its countless drops. The proximity of crystals does not allow one to conceive the innumerability of sand. But the quantity of flakes in snow impresses multiplicity on the viewer with its stately fall. More flakes than every soul that ever lived upon this earth. More flakes than every word in every book ever written. In this relentless torrent could be every letter, from the cuneiform of old Assyria, through Hebrew, Aramaic, Greek and Latin – all pristinely formed and graceful in flight but descending to annihilation in black asperity… *In Eleon, Hyla and Ocalea, and Peteona and the stately streets of Medeon, Copæ, Thisbe full of doves. And Noah begat Shem, Ham and Japheth and Cush begat Nimrod and Mizraim begat Ludim and Anamin and Lehabim and Naphtuhim. Amygdaloid and anthracite, clinkstone and belemnite, galena, mica and colite. Obsidian, porphyry, pozzuolana and pyrite, schist and silex.*

It was still snowing at half past four in the morning when I went to the kitchen to cut off my hair with the scissors.

FIFTEEN

Sunday. I woke to a film of ice on the inside of my windows. The snow had stopped and the sea was still. I went down to breakfast in my uniform and found Principal Bartholomew on his knees firing the stove. He turned and looked up at me.

"What happened to you, Mister Meakes?"

"Sir?"

"Your hair. I have just finished cleaning it out of the sink and from the floor. You look like a prisoner."

"Yes, sir. I couldn't sleep."

"Well, you might try reading a book if you can't sleep. A keeper should appear neat and trustworthy in his uniform – not like a condemned man."

"I apologize, sir. I suppose I started trimming and cut more than I intended. It was only later when I saw myself in a mirror…"

"Very well. But I will have to write a report. Whatever our circumstances here, the regulations must be followed."

Our circumstances.

"Do you think the boat will come out, today, sir?"

"Only the Commission knows when it will come. In the meantime, we continue according to our duty. Will you go down to the provision store and fetch ingredients for breakfast?"

"Of course, sir."

I descended, passing through colder and colder zones until I could see my breath as vapour. I put eggs and bacon in a hessian bag and slung it over my shoulder to ascend. The hard-tack locker appeared exactly the same, but I needed to reassure myself.

The bottle message was there exactly as I had left it. I pushed it further back under the neat piles of ship's biscuit and closed the locker.

Raised voices from the above paused my thoughts and I ascended with the bag.

Mr Adamson was standing in the kitchen doorway. He was not wearing his uniform.

"So write your darned report!" he said. "What consequences will there be?"

"That will be for the Commission to decide," said Principal Bartholomew.

"They've already decided to take me to shore. They can't prosecute a man for not wearing his uniform. I won't hang for it."

"It is your duty. I am wearing my uniform. Mister Meakes is wearing his. Are you better than us? Or just prouder and more arrogant?"

Mr Adamson turned to look at me. His gaze was one of pity and derision. "You look like a plucked chicken with your hair," he said.

"I will prepare breakfast," said the principal. "You will change into your uniform, Mister Adamson, and then we will meet in the library for the service."

"I will not change," said Mr Adamson. "Nor will I be attending any service. I'm finished with all of that nonsense. I am tired of it. Let them take me when they will. Until then, I'll live unmolested like a man."

"Then you will not eat breakfast."

"I can make my own breakfast."

"No. If you wish to consume the Commission's provisions, you must adhere to the Commission's regulations. Those regulations state that on a Sunday—"

"Then I will pay the Commission for my bacon if they

begrudge me tuppence worth. I have coins in my pocket. Wait…"

"You are being ridiculous."

"*I* am being ridiculous? Look at you both wearing your stiff uniforms on the inside of a frigid column twenty miles offshore. Nobody can see you! Nobody knows!"

"No sin is invisible."

"*Sin*? What sin? I want to eat my bacon dressed like a man. Where is the dignity in these rules imposed from afar?"

The principal took a ring of keys from his pocket and selected one.

"Don't do this…" said Mr Adamson.

"Mister Meakes," said the principal. "Take this key. I want you to go down to the provision store and lock the remaining bacon and eggs in the large strongbox by the south window. Mister Adamson will have no access to them until he agrees to obey the Commission's regulations."

"Don't do it, Meakes."

I did not want to put myself in the middle. Besides, I agreed with Principal Bartholomew. *We* were wearing our uniforms and continuing to do our duty. Why should Mr Adamson escape? I turned to descend.

"You will regret this, lad. Do you hear me? Meakes!"

I had wondered about the large strongbox in the storeroom. It was the only place in the lighthouse, other than the Commissioner's door (and now the principal's), that had a lock. When we had searched together for the missing morphia, neither the principal nor Mr Adamson had mentioned looking in the strongbox, as if both knew the morphia could not be inside.

The key turned easily. The heavy metal door swung open with a gritty sigh. It contained bottles of alcohol: wine and whisky. These were presumably for important visitors or for celebrations such as Christmas.

I moved the eggs and bacon into the locker, having to rearrange the bottles to make enough space. However, on returning to the kitchen, I found Mr Adamson seated at the table in full uniform and staring at the principal's back with an expression of tense loathing.

The principle turned from his labours at the stove. "It seems Mister Adamson will be joining us for breakfast after all. Might I trouble you to bring more eggs and bacon, Mister Meakes?"

I returned to the store without comment.

* * *

I write this with the stain of blood upon my hands. I dare hardly narrate the events that have occurred since my last trivial entry, but I do so in the hope that there may be a true record.

I was in the light-room store sorting cleaning materials. I had become distracted by a tool log near the workbench and was marvelling at the range of instruments available. Drill bow, hand saw, plane, adze, axe, pliers, joiner's hammer, wooden mallet, marline spikes, iron set square – all were neatly affixed to the circular wall in spring clamps. I was trying the joiner's hammer for size when Mr Adamson entered the store like a gust of wind.

He was brandishing the bottle message.

"What is *this*, Meakes?"

"I don't know… How could I know?"

"This is calumny, Meakes. This is defamation."

"I… I don't know what you are talking about."

"You think I'm an idiot, don't you? You think you can skulk about the lighthouse without anybody realising. You think you know me. Well, here's something you obviously don't know: I *like* ship's biscuit! I like it with a cup of tea for my supper."

"I really… I have no idea what you are holding."

"Pathetic, Meakes. Pathetic." He held the letter up and read from it: "… *He is a criminal. When last on shore, he drunkenly killed a man but fled before anyone could identify or restrain him. He is a fugitive at Ripsaw.*"

"I found that letter. It was in a bottle by the rock."

A blink. "You found a bottle addressed to you in a bottle by the rock? Can you hear yourself?"

"I can assure you it is quite true."

"I won't stand for these baseless accusations. I don't trust you, Meakes. Not after the business with the commissioner. I'm taking this directly to the principal." He started to fold the letter.

"No! Give it to me! It is mine. It is addressed to me."

"How could it possibly be addressed to you if it was thrown in the sea?"

"It is my property." I snatched for it but missed.

"Forget it, lad. I know your game. You want to destroy the evidence."

We shuffled around the workbench. He noticed that I was still holding the joiner's hammer.

"Ah, so it's like that, is it?" He snatched the hatchet from its spring bracket and brandished it. "Stop this nonsense, Meakes."

"I will not!"

"So help me God, I will strike you!"

He wildly swung back his arm.

That's when it happened.

Principal Bartholomew was entering at that very instant, no doubt to investigate the fuss. The hatchet hit him square on his crown. He paused momentarily, stunned by the blow. Blood began to flow from his hairline down the side of his nose and over his lips. He dropped to the ground.

"What have you done? You've killed the principal!"

Our tools clattered to the ground and we rushed to attend the fallen principal. His body was twitching alarmingly.

"He's not dead," said Mr Adamson. "But he's in a bad way."

"We should signal the shore station. We should show the signal ball."

"And what, lad? They've missed low tide today. They won't come out after dark. We'll have to put him to bed and signal shore first thing tomorrow."

"He could die before then."

"That's the reality at Ripsaw. Bartholomew knows it. We all know it."

"If he dies…"

"He's not going to die."

"But if he dies… You may hang for it."

"Hang? It was an *accident*, Meakes."

"*You* struck him."

"During an argument with you. If anybody hangs, it will be both of us. It looks bad. After the commissioner. After Spencer. They would hang both of us."

The principal was very pale. He had stopped jerking but was entirely immobile. There was a lot of blood on his face and on his clothes. Carrying him two levels down to his bedroom would be very arduous. It occurred to me that it might not be the first time Mr Adamson had carried a body through the lighthouse.

"Hold his head. I'll get bandages," said Mr Adamson.

I looked at him and in that moment I felt I could read his thoughts: *Wait until dark and throw the principal to the sea.* It would look suspicious, certainly but there would be no body and no proof. Even if he was later washed upon the reef or the shore, what would it show? A head injury consistent with a fall. Wasn't the principal always up on the balcony playing with his wind gauge? It was slippery after the snow. Perhaps we could inculpate the principal regarding the commissioner's disappearance…

"Meakes! Concentrate. Hold this end of the bandage and I will wrap it. That's it. Now, support his head. Lift it a little more. Good. I think he's stopped bleeding."

That may have been true, but the principal's face was oversized with coagulate gore, his white hair clotted with it. Banquo at the dining table.

"All right, Meakes. I will tie this rope around his armpits and lower him down the stairs. You go down to receive his legs."

I went down and waited for the dangling figure to descend, its lifeless feet shuffling and slipping off the steps. In order to prevent another fall, I had to embrace and support the bloody body, besmearing my own clothes and hands. His sticky face was wet against my cheek.

Thus, with much grunting and muttered expletives from Mr Adamson, we managed to carry and drag Principal Bartholomew to his bedroom, which was locked. Mr Adamson had to look through the unfortunate man's pockets to find the ring of keys. We looked like two murderers there, blood besmirched and robbing our victim. All of the clumsy manoeuvring had started the bleeding again and the bandage glistened. The air was sharp and coppery.

"Should we try to revive him?" I asked as we stood, finally, in the bedroom looking down at the body laid out on the bed.

"No. If he wakes, he wakes. Sleep is good for him. We've done all we can. And you should wash yourself, Meakes. You're quite a sight."

"What will *you* do?"

"I'm going to sleep. With the principal like this, we'll have to do longer watches tonight. I advise you to do the same."

"You can sleep? With the principal possibly dying?"

"What else so you suggest, Meakes? Praying? Pray if you like. I'm going to rest."

He left.

I went to the mirror in the principal's room. My cheeks and hands were badged with blood. I saw my blanched reflection at a different time, tricked with blood, each droplet fresh and ruby bright, runnels of it tickling down my neck and arms. It will have blood, they say. Blood will have blood.

I washed my face and changed my clothes. I scrubbed the light-room store's stone floor. But still I could not expunge the smell of it. It seemed Ripsaw was a charnel house.

It seems so still, as I sit here writing in the library.

I cannot stop thinking of the principal lying there below, his face a viscous mask of haematite, his sanguineous crown still stiffening with its dudgeon gouts of blood. The herring gulls scream murder in his name.

They say that before Caesar fell, the graves stood tenantless and the sheeted dead did squeak and gibber in the streets, and the stars were with trains of fire, and there were dews of blood, and disasters in the sun, and that the moist moon was sick with eclipse.

Something has changed at Ripsaw. The column leans askew.

Something is unbalanced. There is a sense of dread. We wait until tomorrow, when we will summon the cutter.

The bottle message is safely folded inside my jacket pocket.

* * *

We ate dinner almost in silence, Mr Adamson and I: birds he had collected from the balcony and cooked into a stew. I did not appreciate the flavour. He, too, ate without any evidence of pleasure.

We had visited the principal in his room, both together and separately. The man looked like a tomb-carving of a medieval king once we had mopped daubed gore from his face and changed his bandages. His skin was stony white and pitted as if by passing centuries. His hands lay crossed upon his chest. His pulse was weak, his breathing weaker. Neither one of us said what we were thinking.

I was first on watch. I lit the stove in the light-room and then the lamp in the lantern. The flame seemed smaller and duller than usual. It was probably due to the freezing air and the chilled pump tubes, but I imagined the lighthouse knew about its principal and was subdued.

I set the lens revolving and stood for a while outside it, watching twilight fold into night and darkness roll across the sky. I considered that it might be my last watch at Ripsaw if the cutter came the next day with replacement keepers. They hadn't planned to take me back to shore, but in the light of recent events...

Was it necessary to grant them access to our castle?

What if we bolted the door? What could they do? There was no castle keep across the kingdom more inaccessible than Ripsaw. No siege engine could breach its walls. No invading force could raise ladders against it. The enormous cost of building it meant that no cannon would ever be aimed at its slender shaft. All they could do is leave us inside to starve. But would we? The fish of the sea, the birds of the air would feed us. The clouds would give us water. They say that certain kinds of seaweed are nutritious.

I was in the light-room, half dozing, when a sense of dread jarred me quite awake. The room was suffused with an unearthly red light so that I fancied myself drowning in blood. I looked to the stove, expecting a fire to have started in its flue, but it was closed and calm. The truth was even more unnerving: the red light was emanating from outside the lighthouse. The sky through the north window was a mixture of carmine and magenta. The light through the mesh ceiling was incandescent.

I rushed up the metal steps to the lantern and into the lens, which had become a great faceted garnet flashing with peridot and emerald sparks. I was inside the bowl of an alchemist's alembic, where magic swirled and where immutable properties transformed against the will of nature. Supernal luminosity was magnified upon me, robing me as cardinal, as jester, as caliph or maharajah.

The light outside was moving, undulating, the sky aflame. Was this Judgement? Was this apocalypse?

I ducked under the lens and went into the lantern. The horizon was decorated with luminous cathedrals: arches, spires, buttresses of vermilion. Viridian ribbons soared as flames. Tourmaline currents swelled and ebbed. Its palette stained the sky as drops of blood in water: whirling, twisting, tinting the medium of night with their cold mineral fire.

I stood quite transfixed at the spectacle, watching the great band of greens and reds writhing through the heavens. Emerald, violet, amethyst. The lantern had become a limpid pool amid a world of darkness and I, the solitary fish within, gaped at a firmament afire.

I spread my arms and thought I saw the holy conflagration swell. Massed celestial armies were contending there beyond: heaven, arrayed in gold, empyreal from before her vanished night, shot through with orient beams, when all the plain covered with thick embattled squadrons bright chariots and flaming arms and fiery steeds reflecting blaze on blaze. It was an angelic conflagration. Azazel, Belial, Mulciber and Gabriel. Abdiel, Ithuriel, Urania and Zephron...

I leaned against the lantern panes, momentarily overcome. The glass was cool against my hands. My reflection, shorn head spiky and features blurred with misted breath, did not seem my own. A short shadow flitted behind me.

"Jimmy? Is that you?"

SIXTEEN

There was no need to signal shore the next morning. The day was clear, the sea calm and the cutter visible through a telescope. I sat waiting with Mr Adamson in the kitchen. We were both in uniform. We had checked on the principal just after dawn. Faint pulse. Barely perceptible breathing.

"They'll be bringing relief keepers," said Mr Adamson.

"But they know nothing of Principal Bartholomew."

"Doesn't matter. They were probably planning to take him anyway."

I waited for him to suggest some mutiny or other strategy to remain, but he sat lugubrious and passive, seemingly accepting of his fate. We had met twice during the night as we exchanged watches and stood together briefly watching the aurora borealis. But he said he had seen it before and went to the light-room to read. The principal's accident seems to have subdued him greatly.

"What do we tell them?" I said. "About his head?"

"What do you mean?"

"Well, it looks bad for us. It is our responsibility."

"You mean *my* responsibility. It was I who struck him. What do you suggest? That we lie? Do you want to claim that he fell?"

"I don't know... I..."

"And what happens when he awakes and tells the full story?"

"Will he awake? His skin is the colour of his hair."

A hard stare. "He has a pulse, Meakes. He's breathing."

"Then going to shore is the best thing for him. He needs a physician."

He nodded, but slowly, watching me.

"Meakes – I want you to give me that so-called bottle message."

"I have destroyed it."

"I don't believe you. I will not have you spreading your absurd lies."

"What does it matter if you are going ashore?"

"It matters because I will have no man falsely accuse me. Very well. A compromise: you can destroy the message. Throw it into the stove now and we'll watch it burn together. That's the best thing for both of us. I think you know what I'm talking about."

"I threw it in the sea. It was the cause of Principal Bartholomew's injury and I could not bear to look at it."

"Meakes…"

"I am telling the truth."

"I think you very seldom tell the truth, Meakes. The Commission knows it. You think they are coming for me and Bartholomew and maybe they are, but it's *you* they're worried about. They've been investigating you."

"You are an eavesdropper."

"No worse than you."

He went to the window.

"The cutter approaches, lad. Here comes your reckoning."

* * *

It was clear that no new keepers were aboard the cutter – just the usual crew and one other man. Another commissioner come to enquire about his predecessor? He didn't look like a commissioner. He looked like an undertaker: thin, grave, humourless. Mr Adamson said he looked like trouble.

Through the telescope's watery gaze, the gentleman was

stern and serious. He seemed unused to being on the sea, judging by the way he held on to the rail, his eyes fixed on the unmoving lighthouse. Indeed, it appeared he was looking directly at my face, though he could not possibly have known which window I was occupying.

We went down to the main door like condemned men and then onto the rock to secure ropes.

"Where is Principal Bartholomew?" called the skipper.

"Injured," I said.

"In bed," replied Mr Adamson at the same instant.

"Injured how?"

"An accident. Can you take him back to shore?"

The skipper conferred with the new man.

"I'll send a couple of men to help with the principal. This is Mister Jackson from London. He's come to visit the house while the tide is low."

They all jumped to the rock and we ascended the ladder without a word being exchanged, though Mr Adamson and I shared glances as we led them to the principal's room.

"Is he dead?" said one of the crewmen. "He looks dead."

"He's very unwell," said Mr Adamson. "I think you'll need to carry him out. There's a litter in the light-room store. I'll show you."

"No," said the "visitor" Mr Jackson. "The crew can fetch it alone. I need to speak to you two gentlemen." He nodded his permission and the crewmembers ascended with downcast gazes.

"What's this about, then?" said Mr Adamson "I don't think you're a commissioner."

"I am not. But I am here at their behest to discern the truth of what has occurred. Now that I am here, I see that there is an additional question about the condition of your principal."

"It was an accid—"

He cut me off with an upraised hand. "I am going to spend an hour or so looking over this house. Then I will interview each of you in turn. I ask that you, Mister Adamson await me in the kitchen. You, Mister Meakes, may settle yourself in the library."

He turned and ascended without waiting to see if we would obey his orders.

Mr Adamson waited until the footsteps had gone up two levels before muttering: "Listen, Meakes. I don't like this one. The Commission has it in for us – that much is clear. They're looking for scapegoats. Tell him whatever you like about the commissioner and Bartholomew, but don't you try to incriminate me in any way, do you hear? In turn, I won't say anything about your morphia or about your bottle message or… Your background. Do we have an accord?"

"My background?"

"Meakes! We don't have time for this. Do we have an accord? Tell the truth, but no mud-slinging or imaginative fancies. That's what they want us to do."

"I have nothing to hide."

"Right. I am going to the kitchen to await him. We'll talk later… If we're still here. I've seen no replacements. And Meakes – I swear I'll throw you from the balcony if you incriminate me in any way. Understand?"

He went down and I went up to the library. I looked out of the weather-side window to check that the cutter couldn't see and dropped the bottle to the waves. I didn't see it land.

And I waited. The commissioner had said that they were planning to further investigate the unfortunate circumstances of Mr Fowler's death, but had he formally communicated this intention before his visit to the house? Or had the loss of his notes marked the end of that enquiry?

I was not afraid. A bloodied cudgel had been found in Tibbotson's bed, and Tibbotson had always been the most unpredictable. He had struck Mr Fowler previously on occasion and was the most obvious candidate. He will likely hang, protesting his innocence to the last. As for the disputed date on my recommendation letter, it was clearly just an error. Nothing to worry about.

"Mister Meakes. I am ready for you."

I stood as Mr Jackson entered the library and seated himself at the table. I thought I could see a roll of newspapers under his arm. The ones from Mr Adamson's bed? He was also carrying a logbook I didn't recognise. Principal Bartholomew's?

"Sit, please," he said. "Time is short."

He did not look at me. Instead, he took a small notebook from his breast pocket and flicked to a page. He read for what seemed a disproportionate amount of time – no doubt some trick to unnerve. Finally, he fixed me with an unblinking stare. His eyes were pale grey.

"What was your part in the commissioner's death?"

"I... I had no part in his disappearance."

"He has not *disappeared*, Mister Meakes. He is dead. That much is clear."

"He was on the balcony and then he was not."

"Do you surmise that he fell?"

"That is the only possible conclusion, is it not?"

"And why would he fall? I have checked the weather logs. There was no wind and no ice that night – only fog. The balcony rail would have been at chest height; he could not have toppled accidentally. Nor was he a man for jumping. Therefore, he was thrown. Did *you* throw him?"

"No! Why... What possible reason would I have to do such a thing?"

"Perhaps to thwart or evade whatever measures he discussed with you in his interview. I understand his notes are missing?"

"Yes, sir. We looked all over the house. The three of us."

"That is very convenient. I will not make another search now – there is no time and I am certain they have been disposed of. Fortunately, there is a record of what the commissioner intended to discuss."

"Yes, sir?"

"Indeed. So I will know if you are lying when you tell me what you discussed with the commissioner in your interview."

He readied his pencil, still staring at me. His gaze was one of practiced scepticism. His gambit was a clever one. Did he really know what the commissioner had intended to discuss? Or was he hoping to use doubt as a midwife to revelation?

"He said that there was a matter of the wrong date on my recommendation letter and that this would be investigated. I said that it was probably an error owing to Mister Fowler's busy life."

"Anything else?"

"Well, he told me about the terrible death of my uncle…"

"Save your tears, Mister Meakes. I think you mean to say the *murder* of your uncle."

I nodded. "Yes. His murder. It seems a resident was to blame. Tibbotson."

He flicked pages. "Yes. Tibbotson, whose bed was found to contain an incriminating weapon. There is just one problem. According to the notes of your uncle, Tibbotson had a dread of blood. The smell of it. The colour of it. He may have struck people occasionally, but with slaps and butts and kicks. A drop of blood and he would faint away. He could not have bludgeoned Mister Fowler and dismembered the body so brutally. Quite simply, he could not do it. Are you feeling all right, Mister Meakes? You have become quite pale."

"Sir… It distresses me to hear the details of my uncle's death."

"His *murder*."

"Yes, sir."

"You were in London when the murder is thought to have occurred – is that right?"

"Yes, sir. Attending the interview at the Commission and for some time afterwards."

"What were you doing afterwards? Where did you stay?"

"With a friend, sir."

"Which friend? Here – write a name and address on this leaf."

I looked at the blank page and the stubby pencil beside it.

I knew I should not hesitate. I wrote a name and an address in London and pushed the notepad back towards him.

He looked at the address dubiously and returned the pad to me.

"I would also like you to fill two or three pages with writing. It is necessary that I have a larger sample of your hand. Write anything you like. Copy from one of these books if you have no idea."

I wrote without thinking:

> *All in a hot and copper sky,*
> *The bloody Sun, at noon,*
> *Right up above the mast did stand,*
> *No bigger than the Moon.*

> *Day after day, day after day,*
> *We stuck, nor breath nor motion;*
> *As idle as a painted ship*
> *Upon a painted ocean.*

"Do you like poetry, Mister Meakes?" he said, on seeing what I had written.

"I read a lot of it at school, sir. It has stayed in my mind."

"Hmm. Tell me about your fellow keeper Mister Adamson."

"What about him, sir?"

"I notice that you are rooming here in the library. Why?"

"I make noises when I am sleeping. Mister Adamson was angry. It seemed the best solution."

He made a note. "You make *noises*? You mean snoring?"

"Yes, sir. That's it. Forgive me. I am quite nervous being questioned like this."

"Did Mister Adamson murder the commissioner?"

"Sir! I have no idea what happened to the comm—"

"Somebody killed him. You say it wasn't you. There are only three keepers here and Principal Bartholomew has an impeccable record at Ripsaw. Mister Adamson had the watch following yours, according to the logbook."

"Yes, sir... But..."

"Would you say that Mister Adamson can be prone to violent outbursts?"

I'm afraid I paused too long before not answering.

He made a note. "Very well. Can you tell me why there is a newly fitted hasp and padlock on the principal's bedroom door?"

"He fitted it himself, sir."

"Why?"

"I couldn't say, sir. Perhaps he was worried after the business with the commissioner."

"Worried about what? That you or Mister Adamson might murder him?"

"No, sir!"

"What happened to Principal Bartholomew?"

"It was an accident, sir... There was an argument... Mister Adamson and I were in the light-room store. It became heated and the principal entered at just the moment when Mister Adamson was swinging a hatchet..."

His pencil paused. "Mister Adamson attempted to strike you with a hatchet?"

"No, sir. He was merely brandishing it, threatening me. At least, I believe so."

"What was this argument about that led to weapons being brandished?"

"Nothing, sir..."

A thin smile. "A man lies insensate with a terrible gash in his head over nothing? You are lying, Meakes. What was the argument about? You know I am going to speak with Mister Adamson directly."

"Sir... Perhaps you don't understand... A lighthouse is a very particular environment. Men are pressed together. An argument may arise over nothing. The last piece of bacon.

A poorly cleaned stove. A thoughtless word. Perhaps I said something about his drinking."

"Mister Adamson is prone to drinking?" He made a note.

"No. I don't know. He doesn't drink in the lighthouse. Only a small beer at dinner sometimes."

"He must be a violent man to wield a hatchet over so slight an insult."

Again, I waited too long before refuting this. He nodded and made a note.

"You have been very helpful, Mister Meakes. I will ask that you now go down to the main door and aid the crew while I talk to Mister Adamson. I know that these lighthouses have strange acoustics and that you may be able to hear conversations through various pipes and flues."

I descended with Mr Jackson following directly behind. There would be no opportunity to exchange anything but a glance with Mr Adamson as I passed the kitchen. I glimpsed him sitting at the table, his arms folded in front of him, but I made no attempt to pause.

I continued down. What would Mr Jackson ask? What would Mr Adamson say? It seemed clear that Mr Jackson was playing us against each other. Would Mr Adamson adhere to our accord and tell only the truth as I had done?

I thought about going into the provision store or the oil store to listen. The flue from the water-store stove passed through both and into the kitchen. But I was aware that Mr Jackson had not yet entered the kitchen. Shrewd man, he was listening to my footsteps to be sure that I had gone down to the water store.

In that chamber, I found the crew with Principal Bartholomew on the litter. They had lashed him to it with cords to ensure that he would not slide off on the precipitous stairways. His bloodied hair was disordered. He was as pale as a corpse.

The crewmembers were attempting to set up the crane in order to winch the principle to the cutter. I showed them how to run out the jib through the lighthouse wall and how to fit it to the base. We then carried the litter to the door and they connected the ropes.

I watched as the litter rose and swung out over the waves: that fragile broken man on a fragile litter, dangling horizontally. This was not a barrel of beer or a sack of grain. This was a man with the feeblest of pulses and an infant's frail respiration. He swayed back and forth. What would he have thought if he had awoken to find himself outside and airborne?

The crew called instructions between boat and rock but I was not listening. I took notice only when the cries became more strident and I looked up to see the crane rope unravelling high up on the jib. It twisted lazily undone until the merest cord held the litter's weight. Then it snapped with a puff of dust and fibre.

The litter fell into the sea and sank immediately, though it was still connected to the boat. I watched it disappearing into blackness. Men were shouting all about me, but I was gripped, imagining the horror of sudden resuscitation in a frigid sea, bound rigidly at arm and leg and waist, descending into the dark as pressure increases on the body, on the lungs. Breathe. Don't breathe. Panic! Terror!

I watched speechless and transfixed as the men tugged at the remaining rope. The litter resurfaced, but with the principal face down in the water. The waves were nudging him headfirst towards the rock.

"Heave! Heave!" called the skipper.

They pulled him finally on board, bone white, his hair like seaweed round his face. *Full fathom five thy father lies; of his bones are coral made; those are pearls that were his eyes: nothing of him that doth fade, but doth suffer a sea-change into something rich and strange.*

"What is happening here?" Mr Jackson was standing beside me. He was still holding the roll of newspapers and the logbook.

"He fell into the sea! Rope snapped!" called the skipper, pointing to the frayed end dangling at the jib.

Mr Jackson looked up. As he did so, Mr Adamson arrived at the door and took in the scene: the soaked body, the rope, the drama.

"I want that rope in my possession," said Mr Jackson. "Someone unfasten it and bring it to me. No – not you, Mister Adamson."

"Why not me?"

"It was you who suggested using the litter and winching the principal out."

His hands went up. "Anyone would have suggested the same! How else would you move him?"

A crewman handed Mr Jackson a coil of rope. He held the frayed end up for scrutiny.

Two crewmembers were urgently wrapping the principal in blankets, sea-spray beading pearl-like on the dark wool.

"Very well, gentlemen," said Mr Jackson. "The tide is changing. I return to shore with my findings. I leave you here to man the lighthouse. My advice if you want it: keep the lamp lighted and the sea safe. In that, you justify the Commission's trust in you."

We cast off the lines and watched the cutter turn about. Not the crew nor Mr Jackson looked back at us. They were either attending to the principal or pulling taut the sails.

"Why didn't they bring replacements?" I said. "Why didn't they take us?"

"You still don't understand, do you, lad?" His head shaking slowly. "Why take us? They already have us in the kingdom's most inaccessible gaol. We're going nowhere."

SEVENTEEN

Ripsaw is altered without the presence of Principal Bartholomew. The difference was immediately perceptible as we bolted the main door and ascended.

The sensation evoked, perhaps, the times when a holy place – a church, a temple – is overrun and desecrated by the pagans, by the infidel. They tear down its sculptures and use it as a stable or a warehouse until, decades later, centuries later, it returns to its original practitioners. But something has gone. The anima. The deity. It is just a structure.

Mr Jackson was the infidel. He poisoned every chamber with his cynical suspicions. He tossed aside reliquaries, scattered chasubles and cracked our stained-glass windows. He carried off our lares.

Now we are just two.

I have thought much about Mr Adamson's comment that we are imprisoned here. It is true that our existence is contingent on the execution of our duty to keep the lamp lighted. Do that, and there is no urgency to replace us; investigations and cogitations may continue. Fail to do so, and they swoop on us in instant retribution: we are taken and replaced. It is a kind of slavery. Our fates are in hiatus as they watch us from the shore.

I put these thoughts to Mr Adamson in the kitchen, but he seemed less interested than I.

"Don't mither me with your fancies, Poet. What did you tell Jackson?"

"As we agreed. The truth."

"He asked me about the newspapers under my bed. Only *you* have a strange mania about those newspapers. Why did he want them?"

"I did not say a word to him about them."

He stared hard. "Let him read them all. I have nothing to hide."

"And... What did you tell him about me?"

"What we agreed. That we were arguing in the light-room store and Bartholomew was struck."

"Why did we argue?"

"What did *you* say was the reason?"

"I said I couldn't remember. Something trivial, I said. I thought that might be the best answer to corroborate whatever you might say. What *did* you say?"

He grinned. "You are a crafty one, Meakes."

"What did you tell him?"

"I said there was something irritating in your character – that I simply don't like you. He seemed to believe me."

"Did you tell him anything else about me?"

"Like what, Poet?"

"About my talking at night... Anything of that kind?"

A grin. "I said you're odd. He could see that for himself, I'm sure."

"Did you see that he also had a logbook with him?"

"Aye. Bartholomew's, I imagine. No doubt the old man wrote everything in it. How you went into his room looking through his things... That will be bad for you."

"And things about you also, Mister Adamson. You don't know what he wrote. Or perhaps you do..."

He stiffened. "What does that mean?"

"Nothing."

We sat staring at the kitchen table. I wished for an errant wave to consume the cutter before it reached shore, Mr Jackson carried down to the abyss with his arms gripping that logbook. But when I looked out the boat was still visible. He would know much more when he returned.

"We must only light the lamp," I said. "That will be our salvation."

"Do you really believe that, Meakes?"

"What else do we do if we don't maintain the lamp and keep the house? Just wait?"

He seemed lost in contemplation, staring at the sky through the east window. I thought he hadn't heard me, but then:

"Who's Jimmy?"

"What?... Who?"

"Your ridiculous bottle message said something like *Have you seen Jimmy?* or *Where is Jimmy?*"

"I have no idea what you are talking about."

"You're a terrible liar, Meakes. You might fool others, but not me. Is that how you persuaded the Commission to accept you in the lighthouse service? With lies?"

"What are you suggesting?"

"You know very well what I'm suggesting, lad. You're a man with secrets."

"Does not every man have his secrets?"

"I suppose he does. As long as one man's secrets don't become another man's problems... Is Jimmy going to be a problem for me?"

"I don't know anybody of that name."

"Right. Right."

"It is time to clean the lamp and the lens. Mister Jackson has made us late this morning."

"You do it, lad. I will organise lunch and empty the ashes."

But I later glimpsed him inside the principal's room. I could have said something, could have challenged him, but he only would have told me he was collecting the ashes from the stove. It was a plausible excuse.

I have spent the afternoon in the library finishing *Crusoe*. The following passage seemed worth copying here:

In my reflections upon the state of my case, since I came on shore on this island, I was comparing the happy posture of my affairs, in the first years of my habitation here, compar'd to the life of anxiety, fear and care, which I had liv'd ever since I saw the print of a foot in the sand...

* * *

The first watch was mine. I lit the wicks, set the mechanism in motion, filled the weather log and stood watching birds hurl themselves to sudden death once night had come. I have done it for weeks but something had changed. The experience felt new.

Of course, now that we are only two, the days are shorter and the watches longer. The light-room can become very cold, even with the stove burning. I was stiff-legged and quite tired when the hour came for Mr Anderson's relief. But he didn't come.

I waited for five minutes and called him on the whistle. Still, he didn't come. I waited five minutes more. I imagined him sleeping heavily.

There was nothing and nobody to stop me going down and rousing him. The principal wouldn't know. The shore station wouldn't know. And yet they had been instilled in me, those two inviolable rules: the keeper should not sleep on duty and the keeper should not leave the light-room unless relieved.

And if Mr Adamson was dead? If a haemorrhage had burst in his brain and he was lying cold in his bed? Would I wait in the light-room until dawn? That would be the responsible act. That is what Mr Fowler would have advised. It is what Principal Bartholomew would have told me. I decided to wait.

I'm afraid I may have slept. I vaguely remember the ventilator's comforting moan and the mechanism bell, both of which have become almost inaudible through familiarity. I remember the soft thud and occasional split beak of the light-benighted birds. A wave, now and then, would slap the tower as a reminder that we were uninvited guests in Neptune's kingdom. All I know is that I opened my eyes to see a young boy standing right beside me in the light-room.

"Oh!" I said. "Who are you? You shouldn't be here!"

He was a very sickly looking boy: pale, emaciated and perhaps a little palsied. His hair fell across his forehead in a damp lick and his dark eyes were ringed with shadow. He was wearing a curious grey suit and seemed entirely unperturbed. My first thought: he looked as if he had just been disinterred.

"How did you arrive here?" I said. "This is quite against the regulations."

A dead stare. "I've been here as long as you, James."

"How do you know my...? Look, young man. This is nonsense. Where did you come from? Did you stow away on the cutter?"

"Yes. On the same cutter you took to Ripsaw."

"You were not on that boat, boy. And do you think I wouldn't have seen you all this time at Ripsaw? You are an imp and a liar."

"It's just a game of hide-and-seek. When you are in one chamber, I am in another. There are always empty chambers. If one is careful, it's possible to slip up or down the stairs to avoid discovery."

"No. No. We have searched this lighthouse twice... No. You must have arrived with Mister Jackson."

"I can prove it if you like – that I have been here all the time."

"Then prove it."

"You have seen my messages, I think. *Lord, deliver me from marrowless inertia.*"

"I have not seen that message."

"But you have seen the others. In the privy. In the kitchen cupboard. I like the principal's leeches. And the birds that crash into the lantern."

"When have you seen the birds? There is always a man on duty when the lamp is lighted."

"Sometimes you sleep. That's my chance. I can sneak about like a mouse. Nobody sees me."

"I can assure you that I never sleep while on duty."

"You were sleeping just now. And when you took your morphia."

"How do you know about—?"

"Mister Adamson is a bad man. Do you know why?"

I stared at this sickly apparition, who spoke to me with such unnerving familiarity. His presence in the lighthouse was not possible, but there he stood with his earnest, pallid face.

"He has a secret," he said. "We can find his secret together if you like. I can creep like a mouse."

"Where do you sleep, boy?"

"Different places. Mostly in the provision store. There's a blanket. When it's colder, in the water store beside the stove. Nobody sees me in the shadows."

"You must remain hidden, boy. You should not be here in the light-room. Mister Adamson must not know about you. Stay in the house's depths. Will you do that?"

"If you say so."

"Go. Go now. Mister Adamson may come at any moment."

He went, offering a weak smile and a wave before descending.

Something in his demeanour unsettled me. Something infirm and pestilent. Whey-faced. Linen-cheeked. There was something tombal about him. He was from a different place.

I thought back to my arrival. Could he really have been a stowaway on that vessel? Where? Under a tarpaulin amid the cargo? If so, how had he entered the lighthouse without anybody seeing? Hidden among the fresh provisions? Hoisted unwittingly inside a bag?

It was not possible. And yet here he was. He had spoken to me.

I sit writing this at the light-room desk. It is three o'clock in the morning and Mr Adamson has still not come. The coal in the stove has burned down and I cannot fetch more from the store without leaving the light unattended.

I know that probably nothing would happen – that I could quickly descend and fetch more coal without anybody noticing. But I must maintain the light. I must not leave the light. I am cold and my legs are stiff.

Also, I don't want to encounter the boy again. I would not like to see his face emerging from the shadows – a thing of shadows itself. If it is true that he has always been here, he has become bolder now that the principal has gone. I preferred it when he was scuttling murine and unseen about the house.

EIGHTEEN

I write this feeling grateful to be alive. Cold has penetrated my bones. Not only cold, but fear.

It started when I went out on to the balcony to relieve myself around four o'clock this morning. I knew I should not do it, but what choice did I have with Mr Adamson absent and the light depending on my presence? I left the lee-side door ajar, unbolted, and spent no more than thirty seconds completing my business.

On returning, however, I discovered the door bolted in the closest of the countersunk boltholes. Had the door blown shut? I kneeled and tried to raise the bolt, but the gap was barely a finger's width: too narrow for any kind of manoeuvring. I remained calm. I went to the weather-side door, which was closed and bolted quite flush with the jamb. The lee-side door was my only source of ingress.

The wind was moderate but bitingly cold, carrying flecks of ice that equivocated between rain and snow. The sea's surface was a wilderness of choppy troughs. I tried again to prise the bolt from its hole with no success. There was no chance of waiting until dawn, or whenever Mr Adamson might notice my absence.

I put my face to the gap and shouted.

"Mister Adamson! Mister Adamson!"

But my voice at the crack was lost to the sky and the air. It was a wave breaking against a letterbox – only a meagre quantity of water entering. I began to kick the bottom of the door, but the thick metal absorbed my blows. Downstairs, they would be no more audible than the beaks of birds against the lantern.

It was only then that I wondered: had Mr Adamson closed the door and bolted it?

Had he discussed something with Mr Jackson that angered him and compelled him to seek revenge against me? Had he found something in Principle Bartholomew's room that cast me in a negative light? It's true that he saved my life in the lantern that snowy night, but my death would have fallen on his watch. He would have looked guilty. Now, it would appear my own fault if I had locked myself out of the light-room and been chilled to death.

I wrenched at the door. I sat on the hard, hobnailed floor and braced my feet against the wall to pull. But the bolt had been engineered to withstand implacable elements. Did I have more force than a tempest gust? Would the metal budge for me but not a screaming squall?

Or had it been the boy? That anaemic spectre pervading the house. That lurking imp. Perhaps this was a game for him: to lock me out and chuckle from the shadows at my increasingly urgent cries.

If I could survive until dawn, I could raise the signal ball and summon help. But the sea was boisterous. The sky was an angry palette. I might wait days until anyone came, snow settling on my body, my fingers frozen to the railing.

Three possibilities existed for ingress, each one as suicidal as the next. I could jump two hundred feet to the sea, swim to the pediment and beat at the main door. The fall would kill me, naturally. Or I could dangle from the balcony overhang and somehow swing in vertiginous terror to reach a light-room window with a foot. Pure fear would assuredly cripple *that* attempt. Or I could climb up on the railing and jump up to the parapet around the lantern. This risked a fall and a broken limb. Or a slip and a plummet to the devouring void.

Was this how the commissioner had died? Trying to gain access to the light-room because the door was locked?

The railing was beaded with moisture and dripping. Slippery. I would have to mount it facing the sea and without any support; I'd have to then pivot to face the house like a funambulist isolated on his wire; then leap, fingers splayed, to grab the parapet, where the full weight of my body would dangle until I could either hoist myself up or feel my hands disjointed.

The view to the sea below was abominable. The tower mocked me with its height. The reef beckoned with its mendacious surf. Nothing to fear here! This whiteness is mere down to absorb your fall. There are no rending pinnacles beneath to smash your bones! Come! Come!

I gripped the rail. It was level with my breast. I could not possibly mount it and stand upon it without falling headfirst to my death. No man could manage that feat of balance. No, not even a circus aerialist could vault atop this two-inch ledge when faced with a horizon of sheer nothingness. One's mind revolts from the mere thought of it. The soul shrivels in fear.

But a thought occurred. I could straddle the railing like a gymnast's horse and perhaps work myself into a standing position from sitting. That way, I could face the lighthouse. If I fell, I'd fall towards the balcony, Better to break a wrist than dash my brains against the rock.

Wait and hope.

Or climb and jump.

I pressed my palms against the cold metal and pushed myself up so that I could swing a leg over the rail. I was sitting on it – the lighthouse on one side, death on the other. I gripped the rail with white knuckles. I was shaking. The vacuity of sea and sky seemed to lure my body and tug at the leg that dangled there. Come! Relinquish your grip!

I tried lifting my foot and placing it on the rail: an awkward position that caused my head and torso to lean towards the house. I could see only one possibility: use that tentative foot and my arms to compel the other foot to rise and then, in the instant when both feet were on the rail, before I had time to topple, use both legs to leap for the parapet.

Blood roared in my ears. My throat was constricted. A cold weight squatted in my chest. I took a deep breath…

I strained with hands and foot to raise my body and the heavy, pendulous leg. I placed the second boot upon the rail and – *Oh God! The fear, the insanity of it!* – I was standing on the rail, balancing twixt salvation and annihilation – my arms held up for equilibrium like a clumsy bird about to assail the light.

I tottered. I swayed. I wavered in stability for the most infinitesimal of moments, counterbalancing my earthly, mortal body with jerking arms and shaking knees.

I looked up at the parapet and this small change in symmetry was enough to provoke the beginnings of a fall. I swung my arms. I flexed my legs. I leaped for the parapet with the energy I had left and felt its metal mesh bite into my fingers.

I clenched my hands. A nail ripped. My body hung like a side of beef from its hook, heavier with every passing second. If I could not pull myself up to a level above my head, I would have to do it all again.

I strained my arms and swung a heel up to grip the parapet. Now I was hanging by two hands and foot. I levered myself with preternatural effort until my hip was level with the metal and swung with all my might to land panting and sobbing beside the lantern panes.

I must have lain there for some moments, wanting to sleep, wanting to bathe in the cold beam that washed over me every thirty seconds. The beam could revive. The beam was light in darkness. Snowflakes kissed my skin. Now I would have to shatter a pane to enter the lantern.

The glass is thick and strong, made to withstand wind, ice, bird-strike and debris flung by storms. I had no tool to break it. My knuckles, my elbows would surly fracture before the pane would. Gross impiety was the only option.

I kicked with the toe of my boot at the broadest part of the triangular pane. As hard as I could. It cracked with a sharp report. Again, and a silver web spread. Again and the pieces tumbled over my foot and lower leg. Salvation!

I crawled over broken shards, feeling the glass slice through my clothes and skin, and fell into the lantern. Inside was warm. Inside, the ventilator whined at the new influx of air. The mechanism droned. The lens' great vitreous eye stared impassively at this bedraggled figure that had violated its *sanctum sanctorum*.

Sleep weighed heavily upon me. My limbs were iron. Gravity held me against the floor. I had not slept for the whole night, and darkness still lay before me. My watch was not over.

I must have slept. When I awoke, it was to a diluted dawn: a fragile and apologetic sky. The sea rolled and spat. Hunger throbbed inside my knotted viscera.

I extinguished the lamp and stopped the mechanism. I raised the counterweight with weary rotations of the crank. I noted the temperature and the pressure. Later, I wondered that I had done any of these things without thinking. It was pure habit. Monks will wake just moments before the bells that call them to prayer. Prisoners learn to associate the rattle of keys with mealtimes.

And I examined the door that had locked me out. The bolt sat comfortably in its bored hole but the arm was not turned sideways and secured in a lateral slot. It looked as if the door had blown closed and the bolt had dropped accidentally. Mr Adamson would have known this. Perhaps the boy, too.

One thing was certain: Mr Adamson had not relieved me. I was angry despite my fatigue. I would go and talk to him.

I did not have to go far. He was not in his room. He was in the commissioner's room – reading in bed with a cup of coffee steaming on the bedside table.

"What do you mean by leaving me on duty all night?" I said.

"Ah, Meakes. You look terrible, lad."

"I waited all night. I called you on the whistle."

He pointed to the wall. "There's no whistle in this bedroom. I will be sleeping here from now on."

"Access to the commissioner's room is forbidden."

"By whom? The principal? The Commission? They don't know where I am, lad. They don't know where I sleep or if I do my watch. They can't see me."

"But..."

"But... the rules. The regulations. I know. But I'm the acting principal now. I'm in charge of this house. I'm king of this castle! And I say that this room is mine. I say that there will no be more watches for Adamson. Nor more cleaning for Adamson. No more ash bucket. Only comfort. Reading. Eating well. You, Meakes – you may do as you wish. Light the lamp or don't. It doesn't matter to me. Live as you please."

"We are responsible for lives!"

"No, lad. Every captain, every sailor is responsible for his own life. Do you really think the Commission is bothered about saving lives? Every vessel in every port in this kingdom pays a toll to pass these houses. How many vessels is that each year?"

"But when they come... When they come in the boat and find you here as dissolute as a sultan and neglecting your duties?"

"What about it, Meakes? It's not a crime to be insubordinate. All they can do is dismiss me without pay. They've been threatening that for so long now... Well, no more!"

"And if they try to prosecute us for Principal Bartholomew? For the commissioner? Two men have died here. Three men."

"I've killed nobody, lad. Accidents and disappearances. These things happen. While they deliberate and collect their evidence, I'll live as a free man. You – you do as you wish."

"We are responsible. We have a duty."

"They chose well when the picked you as a keeper, Meakes. But think about it for a moment. When does the light ever go out for want of a witness? It can't go out! It's not necessary for man to be there in ceaseless vigil every night. If the oil pump breaks, the bell stops ringing. If the light goes out, we can see it from the bedroom window. You... You and old Bartholomew – you're like those ancient priests offering their idols sacrifices of blood and fire and prayers. And were their battles always won? Did the plague pass safely through their lands? Did the storm leave ships undamaged and souls undrowned? Were people saved from being slain and exploited and abused? *Of course not!* They were praying to an effigy! They were pleading with a stone! Their sacred rites were fantasies that existed only in their dreams. Wake up, Meakes! Light the lamp if you must, but don't nurse it. Don't make it your idol."

He had become quite red in the face. I had thought were now just two here in the lighthouse, but now I see I am one alone. I, and the boy lurking in the depths.

NINETEEN

The weather has turned worse. The pressure is falling slowly day by day and the wind is increasing. Sight of land is often lost amid the speeding spray. Waves beat about the bottom of the column like a man interred alive and thundering at his coffin for salvation. I hardy hear them now. Only the heaviest impacts compel me to pause momentarily as plates rattle and glasses tinkle.

Rain has lashed us for days, switching its assault according to the wind direction. I like to stand in the lantern and watch the deluge strike the panes in spewing gouts, cascading in silver frills and leaving liquid lacework dripping. The drops quiver lonely, seeking others to conjoin and swell and weep together down the glass. I have passed unmeasured time in this manner.

Likewise with the sea, which is a canvas forever in transition. Its brushwork swirls in bottle-green and turquoise, sapphire and cobalt, slate and charcoal. Crests fleck phosphorescent in the night. Waves heave and roll and crash against the tearing reef. Here, nature rages at the artificial imposition of man.

I have not relinquished my responsibility to the lamp. I cannot. I know that routine is good for me. The bottle message reminded me of as much. Routine and order. Every night, I ascend and light the lamp. Only now, I have fastened the kitchen hand-bell to the light-room trapdoor so that I can hear if anyone enters. I leave a chair between the balcony doors and the jamb to prevent closing, accidental or otherwise. I am the only acting keeper, but not the only actor in this drama.

I often wonder how they view the lighthouse from the shore station. Are their telescopes trained on us at all times? Do they see this slender column and imagine a nest of murderers within? Do they wait for a tiny figure to appear on the balcony, or watch for shadows passing at the windows and comment to each other: there is one of them! There is one who threw the commissioner to his death and assaulted poor old Bartholomew. Do they watch the lights move as man passes up or down with his lamp, and do they postulate what fresh horrors must be afoot? We are ants to them, going about our puny business. But we are mostly hidden beyond sight. They must use their imaginations.

Assuredly, they cannot imagine the changes that are occurring here. As the elements threaten, Mr Adamson, likewise, has become unsettled. Initially, he was merely grumpy and uncommunicative. Now, it transpires that he has used the principal's keys to gain access to the strong box with its bottles of wine and whisky.

He spends all day asleep or crapulous, moving between bedroom, provision store and kitchen: a king in exile, his greatcoat around his shoulders like a cape. He does not wash. He eats whenever he likes, including at night when I am on my watch. The cooking smells rise with the house's respiration.

He is a different man. Ardent spirits will do that to a person. Sometimes, when he approaches the apogee of intoxication – before he lapses into incoherence and then unconsciousness – he assails me with diatribes and orations. Thus was it this morning, as I returned weary from my watch to make some breakfast. He was sitting at the table with his quasi-regal cape, a bottle of wine and a cast-iron goblet. All he lacked was a crown askew atop his matted hair.

"Why does anyone become a keeper, Meakes?"

"I am tired, Mister Adamson."

"Why did *you* become a keeper?"

I did not answer. I was learning it was better not to agitate him.

"It's no life for a man, Meakes. One rusts one's life away out here on the rock. Waiting. Waiting. Waiting for the sun to come. Waiting for the oil to burn so we can refill it. Soiling the lamp so we can clean it. It's futile! It's a punishment. It's purgatory. Our entire existence is inertia."

"Then why did *you* become a keeper?" I said.

He drank from his goblet and refilled it. "The same reason as anyone. But there's no use. You can't escape. You can't escape, Meakes. Not here and not onshore. Do you see? We're all our own lighthouses. We're all trapped in the lanterns of our own towers, waiting for the oil to run out, trying to withstand the constant buffets and billows… Prisoners in… Inside our dreams."

"Now *you* sound like a poet," I muttered.

"What, lad? What did you say?"

"Nothing. It was nothing. I was thinking what to eat."

"Well, the bacon is finished. If you want bread, you'll have to bake it."

I thought of asking him about the boy. It seemed likely that Mr Adamson had seen *something* – some shadow, some fleeting impression. It was not possible that the boy could have evaded the attention of every one of us for so long.

Spencer. Spencer had seen the boy that night on the balcony. Spencer who was now dead from asphyxiation in the lower chamber. What had he written? *I saw again a dark shadow of small stature like a boy.* But the child had told me he'd arrived with me. Spencer was already dead.

"You have that look again," said Mr Adamson.

"What look?"

"You know what I'm talking about, Meakes."

"I'm sure I do not."

He drained his goblet and winked. Banquo's ghost with bacon fat.

* * *

They say that everything that may be said or thought has already been expressed – only lost and repeated through the ages. The Greeks intuited and conjectured our scientific advances through logic alone. The Egyptians and Babylonians understood the stars and geometry before Newton's brilliance. The Renaissance alchemists pulled aside the veil of nature before religion silenced them. But secrets remain undiscovered. Profundity lies in plain sight if we know where to look.

I am reading almost indiscriminately now. Homer and Milton. Psalms and fiction. Dictionaries and encyclopaedias. Sometimes, I find myself caught in the eddy of a thought that sends me circling and circling within a paragraph, looking for the way out. There are labyrinths of meaning in which one must stop and retrace, re-read and search for the thread. This afternoon, I found myself caught in the vortices of an idea in whose shallows I languished, while aware of depths that still escaped me:

Language being the leading instrument by which men communicate their thoughts to one another, it is to it that we undoubtedly owe the most important improvements of which our intellectual character is susceptible. Each quality is an independent object of knowledge: but the ideas of different qualities are strongly associated in the mind, and the activity and versatility of its operations produce a proneness to conjoin each one that comes into view with others conceived to be collateral.

"What are you reading?"

I started at the voice directly behind me.

I turned. The boy. He was still dressed in his little burial suit, tarnished-pewter shadows in the hollows of his cheeks and around his eyes.

"You shouldn't sneak like that," I said. "You frightened me."

"But I'm always here."

"You know what I mean."

"You oughtn't to read. Don't you remember what Mister Fowler told you?"

"You know Mister Fowler?"

"Of course I do. He told you that reading excites the mind and overheats the cerebrum."

"Well, I have finished my work for today. This is my reward."

"But you oughtn't to."

"Don't you know that Mister Adamson is about? If he sees you, I won't be responsible for his actions."

"He won't see me."

"He might. He is very unpredictable these days."

"I can kill him if you like."

I looked hard at this devilkin. His face bore all the signs of candour and intent.

"Don't speak of such things," I said.

"It would appear an accident. Nobody need know. A fall. A slip. A piece of bread inhaled at night while he's intoxicated…"

"Stop, child!"

"An atmosphere of only five or six per cent carbonic oxide can kill a man as easily as him falling to sleep. He will not even realise it."

"How do you know such things?"

"There are worlds of knowledge even in this small library."

"Well, do not think of such evil. Do not suggest such things to me."

"He is a bad man. He is dangerous for you."

"Mister Adamson is rough and rude, but he wouldn't hurt me."

"And that business with the hand-crank? And all his derision? And locking you outside the light-room?"

"That… The last one was an accident, I think."

"You should thank me."

"I won't countenance what you suggest, boy."

"For the commissioner, I mean. You should thank me for that."

"What? What are you saying?"

"He was bad for you. He doubted you."

"What do you know about the commissioner?"

"He fell. He was heavy, but I gripped him by the ankles and toppled him right over. He fell into the big pillow. The fog, I mean."

I stared.

"His note-case went after him, but I burned the notes. Just ashes now. Ashes at the bottom of the sea."

"You're a murderer!"

"We are all murderers, James. Only the vagaries of circumstance direct whether we act on our true natures."

"I… I don't agree at all."

"The cutter is coming."

"What?" I had not seen him look out at the sea.

"Look. Here it comes."

I stood and went to the window. The cutter was indeed coming out despite the heavy weather.

"They are bringing replacement keepers," said the boy. "Your time has finished here at Ripsaw. You should prepare your chest."

"But I have done nothing wrong."

"Principal Bartholomew is dead. If the loss of blood did not kill him, the sea will have. You and Mister Adamson are both to hang."

"It was an accident!"

"And the commissioner? And Mister Fowler?"

"You are a demon child!"

"I can help you."

"Go! I cannot stand the sight of you."

There was a cry of surprise from below.

"Meakes! Meakes! They are coming, Meakes!"

Mr Adamson. He was coming up the stairs from his *boodour.*

"Hide, boy!"

"They are coming, Meakes!" panted Mr Adamson at the doorway. He swayed drunkenly. "I am going up to the balcony. If they try to take me, I will jump. I swear it! They won't take me."

"Mister—!"

But he was gone, banging clumsily upwards.

"The boat will turn back," said the boy, again at my side.

I ignored him. That was the best approach. He would disappear if I ignored him.

"Look to the south-east," said the boy, standing at that window and pointing. "See the black bar of clouds? A squall is coming. It'll arrive before they reach the lighthouse."

I watched the boat. Evidently, the skipper had seen the same. It started to put about.

"Blow, winds, and crack your cheeks!" shrieked the boy. "Rage! Blow, you cataracts and hurricanes. Spit, fire! Spout, rain! You sulph'rous and thought executing fires, vaunt-couriers to oak-cleaving thunderbolts…"

A curtain of rain descended to envelop the cutter in shifting gauze. The sea's surface was chisel-gouged, spray splintered. Louring clouds roiled.

"We are lords of the sea!" crowed the child. "Howl, howl, howl, howl!"

I thought I heard a banshee wail from the balcony. The birds, perhaps, protesting at the sudden tempest. Or Mr Adamson, deranged.

I tried to ignore them both. Too much noise. Too much distraction. The circling room was becoming oppressive.

I selected a newspaper at random from the pile and tried to focus on the words.

Cambricks, thread lace, German linen and bed ticks. The accused was seized with a fit. Aberdeen-built fast-sailing copper-fastened barque. The Mocmain patent lever truss. Belladonna for whisky. Seventeen centenarians. Charles Frederick Kenward, Cheriton, Folkstone. Sugar in tierces. Twelve chapters on Nervousness of Mind for those suffering from depression of spirits, confusion of thoughts, groundless fears, unfitness for society, failure of memory, delusions, sleeplessness, restlessness, wretchedness, indecision, giddiness, suicidal thoughts, fear of insanity. Good useful shirts. Fine strong shirts. Full dress shirts.

TWENTY

Morning arrives without light. The sky is heavy, the sea vexed. Sleet and hail patter against the lantern, sliding down the panes. Out on the balcony, my breath steams and the air stings my cheeks. By the clock, it is day, and yet dark night strangles the lamp. Is it night's predominance, or the day's shame?

I have ventured out a few times during the night, hoping that the chill would cure my soporific fug. Still, I believe I must have slept for moments. On one occasion, I thought I saw the boy's shadow standing at a window, but it could not have been. The hand-bell fastened to the trapdoor didn't ring. Nor, of course, did Mr Adamson make any attempt to relieve me.

He haunts the house. Not like the benign presence of Principle Bartholomew, but like a tortured spirit trapped inside this jar of stone. His wine and spirits have quickly run dry and he is enraged, bellowing taurine, haranguing the shore through the windows. I've seen him emptying every drawer and cupboard in the principal's room in search of hidden stores or keys to secret sources.

I have pondered much on his wild intention to throw himself from the balcony yesterday. What motivated that outrageous threat? Has the alcohol provoked some imbalance in his brain? I know that many men have been tipped from steady equilibrium by excessive drink. Or is it something else?

There is a pamphlet in the library, a souvenir from the

Fire Monument in London – another lofty column erected in a wilderness, but a wilderness of people and buildings. It is almost exactly the same height as Ripsaw and has a lamp of golden flames upon its peak. People are drawn to it for the views, but also to leap unto their deaths.

The catalogue of these few suicides are interesting. Not a soul considered taking his life from the viewing gallery during the first 121 years of its existence, despite the railing being low and there being no other impediment to jump. The occasional fellow fell by accident, but a baker was the first to take his life on purpose. That was 1788.

The next unfortunate case was in 1810 when a melancholy diamond merchant decided to end his life. And here the pattern emerges, for the very same year saw another baker plummet. Two deaths in 133 years, and then two within months of each other. Coincidence?

The next was a daughter of a baker in 1839 – an intermediate period that seems arbitrary enough. But then a boy of fifteen years was next to jump barely a month afterwards. Two in the selfsame year!

What persuaded two people in 1810 and two in 1839 to end their lives in such a grisly, violent and dramatic way? To count the seconds of paralysing fear as the street rushed up to destroy them? To dash out their brains and smash their bones before the horrified crowd? What might explain this statistical anomaly?

Imitation. Emulation. Influence. Incredible as it may seem, an idea may be put into a man's head merely by being propagated at large. A story appears in the newspapers. It is hotly discussed in the streets. The incident attains a kind of fame or infamy. And someone carrying the seed of self-destruction is drawn to that same method, though countless opportunities exist. Why is Waterloo Bridge more notorious than any other in London for its suicides? For no other reason than that so many have already used it so.

One might also ask why so many bakers, or those related

to bakers, launched themselves into the aether from the Monument. Simple proximity. That area of London was where the bakers congregated – indeed where the Great Fire itself had started at a baker's. The man who seeks oblivion does not want to travel far to the site of his end. It would give him time to change his mind or meet an understanding soul. The Monument stood there against the sky as a perpetual choice.

I saw a similar phenomenon myself in Mr Fowler's house. His gentlemen were delicate weathervanes of sensibility. If one of them put his hand through a windowpane and screamed and bled, the effects of that accident would ripple through the house. Parkinson would rush gibbering to his wardrobe. Mayhew would gnaw himself raw. Cuthbert would shriek about his pudding being full of cyanide. And Tibbotson, of course… Tibbotson would commit some outrage that stirred the whole cacophony to ever greater heights. Some days, it seemed that the storm would end in murder or collective self-destruction.

But Mr Fowler was wise. He understood what lighthouse-men know: the greatest waves strike after the storm is over. They have grown and swollen in the fury of the wind and in the ocean's embryo. They travel from a distance, rolling, massing, hunching their great shoulders to assail the slender tower. He knew that the worst might arrive in that frail aftermath and strike *him*, slender tower that he was, light-giver that he was amid a sea of darkness.

Thus: Mr Adamson. A rational man. A man not given to fancy. And yet he has inhabited this house while his fellow keeper Spencer suffocated and was strapped to the balcony rail; he has experienced the strange and fatal disappearance of the commissioner; he has witnessed the sanguinary and submarine travails of Principal Bartholomew who fell into the sea. All of this, and he has also had to endure the interminable uncertainty of his fate, waiting for the cutter to come out. Might not all of this turn the tides within a man's tranquillity and tempt him to copy events unfolding close to him? Even a man of such telluric and unsophisticated tendencies? Might even he be roused by this declension of sorry circumstance to the riotous madness where he now raves?

Yesterday afternoon, I encountered him asleep on the kitchen table. He was snoring, the noise reverberating through the wood. His cast-iron goblet lay on its side with a trickle of rusty spirit at its mouth. The smell of stale sweat and whisky breath were repugnant. I stood and watched him breathing.

"Now is our opportunity," said the boy, squatting by the coal store.

I paid him no heed. That is what he wants.

"The heavy frying pan would do it," said the boy. "Or the serrated knife drawn quickly 'cross his throat."

I did not reply.

"The carving fork. One tine could pierce his temple as smoothly as through butter. A spasm. A sudden liquid cough... And finished."

I left the kitchen. I could not spend another moment in his morbid company. I had to sleep. It seems I always have to sleep. *To sleep – perchance to dream. A great perturbation in nature, to receive at once the benefit of sleep, and do the effects of watching!*

* * *

With the nights growing longer, the lighthouse is using more oil. Today, after cleaning, I had to go down to the oil store. On a calmer day, I might have rigged a rope and pulley to hoist it up the outside of the tower to the balcony. But the wind continues fierce and I didn't want to risk smashing a window or losing a canteen.

Going down meant entering the boy's territory. It is darker down there with fewer windows. It is also practically beneath the sea with the waves currently running so high. Billows redound thunderously from the walls, seeking impossible ingress through dowelled and dovetailed masonry mazes.

The flood is tireless. Eternal repetition is its nature and its ultimate triumph.

I passed the provision store with its perfume of overripe fruit, cold iron and oats. He was not there. I entered the oil store with its horseshoe of separate cisterns and its glistening coal. He was not there. Indeed, there was no sign of him: no wrinkled blanket or foetid juvenile nest.

I filled my canteen with care, spilling not a drop. The boy's absence perturbed me. I had passed down the lighthouse from the lantern and not seen him anywhere, assuming he was not hiding inside the principal's room or in the commissioner's room with Mr Adamson. He could not have slipped past me on the stairs. Therefore, he had to be in the water store below. In the lighthouse's very bowels.

I left the oil canteen and went down the stone staircase. The sea was a rumbling cannonade fulminating against the lighthouse base. Spray hissed beyond the main door and I imagined the dripping mandibles of some manxome foe. *'Twas brillig, and the slithy toves. Did gyre and gimble in the wabe.* But the boy was nowhere to be seen. Only the squat cast-iron water tanks. I lifted the lid on one and watched fascinated as the surface responded to the tower's vibrations in quivering quicksilver.

On such days, the lighthouse seems alive. It shakes and mutters, wainscot creaking, crockery clacking, draughts whistling through window cracks and gasping thorough the ventilator. The sea, too, has its personality and speaks with many voices. I listened to the slaps and gurgles, the massy impacts and the water's chuckling dissipation. Listen long enough, and words materialise in the vortices and convolutions, the wash of rushing elements – a tumbling, random lexicon. Whittawer hypabyssal. Syncope bursiculate zerumbet. Onychomancer hellebore. Elytrum murrion. Areopagitic. Tephritic. Nephritic. Protomartyr protomartyr somnolescent sesterce.

I can make no sense of the words. Perhaps they are

the cries of countless drowned souls trying to be heard. Shipwrecked men. Fallen keepers. The commissioner. Principal Bartholomew, who had surely left his soul amid the reef's hidden fissures.

But there was something else: a tapping that was too regular for wind-driven drops. A fragile knocking, rather, as if a person was requesting access at the main door.

I opened the inner door. The vestibule floor was partly flooded: a dark mirror that reflected me reversed. It shimmered as I trod through it with the lamp, fearful of the din without. And still there was that too-regular tapping from the main door. The boy? Had he somehow trapped himself outside the house and even now was cowering on the rock?

I approached tentatively. Water was washing constantly at the door and, despite the finely engineered sills, was seeping inward. The stone trembled beneath my boots. I pressed an ear against the sturdy wood. A tiny, vanquished voice.

"Lord! Lord! Lord deliver me from this lowly hell!"

I am ashamed to admit that I paused. Something in me did not want to let him in, this malign child. This shadow. I could have attended to my business with the oil canteen and let the sea take him to its twenty-fathom embrace. Nobody would have known.

"Lord! Lord! Lord save me from this howling sea!"

I searched myself for Mr Fowler's counsel: the gentle voice that so often confirmed what I should do. But there was nothing. Only the clamour of the waves and wind.

I unbolted the door below. I unbolted the door at the side. I waited for a pause in the ecstatic bursts of water and pulled open the door a fraction. But what I saw was not the dripping boy hunched freezing there before me.

Instead, there was a seaman's chest bobbing irregularly in the foaming spume as if something heavy was at one end of it. The sea lifted and dropped it, washed over it, subsumed it, but it resurfaced again with a garland strand of bladderwrack about it. Mr Fowler?

"Lord! Lord! Lord deliver me from this lowly hell!"

The sky darkened and I realised I was staring into the colossal face of a suspended wave about to break directly upon me, its phlegmy trough ribbed taut, its shoulders hunched, its crest crowned with flinging fingers. The weight of it would surely crush me.

I crashed the door closed and rammed the bolts home with shaking hands. I was still bending over when the billow crashed against the pediment and shot through the fine gaps around the door. I felt myself inside a drum as the boom stunned and made the entire floor shiver.

I backed away from the door, wading through water, and closed the second door against the vestibule. Against the invading sea. I took my oil canteen and ascended to the light and warmth.

In the kitchen, where Mr Adamson was still insensible, I looked out of the window. The seaman's chest was still there, rocking and tottering in the surf. The herring gulls swooped and circled madly, their shrieking call a sob, a scream, a manic laugh – a sound I have lived with and woken up to many times. *And graves have yawn'd, and yielded up their dead.*

"What's that?"

Mr Adamson, standing now. Bloodshot, dribbling, one side of his face red where he'd been resting on the table. He was looking out of the weather-side window, pointing.

"A bark," I said. "It's a bark."

"It's too close. It's going to strike the reef. Can't they see us?"

"The telescope," I said, and rushed up to the light-room.

TWENTY-ONE

The fore and mainmast sails were close-reefed but all the other spars were bare. The vessel lay broadside to the waves, which were attempting to subsume her while driving her closer to the reef. There was a lot of activity on deck.

Mr Adamson arrived in the light-room and took up another telescope. "As I thought. She must've lost her rudder. At the wind's mercy. She'll be wrecked for sure."

I moved my scope in the direction of the wind and saw the reef's boiling cauldron. All was curiously silent through the magnifying lenses: the breaking waves, the straining cables, the wildly gesticulating mariners. Is this the view our Creator has as He observes our little wars, our games of progress, our passing aeons and eye-blink civilizations – all dumb-show drollery? *Though this bark cannot be lost, yet it shall be tempest-tost.*

"What can we do?" I said.

"*Do*, lad? We can only watch and hope the wind takes her past or through the reef."

We watched as breakers overwhelmed the gunwales and as the twisting ship exposed her canvas to the wind. The sailors had begun to throw things overboard to lighten her draught: barrels, chests, chain. Her foresail ripped free of its cords and flapped maniacally.

"I wonder if that's whisky in the barrels?" said Mr Adamson.

"Men may die and you are thinking about drink."

"Men will die. Men will live. There's nothing I can do to change it. Why don't you pray if you think it'll help anyone?"

I closed my eyes but could not will a prayer. There was only the reef and the wind and the ventilator echoing inside my head.

"Ah, they're climbing the rigging," said Mr Adamson.

"Will they unfurl more canvas?"

"No, Poet. They know they're going down. They want to get above the waves."

Men were scuttling up the ropes and embracing masts or spars. If the ship went aground, they might survive, clinging like limpets, until the storm abated and someone could rescue them.

"We might have to take them in," said Mr Adamson.

"Why?"

"What a question, lad! Because they'll be at the mercy of the sea. Because they'll be drowning. Would you leave them to die, watching them through your telescope?"

"No. I meant only to say—"

"Are you afraid they'd dirty the lamp with their fingers? That they'd consume too many of our provisions?"

"No. It's not that."

"Just think: it's an opportunity to redeem ourselves. If we save some lives, if we make Ripsaw a sanctuary, the Commission may look kindly on us."

"You have changed your opinion about the Commission."

"I'm thinking about myself."

"Of course."

He pursed his lips but made no reply. He was thinking of the whisky. I saw his telescope following the barrels. He was calculating if the waves would bring them within reach.

The ship was moving ever closer to the reef, pushed inexorably by the wind and the waves. Crewmen clung to its spars like withered apples to winter branches. How ironic for them to have Ripsaw standing witness to their plight: the great protector, the light of warning, the granite sanctuary…

But completely impotent in its rearing height. It mocked their imminent demise.

"Any moment now…" said Mr Adamson.

It was not pity or fear in his voice. Rather anticipation, expectation. I would condemn him for it, but Mr Fowler said that an appetite for horror lurks in every man. We know we should not look. We do not want to look. We look. Is there pleasure in the misfortune of others? Is it gratitude that we've escaped a similar fate? Or do we like to see our worst imaginings made real?

The vessel was now at the very lip of the reef, broadside to the ecstatic foaming rocks. The masts swayed. The ship tilted.

"Aye, that's it. She's struck."

For a moment, the bark stayed as she was, leaning queasily. But it was impossible to remain balanced on the reef's gnarled shelf. The relentless waves were crashing and crashing against her hull, breaching her gunwales. She rocked and juddered. Men fell from their perches to the deck, to the sea. The main mast splintered low down and tried to fall but was entangled in its cables.

"It is horrible. Horrible!" I said.

But still I watched as men tried to lower lifeboats from the twitching ship. One boat succeeded and threw off its lines, but was cast almost instantly against the reef, overturning and disgorging bodies to the surf. Another broke free of the drowning mother and its oars raked desperately for escape, but a jealous billow erupted fully within and sank it at a stroke. Oars floated. Men were mustard seeds bobbing in the torrent.

"And now the vessel," said Mr Adamson.

The bark shuddered as its timbers stove in and were excoriated. It crumpled on its beam ends, the remaining masts toppling towards the sea, the keel rising. And still the waves crashed and crashed and crashed pitilessly. Flotsam spewed with fractured planks and prostrate mariners. Spray sprang gleefully around the stricken ship.

"What are those men doing?" I said. "There by the foremast."

"They're tying themselves to the ship, lad."

"But why? It's going under!"

"You don't know the sailor's mind, Poet. A sinking ship is more like land than the abyss. But look – another boat is loose."

Indeed, a third lifeboat had managed to make some distance from the ship, though it was being carried into the very boiling centre of the reef. It spun and heaved amid the frenzy, its oars entirely futile. Brine poured over its sides and, like the others, it sank away, leaving men frantically adrift 'midst demented gyrations: clothes soaking, boots filling – swept across serrated rocks that fractured bones and dashed out brains for a terrifying few seconds until contracted lungs could no longer bear the pressure and swallowed sea while screaming.

Meanwhile, we watched dry and warm and safe via the hygienic impassivity of telescopes. I did not differentiate bodies from timbers. All were dead. There was fascination in the ship's slow destruction, caught between hammer waves and anvil rocks. There was determination and perfectionism in the urge to annihilate completely, or at least reduce the thing to the smallest masticated parts.

"Do you want to go fishing?" said Mr Adamson.

"I beg your pardon?"

"There are men in the water. If they make it to the lighthouse, we should offer them the chance of salvation."

"But I was nearly drowned when I tried to open the door earlier."

"That's why we'll go fishing. Come, I'll show you."

His idea was ingenious in its simplicity. We ran out the crane jib and attached a line whose "bait" was a bobbing cork lifebelt. Higher up, and level with the aperture in the lighthouse wall, we attached the kitchen hand-bell I have been using in the light-room. The theory: any mariner who could reach the lighthouse would see the line and swim for it, whereupon his violent tuggings would ring the bell and alert us. This way, we didn't have to risk our own lives at the open door.

True, the occasional gust or enthusiastic wave would ring the bell, but only once and only faintly. A sailor grappling for his life would set the clapper ringing madly. We left all of the trapdoors open so that the pealing bell would carry up to us. We were fishers of men.

And so we put the kettle on for tea. Not only for ourselves, but in anticipation of possible guests. We waited at the kitchen table, sensitive to every sound. The clang of teaspoon in mug. The scrape of sugar bowl on wood. The occasional splutter of the ventilator.

"You can tell the truth now," said Mr Adamson, leaning back in his chair. He looked quite dreadful after his drinking odyssey: eyes yellow, face red, hair still unwashed.

"What do you mean?"

"It was you, wasn't it? *You* killed the commissioner."

"I will admit no such thing. No death has been proved. Only disappearance."

"Yes, you've been very clever about that. But it wasn't me and it wasn't Bartholomew. Who else would it be?"

"It was an accident. I am convinced of that. The other day, I locked myself out on the balcony..." I watched him carefully for any sign of guilt. "And so I know how easy it might be to fall."

"But easier to knock on the door, especially when there is a man inside the light-room."

I said nothing. I sipped my tea.

"I'm not trying to incriminate you, Poet. We are in this situation together. They blame me for Bartholomew. They see me as guilty. We are both equally guilty, you and me, in *their* eyes."

I could see what he was trying to do, though he was not being very subtle about it. He tried another tack.

"It was a grisly story about Mister Fowler, eh?" he said.

"What do you know about Mister Fowler?"

"Calm yourself, lad. You're not the only one who likes to nose about the house for secrets. I looked at the commissioner's notes while he was with you in the light-room."

"So it was *you* who took the notes! All of that charade looking for them—"

"*Listen*, Poet. I read them, yes; I didn't take them. I have no idea what happened to them after my watch. After *your* watch."

"They were private. That was private information."

"Don't talk to me about privacy, Meakes. You of all people."

"What do you mean by that?"

He shook his head and chuckled. "You're quite incurable."

A shadow appeared at the doorway behind Mr Adamson: the boy. He drew a finger purposefully across his throat. I blinked to hide my stare.

"Anyway," said Mr Adamson. "Poor Mister Fowler, all dismembered and put in a seaman's chest like that. Quite barbaric. But it wasn't Tibbotson. No. It seems Tibbotson was made a scapegoat."

"You don't know Mister Fowler. You don't know Tibbotson. You only read some notes. Nobody knows the truth of what happened."

"I'm sure not. At least, not yet. Mister Jackson is a sharp one. He will find the truth."

"He has your newspapers."

"Ah, yes. The mysterious newspapers. What will he discover in those illicit newspapers, Meakes?"

"I don't know. But he is a sharp one as you say."

"Do you know why those newspapers were under my mattress? Shall I tell you? It's a dark and scurrilous story! I spilled water on my mattress some weeks ago and, in order to avoid sleeping in the damp, I flipped the thing and put newspapers under it to absorb the moisture. I must have then forgotten to retrieve them. Did you notice that the paper was crinkled?"

I thought. The paper *had* appeared somewhat crinkled. But it was a shrewd defence from Mr Adamson. Quite credible.

"So why did you choose issues from June alone?" I said.

"Because when I grabbed a handful of them, they were in date order! That's how Bartholomew liked to keep them. I'm afraid you're sorely lacking in detective skills."

"But Mister Jackson took them. He must have thought—"

"*Did* he? I haven't looked. Or perhaps he had something else rolled in newspaper. Or perhaps they were *his* newspapers."

The boy stood squarely in the doorway, scandalously bold, miming a slow stabbing action. His eyes were turbid pools of hate.

"A seaman's chest with a dismembered body inside must be awfully unwieldy. A man would need a cart or wagon to transport it to the river, don't you think?"

"I remind you that you are talking about my uncle – a man I dearly loved."

"Who do *you* think killed him?"

"I could not possibly say."

"But he kept a house for the insane, no? I expect such men can be dangerous."

"Nervous complaints."

"What?"

"Not insane. They had nervous complaints or eccentric characters."

"An interesting distinction."

"You don't know. You are not a man of science."

I did not look at the boy. I could not look at him.

"And you, Meakes? Are you a man of science?"

The hand-bell rang. We paused.

It had been just a single ring. Possibly a wave. Possibly the wind.

We waited. It rang again. And again and constantly.

"We have a fish on the line!" said Mr Adamson.

The boy vanished from the door. We went down.

TWENTY-TWO

"Ready?"

I nodded.

Mr Adamson opened the main door and a gust of spray immediately lashed our faces. A large wave had just erupted round the column.

"There! Do you see them?"

Four mariners: tiny figures in the roiling crests. One of them was clinging to the lifebelt, his weight straining the cable taut.

"Reel him in!" shouted Mr Adamson over the wind's din. He readied the boathook.

I set to work with the winch, the hand-bell ringing erratically all the while. We were saving lives, but my thoughts were wayward. Where would they sleep, these strangers? How long would they have to stay with us? Until the weather calmed? All winter? It was possible that some of them were already dead, or would die from their exposure to the sea.

"That's enough!" called Mr Adamson.

He used the boathook to pull the exhausted fellow closer to the doorway. "Give me some slack!" he called.

I released more rope and he landed his fish, but evidently the fish would not release his mortal grip on the cork lifebelt.

"Let it go! Unlock your arms! Your mates are still out there drowning!"

They surely could not survive much longer in the

convulsing waves, their saturated clothes weighing their limbs and willing them to sink into darkness.

"More rope!" called Mr Adamson. "Reel him in!"

Three more times we repeated the process – spray and billows constantly attempting to enter – until four wet sailors lay inert or writhing half-frozen in the puddled vestibule.

"We must get them upstairs and warm them," said Mr Adamson. "We'll need extra blankets from Bartholomew's room. We'll need to fire the stoves. Don't just stand there, lad! Help me to undress them."

And so began the laborious process of removing clothes that clung determinedly to pale and malodorous bodies. The sailors did almost nothing to help, exhausted as they were. We had to half-hoist, half-carry them one by one up the staircases until we were gasping and perspiring with effort.

None of them showed signs of dying.

* * *

I sit writing in the library and I sense that the equilibrium has changed. It is as if the horizon is skewed, the tower leaning. Four new presences now inhabit this column: two in the keepers' bedroom and two in the principal's room. All are swaddled in blankets and have been filled with hot, sugary tea. Rum is kept for these sorts of emergencies, but Mr Adamson has drunk the lighthouse dry. For now, they sleep.

The sea around is littered with debris from the wreck: bales, barrels, boxes. Spars, timbers, bodies. Occasionally, there is a different kind of impact as something solid hits the lighthouse. Nobody knows the vessel has gone down – nobody but us. We are invisible out here in the drifting spray. Only when the ship fails to arrive in port, only when the corpses start to reach the land – only then will the loss be surmised. In time, families will know that their sons or brothers or fathers or husbands were lost on Ripsaw reef. They will try to imagine it. They will recall the etchings and the paintings they may have seen of sculpted waves, dramatic skies and men clinging to beams. But these visions will forever be the matter of their dreams and imaginations. Only two people saw the real work of art. Only Mr Adamson and I will know the truth behind the stories and the guesses in the press, or the faulty recollections of surviving crew. There is something satisfying in being the only one to know as everybody else investigates and builds assumptions. There is peace of mind when no other witnesses exist. One may tell, or one may keep the secret.

Four mariners. They are not of these British Isles, but from somewhere such as Holland or Iceland or Denmark. They understand something of English, but cannot communicate as yet. They are men – I can offer little more in illustration for the present. One is hairy, his back and chest like a pelt. One has a blonde beard. One is fatter, with a bulbous wineskin gut. The last is slight and very young – perhaps the ship's boy. Doubtless, they have names.

How long will they stay here at Ripsaw? How long will we have to live with these interlopers? We can signal shore for aid, but the weather has now fully entered its hibernal phase. The cutter might not come out for weeks. Weeks sharing just a few chambers with these men who do not understand the house, who will deplete its resources and contaminate it with their smells. It was thus at Mr Fowler's house, where each new arrival would disrupt the delicate clockwork of routine and throw us into chaos.

Mr Adamson has become quite maniacal about attempting to reclaim barrels from the sea. He believes them to contain whisky or wine and has been down at the main door trying to hook or harpoon or net them any way he can before the wind and currents carry them ashore. I wonder if he has seen the sea chest that I saw. None of this bodes well. I feel myself a lean-looked prophet suddenly enrapt. I see that this day augurs ominous. It whispers fearful change. When or how, I cannot say.

I pass my time reading in the library.

The ancients knew of many ways to see the future and uncover secret knowledge. The Hebrews practised divination with a holy cup, through examination of entrails, or by the selection of denuded arrow shafts. Some sought occult wisdom in a holy book, opening a page at random to see which signal word was beneath the thumb. The Persians favoured readings of the ovine speal. For many, a sieve suspended from scissor points would sway to speak its wordless wisdom. The Greeks, however, were the genuine masters of augury and omen. A ring suspended on a cord was called dactylomancy and would twist or sway according to truth's impulsions. Chilomancy enquired into the hidden power of keys. Pyromancy, and its brother capnomancy, stared within the fire for answers in the shapes of flames and curling smoke. Onieromancy revealed visions in our dreams, cleromancy in the throwing of lots or dice. Cledomantic practitioners, meanwhile, focused on the veiled mystery of chance utterances, whereby an innocent speaker (a child, an overheard passer-by) voiced a word or phrase that meant nothing in particular to them but contained some fortuitous consonance or pattern in the heeder's heightened attentions. A clue. A sign. A warning hidden in the random flow of words.

I have not seen the boy. It seems inconceivable that he can remain unseen with such a crowd of men inside the house. He will have to skulk about the tanks and cisterns like a rat if he wants to remain unseen. Frankly, I am content not to see his sickly countenance or have him appearing at my side to mutter darkness in my ear.

When finally the sailors find their strength, it will be necessary to acquaint them with the house and make clear the rules and regulations. No access will be permitted to the light-room or lantern. They must not take anything from the provision store, nor trespass in the light-room store. Their world will be the kitchen and their bedrooms: three chambers only.

Will they suffer from this limited containment? Will they be oppressed by the stationary nature of the house, whose colossal mainmast takes it nowhere? Or will they be accustomed to the restrictions of life on board a vessel? Many keepers came to the service from the sea. Some will return to it.

* * *

On my watch, I lighted the lamp and set the mechanism moving. I noted barometric pressure and temperature in the logs. I stood in the lantern and watched the rain against the panes. Occasionally, an enormous billow would break against the column and spray the glass with spindrift. The beam picked out hectic precipitate.

I have been thinking much about divination and how the truth surrounds us with Delphic detail. The signs are everywhere, but reading them eludes us. Patterns exist but we see only every third or fourth increment. What appears mystery in inchoate form is revelation in totality.

I descended to the light-room and took up the watch log. I flicked to the entry I had seen from Keeper Spencer about his curious glimpse of a boy-like shadow on the balcony. I was about to read the entry again when I noticed that my thumb was placed over a word: *cowl*. Spencer had heard a rattling and gone out to see if there was a problem.

I ran my thumb over the page edges and opened the book randomly. It was an entry from Principal Bartholomew about some transformation in the weather. The word under my thumb: *slowly*. And again, towards the front of the logbook before either misters Spencer or Adamson were resident. An entry about a notable storm. The word under my thumb: *howling*.

I felt the mystery focusing itself as Ripsaw's lens gathers multiple rays of light into a beam. Signs. Patterns. The boy's hidden messages: *Lord, deliver me from this… windowless pit / dark knowledge / marrowless inertia / lowly hell / howling sea.* Every phrase contained the same lexical trinity, the same concealed clue.

Owl.

Ovid's dire omen of mortality. Lucan's sinister bubo. For Pliny, a perverse fowl both inauspicious and funereal. Ominous and fearful. Presager of death. I had encountered that tawny owl in the lantern and seen in it some memory of a face I'd known – a message coming to me through the fog and filthy air. But a message from whom? Saying what?

I went up to the lantern, where wind and rain expectorated at the glass. Only seabirds were circling the house, their angled wings brief lightning bolts in the beam. What message did the night bird have for me?

"You know," said the boy.

I turned but could not see him. "Where are you?"

"You saw the eyes. You recognised the kindly face."

"Are you inside the lens? Get away from there. You shouldn't be in the lantern!"

"You know who. His eyes were sad. He was disappointed with you, James. Such betrayal."

"Will you stop plaguing me, boy! A lighthouse is no place for you."

"It is no place for *you*."

"When I find you, boy, there will be—"

"These mariners are a pestilence upon the house. They must go."

"The cutter will come out to collect them."

"No, James. They will die here."

"They are our guests. This is their sanctuary."

"There are contaminants. This is their shambles."

"No."

"I can kill them for you."

"No."

"It will appear nothing but a series of accidents."

"No."

"Do you know who the owl is? Think about it. You know."

"No."

"Yes, you do, James. Yes, you do."

"Be gone, fiend! Away, malignant incubus!"

I charged towards the lens and entered, but he had slipped away. There was only the lamp patiently burning, the mechanism turning slowly, the ventilator growling low amid the crazed elements.

* * *

The situation is intolerable. I came to breakfast this morning and discovered a bacchanal in the kitchen. The four mariners had risen and were enjoying breakfast with Mr Adamson – all red-faced with cheer and well fed with toast and oats and eggs. The stove was stocked, the windows closed and a pungent, gamey reek was rising from the gathered stags.

"Ho! Look who has joined us," crowed Mr Adamson, who had neglected once again to do his watch. "This is Keeper Meakes, formerly Apprentice Meakes. He is a poet!"

The others cheered and rose to pat my back, thought it seemed clear that they had understood his gusto more than the sense of his words. They muttered briefly to one another for a composite translation. Evidently, I was a poet.

"You are drunk," I said, noting a barrel of something that smelled like brandy by Mr Adamson's feet. All four iron goblets were on the table.

"I find my Danish is more fluent with a glass or two, lad… If Danish is what they talk. Cheers, boys!"

They raised their glasses raucously.

One of them, a sunken-cheeked thing and very young, noted that I was not drinking and indicated that they should seek a cup or glass for me. Blond Beard offered his own goblet with a hand across his heart in what I interpreted as a grave expression of gratitude. Bulbous Gut stood in salute. The Ape – evidently too inebriated to stand – offered a gaze somewhere between befuddled and profound.

All were attired in a tatterdemalion motley of surplus and borrowed clothing. The principle's trousers folded triply at the hems, Spencer's woollen jersey, sundry lendings from Mr Adamson's wardrobe, and, I noted, items from my personal chest.

"Mister Adamson – I need to speak with you."

"Speak your mind, lad. We're all friends here. And they barely understand a word."

"Outside. In the stairwell, if you don't mind."

"I have to tell you that I'm drunk, Meakes. It's easier to speak while seated."

I looked around the sordid kitchen with its dirty plates, scattered breadcrumbs, cloven eggshells and sticky stains. The windows were opaque and dripping with condensation. It smelled like a low harbour-side bar. Wordlessly, I went to the stairwell to await him.

I heard the mood shrivel inside. Whispers and mutters. Interrogative tones. "Don't worry, mates," said Mr Adamson. "He's our ship's boy. I'll talk to him."

"What's this all about, Mother?" he said when he emerged.

"This is unacceptable."

"What's unacceptable, lad? I find it very agreeable."

"We cannot feed four extra men like this. It's not a banquet."

"Do you suggest we starve them?"

"And lighthouse regulations forbid drinking of wine or spirits except during visits from dignitaries or at Christmas."

"I won't tell if you don't. And what difference does it make if we drink. *You're* the one minding the lamp and you're as sober as an apostle."

"Don't you see? They are polluting the house. We cannot have the windows closed like that in the kitchen. The moisture will rise. The miasma of unwashed flesh will rise and soil the instruments."

"*The miasma of unwashed flesh*? Lord!"

"They cannot stay."

"And what do you recommend? Toss them back into the waves? Throw them off the balcony, perhaps? Lock them in irons in the water store? We're all trapped here for as long as the weather lasts. Nothing will change that. These men aren't keepers – they can drink if they want."

"But *you* are a keeper."

"Am I? The Commission intends to dismiss me as soon as they can bring a replacement. I will not be paid for this current duty. I am a lighthouse-man only in the most literal sense of living in a lighthouse, but I am not employed as such and am not considered one."

He was grinning. That one may smile, and smile, and be a villain.

"We need to establish some rules," I said. "Some limits."

"There is a book of them in the library, Meakes. We don't need more."

"I mean rules for the mariners. They should not enter the light-room or the lantern. There is no reason for them to venture there. Nor have they any reason to be in the library if they cannot speak English. Besides, it is my room."

"*Your* room, is it?"

"It is my room, yes. Will you communicate these things to them? You are, after all, the acting principle."

"Flattery, Meakes?"

"I meant only—"

"I know what you meant. You think you are sly, Meakes, but I *see* you." He tapped the corner of his eye. "You are not in your Bedlam now. I am not your Mister Fowler."

"You assuredly are not. *He* was a gentleman."

"He was chopped up like cat meat and packed in a seaman's chest."

I could barely breathe.

"I cannot speak to you when you are intoxicated," I said.

"Then save your breath, Poet, because I plan to drink for the duration of this weather."

I went up to the library and lay on my bed. The boy stood silhouetted against the window and spoke to the sea. "Come, thick night, and pall thee in the dunnest smoke of hell, that my keen knife see not the wound it makes, nor heaven peep through the blanket of the dark, to cry 'Hold, hold!'"

I closed my eyes but the darkness was red. I pressed my hands over my ears but the screams would not stop.

TWENTY-THREE

The weather continues bad. Principal Bartholomew's storm glass in the light-room has been stirring, the pale matter in its base slowly creeping feather-like up the tube. The lantern glass streams and shivers with wind and rain. Billows batter and protest about the tower, speckling and spitting at the higher windows.

I have closed all storm shutters below the kitchen. Now those chambers languish in perpetual shade. One must enter the dungeon with a lantern, facing a nether world of jerking shadows, cryptic glints and proximate thunder. The superstitious mariners have conceived a mortal fear of these catacombs and refuse to descend even for food and drink.

Indeed, their trepidation in the house has magnified as the strumpet wind and enchafed flood have grown in boldness. Accustomed to a vessel that flies before the wind and turns its keel to better accommodate the waves, they sit stunned and stationary inside a tower that shows flat granite cheeks to every blast. We are living now amid a yesty battlefield in which cannons assail our keep at every moment, rattling our crockery and setting every beam a-creak.

Naturally, they have been numbing their dismay with drink, Mr Adamson their liege. *He* has returned to the role of dissipated king, his watch-cloak about his shoulders, his iron goblet in hand, his loud pronouncements welcomed with wine-fuddled and uncomprehending glee. They are his jesters and his courtiers, his sycophants and counsellors.

I encounter them in stairwells as they move aimlessly between their bedrooms and the kitchen. They traipse about the house like tourists who have long since lost interest in their destination, having seen and done everything that this London or Paris has to offer. One museum is much like another. The Seine is as wet and as dirty as the Thames.

Young Sunken Cheeks has attempted to engage me in social intercourse with his limited English. Perhaps he sees me as his coeval, I having arrived here as an apprentice keeper. Perhaps he detects some sensitivity or sensibility in me that is lacking in his throaty and boisterous shipmates. There is some yearning in his eyes, some vulnerability that disturbs me. He could have been one of Mr Fowler's men. I wonder what his infirmity may be and why he seeks me to express it.

Yesterday morning I caught him in the library with a book and flung him from the place. He stuttered something about wanting to find a word in the dictionary, but I will not have him in the place. That was always the rule at Mr Fowler's house. For every man his own protected space, inviolable and private. Flouting of this rule caused conflict, and conflict is a canker that grows hidden until it bursts as violence.

The others seem to know – or have been told – that avoiding me is preferable. Blond Beard is evidently uncomfortable and nods to me in silent greeting if we pass. Bulbous Gut began by trying to shake my hand or embrace me at every opportunity, but my horror at these advances was clear. Now he merely scowls. The Ape, meanwhile, has barely left the kitchen and spends most of every day sleeping or insensible with drink. He smells like a bloated corpse in some Levantine alley.

I am weary. I alone continue the nightly watches and enjoy the relative solitude of the upper levels. With the trapdoors closed, the ventilator breathing and the wind roaring, I can occasionally forget that the others exist. I am among the tower's battlements where I can repel all invaders.

But I am grievously tired. I try my best to stay awake at night, remaining on the chair so I will fall if sleep attempts to take me. Or I go out to the balcony, where the wind casts pins of rain or grape-shot hail into my face to wake me. During the day, I seek repose in the library, but the Dionysia continues raucous as long as salvaged barrels remain undrunk. After cleaning and emptying the ash bucket and maintaining the stores in good order, I can barely keep my eyes open. My head is heavy. I walk as if in a dream.

The owl has not reappeared. I spend hours in the lantern circumambulating the lens, but only seabirds gyre about the glass. What the feathered prophet might tell me, what message it may bring from beyond, I cannot say or guess. I recall only its large, black eyes and its bearded, astragal-framed face. It came out of the fog, out of the darkness, to this light. To me. To condemn? To forgive?

There is some connection, some strange affinity, between owl and boy. One is the harbinger of the other. I have not seen the boy since he appeared in the library. I imagine him in the tower's windowless stygian depths, scuttling rat-like, muttering dark incantations.

* * *

Outrage! Sacrilege! Blasphemy! I am fresh returned from the water store, where I was obliged to use the privy. It was there I noticed a stack of pages skewered on a wire hook for the benefit of wiping. Dictionary pages. Shakespeare. Some barbarian had selected the fattest volumes for their desecration and torn out pages thoughtlessly.

I went first to the library to verify the crimes. There, I saw the riven paper and the ragged spines. The books had been replaced in the wrong locations. There was a smell of humid dog. Bulbous Gut. He had posseted and curded the purity of this place, like eager droppings into milk. Mr Adamson would have to answer for this.

"What do you want me to do?" he said, bibulous and

languid in a kitchen chair. The other swine were snuffling in their beds.

"The library is a prohibited area."

"Poet, Poet," he sighed. "Think of it: these men are gaoled here and limited to just four rooms, mine included. Imagine their sense of confinement and frustration. They aren't keepers. They didn't volunteer for this. They have no purpose here."

"The books do not belong to them."

"Nor to you, lad. Ripsaw is not your lighthouse. You're just another working part of it: another cog, another valve, another door or window. When one part breaks, there's always a replacement. Even Bartholomew – even he can be replaced. You and me, we're jars of jam or bottles of vinegar. If one falls from the shelf and shatters, there are five more. Ten more. Accept it. Admit it to yourself. Or are you one of those always complaining that life's not fair? The whole world must change because you are at its centre? Is that it?"

"You implied something earlier – something I would like you to retract."

"Did I? What did I imply?"

"That I was involved in some way with the death of the commissioner."

"You said he fell in the fog."

"New information has come to light. There is a boy here in the lighthouse. He told me that *he* pushed the commissioner from the balcony."

He looked at me. Intoxication drained from him. Sobriety paled him.

"A boy," he said. "In the lighthouse."

"Yes. It was also he who disposed of the commissioner's notes. He burned them and threw the ashes in the sea."

He continued to stare.

"This boy," he said. "Where does he sleep?"

"In the lower chambers, but I have not seen him recently."

"And how long has he been at Ripsaw?"

"He says as long as I have. He says he came on the same boat. I admit… I admit I am very dubious about that part."

He had not blinked for some time. Evidently the news had shaken him.

"Can you explain to me, Meakes, why I have never seen this boy?"

"I asked him the same question. He says he eludes us, that he is like a mouse."

"And you have spoken to this boy."

"Indeed."

"What is his name?"

"I don't know. But he knows my name. He knows your name."

"Perhaps his name is Jimmy?"

"No. I don't know. I have not asked him."

"Do you know where he is now, this boy? Can I meet him?"

"Not unless you can find him. I have not seen him."

He slowly rubbed his chin with thumb and forefinger, fixing me all the while with unwavering attention.

"Mister Meakes… Do you think this boy is a danger?"

"Why do you ask?"

"You're telling me he killed the commissioner. Might not he threaten you or me?"

"I don't know… I don't know. Sometimes he says things."

"Meakes. I want you to think carefully. Have you ever seen this boy before? Before you came to the lighthouse, I mean?"

"I don't believe so."

"But he knows you. He knows your name."

"Perhaps he overheard it. If he is here all the time…"

"Do you think I might speak to him? Shall we look for him now?"

"It will be difficult. He hides."

"He cannot hide in a lighthouse with six other men in it. Shall we look now? We can start in the lantern and work our way down."

"He passes on the stairs. He told me… But no. I see from your face that you do not believe me."

"I don't know what to believe, Meakes. I'm sure that *you* believe it."

"I have spoken to him. I have heard him and seen him."

"Very well. Then we'll keep a look-out for him."

"You don't believe me. You are merely humouring me."

"Meakes – you're tired. You should sleep."

"I am grievously tired. It is true."

"I'll talk to the mariners. I'll make them understand that they mustn't take any more pages for the privy."

"Thank you. Thank you. I must sleep."

I went to the library and slept like the dead, woken only briefly by some hollow hammering. I revived fully only half an hour before twilight – just in time to prepare. It seems my body has become accustomed to the rising and the falling of the sun.

I prepared sandwiches to sustain me for my watch and on ascending to the lamp I noticed that the hasp and padlock had been removed from the outside of the principal's door. Mr Adamson has affixed it to his own and was adjusting it as I passed. Evidently, he *does* believe in the boy's existence, for he has positioned it on the inside of the door.

* * *

It occurred to me while in the light-room that I am once again living in a house of eccentrics. There is Mr Adamson, who fluctuates between sobriety and drunkenness, between bawdy and boorish. Sometimes the dissipated king, sometimes the melancholic misanthrope. A Richard. A Lear. He is a man of controlling appetites and limited control.

As for the mariners, they mask their fears and frustrations in gross inebriation. Many conceal themselves thus. It was Mr Fowler who told me that most men live within a drama they construct for themselves. We are all characters, he said, in the tragedies or comedies of our own making – living a role, mistaking reality for stage because reality is frightening and disordered. The problems come when we must play our parts in other people's dramas, whose plots don't coincide, whose acts have different rhythms, whose heroes are often villains. What then is the denouement? Something must be forced. Something must be broken.

But we lack a Mr Fowler here to provide a guiding wisdom, a voice of tranquillity. He gave each player his own scene, his own stage, where he could feel safe. Not to perpetuate illusions and augment the world of fancy, but as a calming influence to effect an understanding of the real world. He encouraged his gentlemen to turn from the jerking silhouettes of their cave walls and gaze upon the sun. Perhaps Principal Bartholomew was our Mr Fowler, but he has gone. I am alone amid the gibbering and insensate *dramatis personae.*

The lantern soothes me. What, at first, were irritants have now become my lullabies: the whirring mechanism, the ringing of the bell, the ventilator's breath – even the wind and pluvial percussion. The lens circles slowly with its dancing prisms and refractions, transforming light from elemental flame to holy beam. In such a way does learning change man's lowly animal impulses into the purity of knowledge…

I may have slept for a brief moment, but was awoken by sounds that shocked me: base, guttural grunting. A cry of surprise or pain. A chair overturned.

I lifted the trapdoor between light-room and the store below. Another yelp. Another grunt. I was caught in indecision – descend and leave the lamp, or sequester myself in the safety of the castle keep?

If I could hear the voices, they had to be close. In the library. I took my lamp and went down to the light-room store, darting glances among the supplies for any sign of the boy's sharp eyes. Still, the commotion continued below: furniture scraping, the occasional gasp.

I lifted the next trapdoor and looked down into the darkened stairwell. The library door was ajar and light shone in the gap.

I approached the door and held up my lamp. I pushed the door with my foot and said boldly, "Now I have caught y—!"

The scene shocked me into silence.

The Ape and Sunken Cheeks. Both naked. The former's body was an ursine horror of glistening pelt. The latter's frail form was pale and doubled over the marble-top table. Both sweating. Both red-faced. Fingers intertwined in voluptuous collusion. Eyes wet with vulgar passion. The smell in the room… The smell of it… The viscous haze…

* * *

"Meakes! Meakes!"

A sharp slap on my cheek. Another.

I opened my eyes to see Mr Adamson above me, brandy on his breath. I was on the floor. I looked around. The others had gone.

"You gave us a scare, Meakes."

"What…?" My voice was hoarse.

"Forget the lamp tonight, lad. It can illuminate itself without you. You need to sleep. Can you get into bed unaided?"

"I saw…"

"I know what you saw. Sailors will be sailors. Sleep. You need to sleep."

"What happened? Why am I…?"

"You were screaming and shouting, lad. Enough to wake the entire house. The others tried to placate you but, well, you had some sort of fit and finished on the floor."

"I was screaming?"

"You haven't slept for days. Let me help you."

"What was I shouting?"

He was avoiding my gaze.

"What was I shouting?"

"Meakes…"

"Tell me."

"You were saying, 'Stop! Stop! Mister Fowler! Stop!'"

"I... I don't believe you. You are lying."

"Perhaps I misheard. Sleep, Meakes. Sleep. I will leave you."

He closed the door behind him. I heard his footsteps on the stairs. I heard the key turn in his lock. I heard the hasp fasten and padlock rattle.

He had lied to me. Assuredly so. I have no recollection of any screaming.

But that smell. That smell lingered in the library. Hot flesh and domination. Another body close and panting humid at one's neck. I was so tired. So tired. Despite my agitation, I was soon swallowed into sleep. But not before I thought I heard a voice – within or without, I could not say.

'Tis now the very witching time of night, when churchyards yawn and hell itself breathes out contagion to this world: now could I drink hot blood, and do such bitter business as the day would quake to look on.

TWENTY-FOUR

I slept fitfully. The elements were angry and billows beat against the tower. The wind itself was thunder. Spray hissed and whispered at the windows. I dreamed I was in a forest in a storm, the branches swaying, the leaves tremulously gossiping. I dreamed I was wrapped in a sheet and lashed to a trunk as a cold inundation rose slowly up my legs.

It was daylight when I woke. My first thought: I must extinguish the lamp to conserve the oil. But such thoughts were overtaken by the cries coming from below. I cast aside the bedding and descended.

Down, past the empty bedrooms. Down, past the empty kitchen. Down, down to the water store where all were congregated in a chiaroscuro scene of lamp and shadow: an atramentous composition of crouching figures round a prone figure on the puddled, stone-flagged floor. Briny hell lashed frantically without the walls.

"What is happening?" I said.

"See for yourself!" said Mr Adamson, holding his lamp to the face of the lying man.

It was the Ape, his countenance cherry-red, his lips purplish and frothing slightly at their corners. His hands and fingernails also seemed deeply purple. He looked like a fallen demon or satyr with his shaggy legs exposed and his trousers round his ankles. I could see no blood.

"Is he…?"

"Yes, lad. He's quite dead."

209

The other sailors stood witness with ominous and superstitious muttering. A death was bad among mariners, but a dead body onboard any vessel was bad luck. It invited storms, and lo! here was a storm greater than the one that had wrecked their ship. They flinched and cowered at each tremendous wave.

"What happened?" I said.

"Look." He stood and went to the stove with his lamp. I saw coke glistening on the floor before it.

"Carbonic oxide," I said. "Was the trapdoor closed?"

A nod. "He must have taken coke from the storeroom thinking it would burn as well as coal. It's easier to carry down the stairs than coal."

"He was probably drunk."

"What has that to do with it?"

"I mean, perhaps he wasn't thinking clearly. What shall we do?"

"What *can* we do? Signalling shore is a waste of time in this weather. They won't be coming out for a week or more."

"Then do we bind him to the balcony rail as you did with Mister Spencer? There are more men now. It will be easier."

He held up his lamp the better to see me. "You don't seem very concerned that a man has died here, Meakes."

"It is shocking, I agree. But I am thinking of solutions."

"His shipmates want to consign him to the sea. At least, that's what I understand. They don't want a corpse in the house. If they were aboard their ship, they would bury him at sea."

I looked at the interior door. More water had seeped beneath it from the vestibule. Waves were convulsing and exploding at the main door. We wouldn't be able to open it unless the wind changed. And even then…

"What are you thinking?" I said.

"The balcony. He is too large to fit through a window."

I looked at the hirsute bulk of the Ape.

"*They* would carry him," said Mr Adamson.

"But what about the Commission? If there is no body as evidence of accidental death, suspicion falls on us."

His expression was briefly incredulous. "Meakes. The Commission doesn't know that we have taken any mariners in. It was impossible to see anything on the day of the wreck. Nor have we recorded it in any log. That is, I haven't. I suspect you haven't either."

His logic seemed sound. "Then I suppose they need to get hold of him."

Thus, with much grunting and gasping that evoked for me unpleasant memories of the previous evening, Blond Beard and Bulbous Gut manhandled and hoisted their crewmate up almost the entire lighthouse length to the light-room. I noticed that Sunken Cheeks was not with us and must have been hiding shame-faced in his room.

Once above, it seemed the mariners expected some kind of service to be read, as happens on a ship when a fellow tar is sent to the abyss. I fetched the Book of Common Prayer and we went out of the lee-side door into the fretful elements, rain and gusts flailing at us, my words scattered to the wind like chaff. Perhaps it was just as well, given my improvisations.

In sure and certain hope of the resurrection to eternal life through our Lord Jesus Christ, we commend to Almighty God our brother… Ape, and we commit his body to the deep: reef to eddy, crest to trough, spindrift to spume. The Lord bless him and keep him. Amen.

They muttered their *amens*, these godless men, and carried him shoulders-and-feet to the railing, where they briefly rested him along its ferrous rod. Mr Adamson and I approached – both drawn, I suspect, for no other reason than the novelty of watching of a body fall from the house into the boiling sea.

A slight push and he was free, turning slowly in the air, falling, falling smaller, accelerating. A yawning trough opened to receive him and he struck the water with a stellate splash.

The wave closed over him – a three-ton liquid sarcophagus – and he was swallowed whole.

"For God's sake, let's go inside now," said Mr Adamson.

Blond Beard and Bulbous Gut went sombre to their rooms but I caught Mr Adamson's arm before descending.

"What is it, Meakes? I'm much the worse for drink. I want to sleep."

"Do you think it was an accident? With the coke and the asphyxiation?"

"What are you suggesting?"

"The dead man – he was one of those engaged in... In those acts last night. Perhaps the young one was unwilling. Perhaps he sought his vengeance in the night?"

"By using coke to provoke carbonic oxide? Who would think of such a method? They share a room, Meakes. He could have bludgeoned his bully while the big man slept."

"But it would have looked like murder, and he the obvious suspect."

He sighed and passed his hand over his eyes. "There's an easy enough solution. Let's ask the lad. He's the only one of them who understands much English. Come on."

We descended to the principal's room. The boy was not there. Nor was he with the others in the keepers' room. Mr Adamson spoke to the remaining two in some juvenile incarnation of English he had apparently developed with them.

"No. They have no idea where he is. They have not seen him since last night. After the... The incident you interrupted."

"Then we must search the house," I said. "He may be injured and hiding scared."

And so began another charade of the kind we had experienced with Principle Bartholomew and the commissioner's notes. No sign of the boy in the light-room store (where potential weapons could be found). No sign of him in Mr Adamson's room, nor in the kitchen. He was not in the provision store, nor in the coal and oil store. We had already congregated in the water store that very morning and there we stood again like explorers in the tunnel vent of some smoking volcano that belched and rumbled under the earth, our meagre lamps probing at the shadows.

Mr Adamson and I looked at each other. He said nothing.

Blond Beard and Bulbous Gut began to jabber incomprehensibly.

"He is not in the house," I said.

Mr Adamson held his lamp up to my face.

"Do you know who else isn't here, Meakes? Your phantom boy. Your Jimmy. Or is he clinging to the rock outside?"

That's when I finally understood it: the boy and he were in collusion. It was a game of theirs to torment me and make me doubt myself. Mr Adamson was hiding him, sending him to taunt me, instructing him what things to say. When the boy told me he had killed the commissioner, he meant to say that Mr Adamson had done it. Mr Adamson had burned the notes after reading them.

His lamp remained at my face. Could he see that I had perceived his duplicity? Could he see that now that I knew his secret?

"Where is he, Meakes?"

"You tell me, Mister Adamson."

"I'm talking about the ship's boy."

"What are you suggesting? I was asleep from the moment you left me last night to the moment you awoke me this morning. Since then, I have been with you. I might ask you where *you* were during the night and after dawn? Evidently, you extinguished the lamp this morning."

Blond Beard and Bulbous Gut watched us. They could sense our disagreement. Mr Adamson continued to affect his look of incredulity as if *I* were the unreasonable one.

"Another possibility," I said. "After planning and executing the death of his shipmate, the young man took his own life from the balcony. Have you thought of that?"

"That would certainly be very convenient, Meakes. No

way to prove or disprove it. No body to be found. Or will you tell me next that our mysterious Jimmy is the culprit?"

"You should know."

He actually laughed. *That one may smile, and smile, and be a villain.*

"What does that mean, lad?"

"I will not say it."

"No, say it. Let's hear it."

"Very well. I know the boy is in your employ. He is your fatal agent."

His smile fell. He studied my face with his lamp.

I saw from *his* face – a play of shadowed hollows – that I had cut to the heart of his deception. He was caught in fear.

"Then where is he, lad? Where is my *fatal agent*?"

"I don't know your stratagems. You are an arch beguiler."

He studied me for a moment longer then lowered his lamp.

"There's nothing more to be done here. Let's go up and prepare breakfast. I'm sure we're all hungry."

* * *

I have spent the day predominantly alone. I cleaned the lamp while they were eating breakfast and ate my own while they were gathered in the keepers' bedroom. Their carousing has diminished somewhat, in part because they are trying to conserve the remaining alcohol, in part due to the unfortunate events with their shipmates, and in part the dismay they feel about the weather.

It is true that the air and sea are warring. The wind waxes mad and moans about the tower. Liquid peaks lash the shaft and crash sissing 'bout the rock. The house quivers with each clapping cannon shot. It is not difficult to imagine that such an ambience might provoke anxiety. Is it better to look out of the window and watch ranks of massy waves break foaming up the column without cease? Or is it better to close the shutters tight and sit in lamplit darkness listening to the battle roar? Imagination, always, creates the greatest timor.

The worst is: there's no escape. The wind's assault is tireless. The rushing crests are numberless. The spirit and the senses cry *No more!* and still the cannonade continues day and night, day and night. The elements will not submit before the lighthouse crumbles. Will solid granite withstand the fury of all Neptune's realm? Will the winds of Jupiter renounce their right to blow where man-made impediments block their way?

The wise man knows that nothing will survive the patience of the elements. No, not even the great pyramids of Egypt, wind-whittled and sand-scoured by the centuries until they too are desert once again. We measure our time in mere seconds against dumb nature's doggedness.

The lighthouse-man does not live in fear. He trusts that the house has already withstood screaming tempests and survived. He accepts that there is nothing to be done when heavens and flood combine. He smiles at the atmosphere's tantrums and waits patiently for them to subside. Where there is madness without, sanity reigns within.

I was refilling the lamp and thinking such thoughts when a shadow flickered through the lens. The owl? Come to complete its oracular message to me? No. It was the gaunt malediction of the boy, his waxy skin now yellowish, his teeth all blackened.

"Don't speak to me," I told it. "Aroint thee, knave!"

I noted that his fingernails were coked half-moons. His trousers were oil stained.

I cried out, "You! You are the murderer! You have killed again!"

He said nothing. He merely pointed to the balcony door.

I turned to look but there was nothing. Only the closed metal door reverberating madly with the fisty wind.

"What do you—?"

He was gone. I went to where he had been standing and my boots crunched on glistening coke dust. Close to the triangular panes, I noted that no birds were flying round the lantern. They knew that worse was coming in a sky of blue-black slate and speeding scud.

Dusk was approaching when Blond Beard appeared at the light-room's wooden manhole.

"You cannot enter here. This place is forbidden to you."

He said something I didn't understand, but I perceived from his gestures that he wished to placate me and explain some point. He ascended another step.

"I said you must not enter."

He was garbling away now in his language and pointing out to sea. I looked. There was indeed a ship between Ripsaw and shore, but it was close-reefed, distant, and in no danger from the reef. I couldn't understand a word of what he wanted to communicate.

He formed a large rectangular shape with his hands and pointed down into the reef's hectic pandemonium. And there I saw a seaman's chest amid the surging swell. It was only intermittently visible in the tumbling convulsions, bobbing and sinking and rolling amid the sawtooth outcrops. Miraculously, it had not splintered and burst its seams to cast its contents on the flood.

"What?" I said. "What are you trying to tell me? It's *your* chest?"

Was he mocking me? Had Mr Adamson sent him to taunt me?

"Did Mister Adamson send you? Go. Leave the lantern. Go!"

He flinched at my raised voice and raised conciliatory palms, but I pointed insistently to the manhole.

There were three of them against me now. With the boy, four. And I, alone, in the castle keep, maintaining the light.

I fastened the hand-bell to the manhole hatch and set about lighting the lamp.

TWENTY-FIVE

Dark night. Unhallowed night. A moonless night made darker by the mourning cloud and the elements crowding at the lighthouse. There was no peace for me in the bell and the mechanism, for the ventilator shrieked and wailed, gasped and gulped and wheezed amid the wind-wrought tortures. Rain hammered. Spray ricocheted. The panes shivered my reflection in the sea's pulsing blows.

Below me lurked conspirators and traitors who would inculpate me as scapegoat, impugn my name and put wild ideas into my head by their venomous influence. Only here in my prismatic eyrie could I maintain myself immaculate and pure beyond their mortal plans.

Pitchy night. Tyrannous night.

Tonight the light-room doors are boisterous, their metal banging hollowly as if a man was trapped outside and beating for his life. The wind whistles outraged through the parapet and drums against the astragals. It spirals up the tower with insinuating eddies and rages at the railing. Seeling night. Howling night. Whittawer hyabyssal. Bursiculate zerumbet. Onychomancer hellebore. It's possible to hear words in all of nature's utterances, but interpreting them is not the work of common men. Only an alchemist or mage or madman can discern the clues and patterns.

There was a fellow at Mr Fowler's house with a mania for reading. He would read everything quite indiscriminately, from encylopaedias to newspapers, train timetables to advertising bills. Poor man, he believed that there was a hidden truth in the infinity of printed words and that, by reading them, he would find patterns invisible to the vulgar masses. Poetry and drama – being of a more ethereal origin – would provide the keys to more mundane works such as shopping lists or apothecary's catalogues. Words were his currency and his passion. He made lists of them, finding shapes and meanings in their columns. But it was an endeavour without end and doomed to the abyss, as when two mirrors face each other and lose themselves in vanishing reflection. His treatment, this fellow, was a daily regimen to fill his time with mundane and repetitive tasks. No reading. No writing. Nothing to overheat the cerebrum or provoke irritation. No feats of imagination or creation. I can't recall what happened to that fellow. He went away, I believe, after some trouble. Men came looking for him.

Words themselves are great dissimulators, shifting shape and significance through time. In essence, they are merely accretions of vowel and consonant, syllable and stress, suffix and prefix. Their roots are deep or barely grown. Say any word a half a dozen times and it turns meaningless: an absurd assemblage of sounds. Take *language*. *Language* from *lingua*, the tongue. Lenga. Lengua. Langue. And *tongue* – tunge, tunke, tonke, tonge, tungge, tongge. Just sounds. Just wet flesh writhing in darkness.

The voices of animals are meaningless to us, but how do we sound to them with our clicking consonants, our lowing vowels, our stammering grammar? Indeed, these shipwrecked mariners are wordless beasts to me. We live in worlds as different as worm and eagle.

The balcony doors reverberate with formless sound. Vibrate. Berate. Vertebrate. I can make no sense of their cacophony. Lamentings heard in the air; strange screams of death and prophesying with accents terrible of dire combustion and confused events. Do the dead speak in the same tongue as the living? Is the commissioner's spirit out there mingled with the wind? Is Spencer's? Is Principal Bartholomew's, crying fathom-deep to questing crests? And the rest? And the rest?

Will all great Neptune's ocean wash this blood clean from my hand? No, this my hand will rather the multitudinous seas incarnadine.

* * *

Banging wood and ringing bell awoke me. I started from my slumped position in the chair. It was light outside but the mechanism was still revolving, the lamp still burning. The wind seemed even more tormented.

"Meakes!"

"Mister Adamson."

His head appeared in the manhole. "Is the other mariner with you? Is he in the lantern?"

"Which one?"

"The blond one. He's missing."

"Missing? Are you sure?"

"Of course we're sure! Don't you think we've looked? Up here is the only place we haven't searched."

"He visited last night. Around dusk. I told him the light-room is prohibited and sent him below."

"Why did he visit, Meakes?"

"I have no idea. He was talking and pointing to a distant ship but I could make no sense of his language. I thought perhaps you sent him up here."

"Why would I send him?"

"I don't know. I could see no other reason."

He ascended fully, followed by Bulbous Gut. They looked around the light-room and saw at a glance that no one else was present. They went clanging up the staircase to the lantern and I watched them from below, foreshortened figures through the mesh. Of course, Blond Beard was not above. They descended.

"Where is he, Meakes?"

"Why are you asking *me*?"

They stood facing me where I sat, sceptical inquisitors. Mister Adamson looked to the balcony doors and beckoned the other with a jerk of his head. They unbolted the lee-side door and had to push it open 'gainst the wind. The churning storm burst in with a gust of spray.

"The lens!" I said.

But they went heedless to the howling. I heard their voices torn to rags.

"Meeee! Eeeee! Meakes!"

I went to the door and looked out. Mr Adamson and Bulbous Gut were crouching at the railing where Blond Beard slumped, apparently dead.

His wet hair lashed about his face. His shirt had been torn or taken off. His lips were blue, his eyes closed. He clung stiffly to the gunmetal rods.

"Is he dead?" I shouted.

Mr Adamson waved a furious gesture: there was no point trying to converse amid the elements.

I watched as they prised him loose from the bars and dragged him into the light-room. Mr Adamson slammed shut the door and bolted it. All three were red-faced and sharp with ozone.

"Is he dead?" I said.

"If he isn't, it'll be a miracle. Has he been outside all night?"

"I am sure I don't know."

"Meakes – you have been here since dusk. Dusk, when you were the last one to speak to this man. The last one to see him alive."

"I must object to your sugg—"

"Meakes! For the love of Christ, can you tell the truth just once? This man couldn't possibly have gone out on the balcony without you knowing. He must have been hammering and shouting for hours."

"The storm is quite ferocious, as you can hear."

He glared at me.

"Perhaps you need to ask the boy," I said.

"The boy? The boy? *There is no boy*, Meakes! There *is no boy*."

Of course, he would say that.

"Meakes... I'm going to take this man down and try to warm him. He's frozen to the bone. Stay here. Are you listening? Don't move from this place. Do your cleaning. I'll return directly."

"Very well."

His eyes fell on the watch log. "I'll take that also and make a note of these events."

"The watch log should not leave the light-room."

"There're many things that shouldn't happen but do. Stay here. I'll return directly."

They manhandled Blond Beard down the stairwell, glancing at me all the while. Evidently, Mr Adamson had already been filling Bulbous Gut with his conspiracies.

I sought tranquillity and order. I extinguished the lamp and fetched fresh cleaning materials from the light-room store. Chamois rag. Linen cloth. Spirit of wine. The stiff-bristle broom. I was the hierophant of this crystal temple, making my ritual supplication to the light.

The view from the lantern panes was opaque with salt spray and quivering rills. The sea was a mountain range new-formed: crest edged, dark scalloped. Heaving. The waves were breaking ever higher up the column and I could feel the wind's pressure on the glass, pushing enviously to get through. The cowl groaned and whined, howled and guttered. Ripsaw's tower is a slender finger raised against the chaos of creation. The finger of St John the Baptist indicating heaven's will.

I wonder how Mr Adamson engineered the egress of Blond Beard on to the balcony. Perhaps I was sleeping and they moved him silently. But how to avoid ringing the hand-bell? How to open the balcony without the gusts awaking me? Sinister activities are afoot at Ripsaw – things I can neither understand nor explain.

I was polishing the lens when I heard the clang and clatter of tools in the light-room store.

"Mister Adamson? Are you below?"

No answer.

"Mister Adamson?"

A hammer echoed sonorously against the manhole hatch. There was a rattle like a padlock in a hasp.

"Mister Adamson?"

I went down to the light-room store. It was empty but there was a smell of men. Some tools had been left disordered on the workbench top. Pliers. The lead ladle. An iron set square. A scattering of nails. I went to replace them in their proper places and saw that the rest of the tools – the saws, the hammers – were missing. Some mischief was apparently in progress.

I went to the manhole hatch… a found it resistant to my pull. I pulled again and a hasp rattled.

"Mr Adamson?"

"It's for your own good, Meakes," came his voice from directly below the deal cover.

"What are you doing? Have you locked me here?"

"You can't be trusted, Meakes. The Commissioner… And now the sailors. You're a danger to this house."

"You have locked me here?"

"I've taken the tools so you can't break through the hatch."

"So… So, I am imprisoned here?"

"You can't be trusted Meakes. You… Well, you've clearly lost your mind."

"You have been planning this—"

"The boy, Meakes. The boy doesn't exist. And the watch log…"

"What about the watch log?"

"It is full of nonsense, Meakes. You have filled it with derangement and fancy. That entry from Spencer– the one about seeing a shadow – it's not real!"

"I read it myself. You cannot trick me."

"*You* wrote it, Meakes! The writing is the same as in that bottle message."

He would not catch me out with that. "Then it's obvious: Spencer wrote both."

"Can you hear yourself, Meakes? What are you saying? That Spencer wrote a bottle message to a man he'd never known? A man who would replace him once he'd suffocated accidentally on the privy? Is that what you're saying?"

"You will not contaminate my mind with tricks, Mister Adamson."

I heard him sigh. "I will bring you food, Meakes. And oil for the lamp if you want it. But you'll remain aloft until the next boat comes out."

At this, a colossal gust buffeted the tower and wailed through the railing. The sea and sky knew that no boat was coming for two weeks or more.

"Then I am your prisoner," I said.

"It's for our protection, lad. And possibly for yours."

I heard him receding down the wooden steps.

So. A prisoner in the tower, confined to these three chambers: store, light-room and lantern. He had taken the tools I might use to dismantle the wooden trapdoor. That was forethought. How long had he been planning this? Since my arrival at the house? I had walked blindly into every one of his traps. Now he would accuse me of the commissioner's disappearance, of Principal Bartholomew's fall into the waves, of the unfortunate sailors. He had me doubly incarcerated in this fortress at the edge of the world.

I went up to the lantern, where the weather raged dark, wasteful, wild. The immeasurable abyss hurled and twisted and threw jealous billows high against the house. Spume flecked, foam strewn, spindrift chidden. The sea lashed in torment.

But I do not feel like a prisoner. Rather, I see myself Ulysses, Diomedes or Pyrrhus expectant in the wooden horse: he whose sable arms, black as his purpose, did the night resemble, his dread and black complexion smeared with heraldry more dismal. Head to foot now is he total gules, tricked with blood of fathers, mothers, uncles...

TWENTY-SIX

True to his word, Mr Adamson has brought me food and drink. I hear the padlock scratching, the hasp clang and a wooden tray appears at the gap. He is careful not to show his fingers or any trace of skin as he places the food on the floor. He has been quite clear with me:

"Listen carefully, Meakes. Any attempt to attack or escape and there'll be no more food. Do we agree? You'll have to live on rainwater and any birds you catch."

Naturally, I agree. It is necessary to appear calm and compliant. Perhaps, in time, he will accept my innocence and seek instead the boy for punishment. *He* – that poisonous imp, that moribund homunculus – must answer for the crimes levelled against me. In time, I will be exonerated fully.

It is difficult to remain at peace here in the tower turret, for the firmament is allied with the flood as they conspire to erase the house from existence. The banshee ventilator's din is quite demented and the wind moans interminably round the granite courses.

I have nothing to read except columns of weather notations and the ship-sighting log with its list of nameless colliers, schooners, skiffs, cutters, lighters, barks, merchantmen and sloops. There is nothing to see but clouds, spray and savage water. I sleep. I wake. I watch Principal Bartholomew's storm tube turn opaque and crystalline.

Twilight. I light the lamp and set the mechanism going. I feed the light-room stove with coal and move my chair closer to its warmth. And I wait for the inevitable. I know he's coming. I have felt his presence.

It seems the tempest has felt his presence, too. The billows now are constant thunder. The tower shakes almost without pause. I remember my first days at Ripsaw when the gentle *whump* of waves alarmed me so. How they must have laughed at my naïvety.

"You have always been naïve," said the boy, just behind me.

I didn't turn. "I've been waiting for you."

"I am always with you. You know that."

"What message has Mister Adamson given you?"

"I don't speak to Mister Adamson. Only to you."

"As you like. You have been busy in the lighthouse. How many have you killed now? The commissioner. Spencer. Two mariners... Or is it three? One of them has vanished."

"James, James – you know where he is, the one you call Sunken Cheeks."

"I do not."

"Mister Fowler told you not to lie. Lies are weeds that grow and grow and suffocate the truth. He would be disappointed with you, James. Look what you have become: a prisoner again. Distracted. Your cerebrum is quite overheated."

"Do not sully his name with your tainted mouth. Be gone, you starveling. You loathsome toad."

"Poor Mister Fowler – bludgeoned by his favourite, by his own nephew. Not only clubbed but chopped. The blood! Oh, the blood! And that sharp cupric smell impossible to wash away. You supped full with horrors that night, James. What man could do such a thing?"

"Go, you morbid harbinger!"

"Harbinger, *I*? You are the death-wreaker, James. You are the fatal shadow. What other fellow would kill his very own—?"

"Leave me, fiend!"

"—Would kill his very own par—"

I spun in my chair and leaped at the pallid spirit, taking his cold throat in my hands. I squeezed and forced my thumbs tight against a gristly tube. Tight and tighter still to stanch the seeping poison of his words.

The foul youth fell. I kneeled on his chest and leaned into my work, but still he spoke calmly and with clarity.

"Convict, murderer, madman…"

"Die! Why won't you die?"

"… Patricide. Matricide. Avunculicide…"

"Lord, deliver me from this infernal imp!"

"… Incendiary. Dismemberer. Decapitator…"

I grasped a handful of hair and beat the child's skull against the stone floor, shaking his fragile form as a dog shakes a rat to snap its spine.

"No more words! No. More. Words!"

Exhaustion overtook me. I realised I was alone in the light-room. The boy was gone. No trace or stain remained. I was on my knees and dripping perspiration. My panting briefly challenged the wind for fury, but the elements would have their say.

A colossal billow crashed booming against the tower. I felt it shake beneath my knees. The mechanism stuttered in its steady hum. The barometer toppled from the wall and smashed against the floor.

A pause. A breath.

And then another strike, but from another angle. The already shaking lighthouse was confounded in its swaying. It lurched. Warping metal groaned. The supporting column shuddered and the great lens heaved sideways, jarring free of its mechanism. Prisms fell and splintered. Shattered shards rained tinkling on the light-room.

I rushed up the stairs into the lantern and gazed in horror upon the afflicted deity. The lamp was still alight, but the lens was tilted, static. Its beams were frozen, misaligned. The ventilator wheezed and swallowed seaspray. The waves had reached the very cowl.

The lens and frame weigh in excess of one ton. Not even

three strong men could lever it back into its clockwork saddle. Nor are there spare prisms in the store for this eventuality.

"Meakes! Meakes!" The voice of Mr Adamson below.

"I'm in the lantern."

He came up the stairs. "My God, what a strike! We have lost windows in the storerooms and the kitchen." He saw the lens. "Christ save us!"

I saw that he was holding the hatchet he had used to injure Principal Bartholomew.

"What can we do?" I said.

"It's broken, lad. We can't do anything. The waves are breaking clean over the lighthouse. We must get you down below. Come. Come!"

"But the light!"

"Damn the light! Do you want to die!"

"I cannot abandon my watch."

We stood in that dramatic tableau for a moment – he gripping his hatchet for defence or attack, I unbalanced by the leaning lens askew. Nature decided for us.

The lantern's weather side exploded in vitreous hail as a great beam smashed through the astragals to lie half in, half out of the hole it had made. Seawater and sand rushed in up to our knees – sand vomited from twenty fathoms deep. The cheated wind burst in with spitting spray. I heard a fog bell ripped from its iron mooring, pealing as it fell.

The lamp was out, the lighthouse blind.

"Down! Down!" screamed Mr Adamson over the wind.

"We must fix the lantern!"

"Fix it? We cannot fix *that*! Down! Down!"

He did not wait for me. I followed him down the steps, through the light-room manhole, through the store manhole to the stairwell outside the library.

Bulbous Gut was waiting with a coil of rope over his forearm.

"You understand, lad," said Mr Adamson. "I cannot have you free about the house."

I submitted to be lashed with sturdy seaman's knots at thigh and arm and ankle to one of the wooden chairs. All four shutters were closed against the storm. The sole illumination was from Mr Adamson's lamp.

"Might you leave the lamp or light a candle?" I said.

"Afraid of the dark, Meakes?"

I did not respond to that. He used his lamp to light two candles, which he placed on the marble-top table in their brass holders.

"Am I expected to sleep upright in a chair?" I said.

"It's uncomfortable, I'm sure," he said. "But so is being murdered and I've no wish to be your next."

"What will you do about the lantern?"

A shrug. "Nothing, lad. What can I do? We don't have panes enough to fix it. As for the lens, it is ruined. That's nothing you or I anybody at the shore station can repair. Men will need to come from Birmingham or London."

"The light is out."

"Yes, lad. The light is out. The light is out. There's nothing you or I could do about it. It's not our fault. The lantern's built for wind and birds – not for ship's timbers borne on mountainous waves. This must be the worst storm since 1703 and poor old Bartholomew is missing it. Or perhaps he lies in bed on shore listening to its wailing and wishing he was out at Ripsaw with his instruments. I don't know." His smile flickered in the candlelight.

"The light has shone from Ripsaw every night for twenty-seven years."

"Well, it shines no more."

"There may be vessels in the straight."

"Only a maniac would be out sailing in this. Besides, how can you fret yourself over drowning sailors when *you've* accounted for more of them than the sea in recent days?"

"That comment is unjust."

He took a step towards me. "Is it? Is it, Meakes? What's your story, Poet? Why did you come to Ripsaw? Was it only to take lives? Or are you a fugitive from crimes committed on land? I wonder. I was joking before about your chopped-up Mister Fowler, but now I'm thinking…"

Bulbous Gut stood watching all the while. He didn't seem to understand anything other than the tone. He was watching a play in a foreign or a dead language: the characters gesturing this way and that, their voices placatory or threatening, cozening or seductive. One is compelled to guess the action and each uncomprehending viewer sees his own play, constructing it from the clues at hand, the inferences, the music of the words if not their real meanings. His experience is as much imagination as the play itself. A new interpretation. A new production. Had Bulbous Gut perceived the *dramatis personae* in our unfolding drama? Did he know about the lurking boy? Could he untangle the concatenating syllables of *Principal Bartholomew*, a character who'd left the stage long before he'd entered the main door on his cork-baited hook? Who was Spencer to him? The Sphinx? The Ghost of Banquo? Hamlet's armoured father stalking the battlements of Elsinore? Had he perceived earlier scenes with the commissioner? How difficult to understand the drama having missed the opening acts! If he left this place alive, what story would he tell his wife, his children, his drinking mates in portside bars? Would this be his *Macbeth*, his *Lear*, his *Titus*? And would they believe a word he said, sailors being so notorious for their yarning? Get away! they'd tell him. A great column in the middle of the sea? A prismatic deity beaming from its tower top? A bawdy king who caught barrels from the sea and ate ship's biscuit and drank brandy from an iron goblet? A tempest preternatural dredging sand from twenty fathoms deep? Get away! Get away! Murder most foul in the asphyxiating privy chamber! Another fellow sacrificed to clouds upon a balcony between sea and sky? Get away! Put down your flagon!

"Meakes? Meakes? You're quite hopeless, aren't you? I knew it from when I first laid eyes on you."

"Perhaps you will allow me some peace and quiet now," I said.

"In *this*?" he said, jerking a thumb at the ululating elements without.

"I have slept amid worse."

And it was true. I had slept through the keening wail of Mayhew as he sought to eat a finger. I dozed as Cuthbert vomited his stomach dry with cries of strychnine poisoning. I was in the very next bed alongside sorry Tibbotson as they wrestled him into the straight-waistcoat for destroying Cuthbert's favourite flowers. What a night *that* was – the whole house a veritable Bedlam! I have slept also with my sleeves soaked stiff and images of horror imprinted on my inner folio. Aye, this tempest could not rival the vast and boundless deep, this seat of desolation, the lightless cavern of my memory.

They were gone. The door was closed. Twin candles flickered. Outside, unseen, the world was returning to the chaos whence it came. Booming. Howling. Screeching. Despite the shutter, despite the window, a draught had infiltrated. Flames fluttered. One guttered and smoked. The room darkened. Shadows quivered in penumbrae.

A cataclysmic gust of wind and spray assailed the shaft. I heard metal squeal and rent in the lantern. The second candle winked out and I was in Tartarus. Stygian gloom – a Cimmerian grasping blind in raven darkness. Sightless night.

The only light was a slender line beneath the door, and this a gossamer of pale gold so fine that the weight of shade might break it. In the library, I saw nothing, though four dozen worlds inhabited that space. Simeon praying filthy on his column; kings Richard and the Henrys; Crusoe on the shore; Gulliver in Lilliput; Achilles in his tent. All watching. The sedimentary and volcanic rocks; the early kings of Rome; the suicides of London; Arthur Pym trapped in the hold. All of us together in the blackness. Aye, and Macbeth's woman, who walked in sleep while washing, washing, washing gore. It stays under the nails, blood, and in the creases of the fingers. The smell of it dwells in the nose and in the senses so that a naked nail or rain-beaded rail whispers scents of sticky death long after terror has elapsed.

I sat in darkness.

Agamemnon coughed.

Leonidas tapped a finger.

Friday's gaze was quizzical.

Iago felt blindly for his purse.

A single drop of water landed on my crown where the hairline meets the forehead. I looked up sightlessly and another hit my nose tip.

Had the double wave strike cracked the tower? Was water working its way between the courses down from the fractured lantern?

Drip.

Drip.

Drip.

Memories of the saline douche. That maddening clepsydra. I could not tolerate another drop. I pushed against the floor and tried to scrape my chair away from torment. I overbalanced. I toppled. I hit my temple against cold stone.

And still the water dripped as if following me. I tasted blood.

And still it dripped, bespattering my face, wetting my eyes, matting my hair. Spraying hot and red.

No more.

I struggled with my bindings. I twisted and contorted like a man writhing in extremities of torture. There was weakness in this chair, in its jointed angles, in its fragile legs. If I could force the whole weight of my body against its frailest points and crack its interstices asunder. If I could splay and split with mortal mass…

A creak. A crack. A cough of splinters. A snap.

Cassandra, in support, threw incense on her sacrificial fire. Lucifer sent Belial – Belial who reigns in luxurious cities where the noise of riot ascends above their loftiest towers, and injury, and outrage, and when night darkens the streets – to guard the door.

Rachitic timbers yielded one by one to breach. Ropes fell loose.

I was free. Free and glisteningly delivered from night's foul womb.

TWENTY-SEVEN

By rekindled candlelight, I found the hatchet left sitting on the kitchen counter in full confidence that I would not escape my bounds.

I hefted it for weight and balance and saw my dull reflection in its cheek: dark, distorted. This same hatchet had cloven Principal Bartholomew's brow and frayed the jib rope that failed him that day he fell into the sea. Blood will have blood, they say.

I ascended the stairway to the keepers' bedroom, my footsteps' quiet creaking quite masked by waves and moaning wind. The room was disarrayed and empty, the rank sweat of enseamed sheets left wrinkled as the sea where Blond Beard and the Ape so recently slept. Their bestial aroma lingered.

Up again to the principal's room, now unhasped and standing ajar. Not a flicker of light showed within. I extinguished my candle with licked fingertips and entered on a filament of smoke.

The lee-side shutter was undone and water dripped a silver-beaded curtain at the window. Evidently, the bloated brute dare not sleep in total darkness. I cast my gaze about the room: Principal Bartholomew's books and charts; his watch-cloak waiting on a hook; draws and doors half-open as if ransacked. The leeches in their jar had climbed and congregated in a mucous mass about the rim. Escape! Escape! they seemed to say, insensate with barometric fluctuation.

Bulbous Gut was sleeping prostrate, snoring lightly, his

mouth open. Accustomed to the rolling ocean, he was not incommoded by the restless weather. If the lighthouse shook, it swayed him as his hammock swung him in the foc'stle. Did he dream? Did he hope? But each man's thoughts are granite-walled and dovetailed tight. The masonry might crumble or the lens be smashed, but still the essence remains obscure.

The hatchet handle was balanced in my hand. The head glinted dully. Poll or bit? Bit or poll? I spun the handle in my palm. Better the poll – a crushing blow. Quick. No blood. *What are you doing, James? What are you doing in my room? Peace, nuncle – be not afeard. But, James… What are you doing with that hammer? Go back to your room; we will speak tomorrow. I am sorry, nuncle, but I must. I must. I must.*

Bulbous Gut was staring madly. He took a breath to yell.

I hammered the flat hatchet poll into his forehead before he raised his arms. A single, fatal swoop. A muffled crunch. His body jerked spasmodically. Bloody night descended on his eyes but his skin remained immaculate. I closed the eyelids tenderly.

What would this look like? A fall? The somnolent mariner awakes in need of the privy. Groggily, he stumbles for the stairwell, grasping blindly 'midst the thunder of the surf. A trip. A tumble. His forehead strikes the floor as a blacksmith's hammer hits the pliant tongue of glowing metal twixt his sturdy tongues, purifying it with bursts of showering sparks and turning something humble into a work of art.

I threw back the sheets, took his furry hand in mine and dragged him from the bed on to the floor. The wax-cloth rug ruched as I pulled him to the doorway and positioned him headfirst atop the staircase to the keepers' room. A pause. I waited and listened to the weather's paroxysms for a fortuitous eruption. A gust, a billow, and a firm shove with my foot sent him juddering down the wooden steps to land squarely on his face, limbs a-tangle, one arm outstretched as if belatedly to break his fall. Efficient. Ordered. No need to clean the walls or burn a mattress. Merely pull the wax-cloth taut, return the hatchet to the kitchen and let the story tell itself.

I ascended to the library with my candle. The shattered chair lay in pieces on the carpet, the rope a Medusa's head of serpents. A problem, then. I took another chair and sat and thought. What would clever Ulysses have done, arch-trickster and beguiler of the gods? He who clung to the underside of sheep, having blinded cyclopean Polyphemus in the cave.

Of course: the stove.

I blew on embers and fed small fragments to the nascent flames. The fire grew and consumed the legs, crackling and seething as the storm sucked air up through the flue. The seat back with a carved likeness of Ripsaw's tower succumbed to orange tongues, but the leather would not burn and merely shrivelled.

Next, the question of my restraints. I could not lash myself convincingly to another chair using the same rope, but I could utilise the power of illusion and distraction.

I took another chair and tied myself securely thigh and ankle. Thereafter, all I could do was loop the rest around my arms and torso the best I could and throw myself over on my side. When Mr Adamson entered, he would find me asleep on the floor, still apparently tied up and evidently having attempted (unsuccessfully) to escape. Perhaps the rope about my arms was loose, but I had clearly given in to exhaustion and despair.

First impressions are powerful. He wouldn't notice the missing chair. He wouldn't imagine that I had been at liberty about the house and returned to knot myself anew. He would see only an unfortunate young man tied to a chair and lying helpless on the floor.

And so I waited, my neck cricked at an awkward angle and my shoulder sore against the stone. The structure shook and trembled but would not yield. Wave and wind and rain and spray assailed it, but it is adamantine – a temple pharos. No elements can crush it.

* * *

Four rectangles of light around the shutters showed that day had ventured to appear. The door was open and Mr Adamson was standing silhouetted in its aperture, wordless, watching me. He looked around the library: at the wrinkled carpet, at the toppled chair, at two depleted candles on the marble tabletop. I fancied I could see his mind working.

So many accidents at Ripsaw. Poor asphyxiated Spencer and those others washed off the rock. The missing commissioner and vanished Sunken Cheeks. Woeful Principal Bartholomew whose end had followed a series of misfortunes. Blond Beard and his fatal desire to take the air. The Ape a victim of mephitic air. And now uncomprehending Bulbous Gut another casualty of gravity. The evidence seemed clear enough.

"Meakes. Are you awake, Meakes? Are you alive?"

"I am."

"The other sailor is dead, Meakes. The last one."

"What has happened?"

He approached and stood over me, still a shadow 'gainst the dim light of the stairwell. I felt that he was studying the ropes and gauging possibilities. The hatchet was in his hand.

"What do *you* think happened, Meakes?"

"I'm sure I have no idea. I have been here all night."

"He appears to have fallen down the stairs."

I said nothing.

"That is, his death looks very like an accident." His eyes upon me were unwavering.

"Then you and I have nothing to regret or fear."

"What manner of demon are you, Meakes? What brought you here? Did you come with evil intentions, or did they grow and fester once you arrived at Ripsaw?"

I said nothing.

The hatchet rose. "Tell me, Meakes – what if *you* were the next seeming accident at Ripsaw? The lantern has been irreparably damaged and you were in it at the time. It would be no shock to learn that you had tumbled to the sea. Just another one of so many fatalities. Your body lost to the waves. Who would know? Who would mourn you? The world is better without you. Without men like you."

"It would look bad for you: the sole survivor."

"It looks bad for me already, Meakes – thanks to your machinations and your conspiracies. The Commission will hang me for Bartholomew if they can. And for their commissioner, too, if one stone gets two birds."

"They don't know about the sailors. Nobody has seen. They can't prove anything about the commissioner."

He looked down at me. "Are you my punishment, Meakes? Have you been sent to castigate me for accumulated sins? Have I lived so badly that I deserve incarceration in this house of wailing winds and madness?"

"Mister Fowler says we are each our own deity. We reward and punish at our will."

"Mister Fowler. Mister Fowler. You killed him, didn't you?"

I said nothing.

Lightning flashed. A pause. Thunder ripped the sky and shook the house.

He went to the window in the stairwell.

"Have you lighted the lamp, Meakes?"

"How could I?"

"It looks like the lamp is lighted. I can see its glow in the rain and spray."

"Perhaps the lantern is burning. The lightning…"

He went quickly up the stairs. I heard him enter the storeroom through the manhole and then into the light-room. Then silence.

I shrugged off the ropes around my arms and worked quickly at the bonds about my legs. Up the stairs, up through the manhole, up through the darkened store.

Illumination shone from above.

The light-room was flooded with celestial light. I looked up at the lantern and saw a cold blaze emanating from the astragals, from the lens frame and the parapet – a pale blue electric phosphorescence that dripped pearlescent with the water that had entered. Flamed amazement.

Mr Adamson was inside the tilted lens. He had neither heard nor imagined my approach. The wind and rain had momentarily paused – the storm's calm eye? – but the sea still thundered spray in through the fractured panes.

"The corposant," I said, appearing at his side. "Saint Elmo's light."

He raised the hatchet, shocked, but saw my reverent wonder.

"Have you seen it before?" I said.

"At sea. Off the mastheads and the yard arms."

We stood together at the centre of a glowing dream. All around us, in the lantern and the lens, holy vapour hissed and sizzled with chill fire. Our faces were pallid with it and our eyes galactic gems. Out beyond, the dark and cloud-raked firmament flashed stuttering white.

"The boy is gone," I said. "We have nothing more to fear."

"Is that right, Meakes?" said Mr Adamson somewhat wearily.

"Indeed. No more lives will be taken. You need not restrain me further."

He gazed at me, an insubstantial spirit in the pallid light.

"I believe we must work together," I said, "if we are to survive this tempest and reach safety. We must be allies."

"You think that returning to shore means safety?"

"You have said it yourself: we are prisoners here. There is nowhere to go except the abyss."

"Some might say you're already there, Meakes."

"Do we have an accord?" I held out my hand.

He looked at it as one might look into a freshly disinterred coffin.

"Very well, Meakes. I suppose you talk sense." He shook my hand.

He was lying.

The heavens flared white and thunder followed instantly – a basso cannonade that shook the house. A fanged pane dropped from its astragal and shattered on the parapet: a spray of glowing sapphires.

"We should descend," said Mr Adamson. "I don't want to be up here in the lightning. I expect we've lost the conductor in the wind."

His words were prophetic.

A colossal violet flash. Blinding. Deafening. A smell of burning phlogiston.

I could not see, hear, think.

A heavy weight against my leg. Burned flesh. Burned wood.

Mr Adamson was at my feet. Dead? Stunned?

An annular section of the lens dropped and smashed. It's gun metal frame had isolated me from the lightning strike, but some part of Mr Adamson must have been touching metal. Perhaps the hatchet in his hand had grazed the frame.

The sky twitched epileptically electric. We had to descend.

I dragged him unceremoniously down the metal stairs into the light-room. I closed the windows and stocked the stove. He would have to stay here until he regained consciousness or died. Meanwhile, I had to check the lighthouse was not burning.

TWENTY-EIGHT

The manhole hatch to the light-room store had been blasted to charred pieces and was smoking still. A scorched and ragged line continued down the wooden stairs, while on the wall a curious fern-like burn pattern had spread.

I followed the trail down past the library and the bedrooms, noting that the inert corpse of Bulbous Gut was marked with a red and ragged slash where the lightning had crossed his back. The skin was melted and cauterised, the shirt left carbonised.

The thread of destruction continued past the kitchen, where many of the cupboard doors stood open, their cutlery, crockery and glassware spewed and lying broken on the floor. A skein of acrid smoke hung head-height in the provision store, though nothing seemed disturbed.

The oil store was quite a mess, however. The cistern nearest to the door had convulsed and ruptured, its riveted seams burst open and the body of Sunken Cheeks half-vomited from within. His head, shoulder and left arm were visible in the lamplight, slick and viscous with the oil. The floor shone stickily with all that had spilled and the air was heavy with its scent.

I continued down to the water store and saw that the brass handrail had been transformed by the sky's ferocity from the gleaming yellow of Principal Bartholomew's tenure to a sombre iridescence. Evidently, the bolt had travelled right along it into the cellar of the house and shattered the final granite step.

The lowermost chamber was two-inches deep in brine – a mirror in the lamplight, quivering mercurial at the tempest's ceaseless onslaught. The noise was apocalyptic. Here was Vulcan's forge with gasping bellows and the constant thunder of massed tilt hammers. Here was purgatory amid the wail of countless souls held to the purifying flame. Here was ten years of warfare on the Trojan plain, the peopled din of sword and spear 'gainst man-covering shield. Here was madness reigning, raging, railing in the darkness edging abyssopelagic depths. Here, on the bare outside of this world, amid black tartareous cold where the firmament spouts cataracts of fire and this house, is the prey and sport of racking whirlwinds. Here, where length and breadth, and height and time and sense are lost illimitable without dimension. Here, unrespited, unpitied, unreprieved we crouch and cower beyond grace.

This is Hell. This, the imprisoning tower of the inward self with walls seven-feet-thick, impenetrable but corrupt and blackened at their core. On this abhorrent rock we stand, victims all, to face the vagaries and whips of fleeting spans – powerless 'gainst tide and season. Toys of fortune. Afflicted, benighted, betrayed. We may close the shutters and bar the doors and build our edifices higher than the flood. We may tantalise the sky with Babel ambition. We may combine our lights and refract beams that challenge heaven. But our mortal feet remain barnacled in darkness and it will seep; it will enter; it will undermine and poison all our play-divinity.

* * *

I write now at the marble-top table in the library. The stove is hot, the shutters closed against the storm. I have laboriously dragged and lowered Mr Adamson here from the draughty, ruined light-room and swaddled him in blankets on the bed.

Bulbous Gut remains dead and firebolt-scarred in the interstitial stairwell. Sunken Cheeks remains unholily baptised in the oil cistern. The lighthouse is dark and I move about it with a lamp, monk-like in these rectilinear catacombs.

Poor Mr Adamson remains unconscious and gravely injured, a livid band all along his left arm and down his back. From this scarlet root extend many of the same fern-like patterns I have witnessed on the lighthouse walls. He is as helpless as a child, yet I have tied him firmly to the bed at wrist and ankle for his own security.

I believe the storm may be abating. The wind has lessened and the rain has stopped, but we are still being battered by the sea. The greatest waves come after the wind has ceased and I wait with trepidation for crests yet higher than the ones that took our fog bells and our lantern glass.

Ripsaw is half-destroyed and lightless – invisible to mariners and to the shore. We are now just a dark column, a slender pencil mark amid a sheet of charcoal swirls and shading. They know nothing of these dramas in the station. They can only imagine what is happening, what has happened, here, and trust to gossip or imagination the events unfolding on the reef.

No doubt they've heard rumours from the Commission and from Mr Jackson. No doubt, they saw the pale, brine-soaked corpse of Principal Bartholomew arrive unmoving on his litter. They've watched the elements grow mad and the lighthouse disappear in their ecstasies. If, sometimes, the house materialises through the spray, they must gaze through their telescopes and study us as villagers once gazed up at the castle on the hill and wondered at the intrigues and the mysteries within.

Could any of them, I wonder, picture the scenes we are living now? The Cyclops lantern blinded. The tower lightning-blasted. The lower chamber flooded. Bodies on stair and in cistern. One keeper insensible and the other enshuttered in perpetual night 'gainst assailing seas.

I am so grievously tired. The storm torments with thump and shake and lashing spindrift. We are inhabiting a place of ghosted absences and timeless expectation. The sea must calm, the wind must stop, and then will come the cutter with its fateful emissaries to take us to that other world. The world of men and streets and gaols.

But before I sleep, I must clean the house and put it in order. A new manhole hatch is required for the light-room. Bulbous Gut, lying further up the house, will have to go off the balcony. Hoisting him up four flights of steps is going to be a tiresome and disagreeable experience without the aid of Mr Adamson, but the mariner must not be here when the Commission arrives. No trace of he or any of his shipmates must remain – not clothes or shoes or evidence of other guests at Ripsaw. They and their vessel must be so erased that only the sea's smooth surface may smile at their passing.

Sunken Cheeks may be toppled down the stone staircase to the water store without much labour and cast out of the main door once the night has fallen. It's true that I may risk a tumbling billow entering the house, but we must dispose of our rubbish and keep the tower clean. The Commission may be pacified provided that their twenty-one flat plates are stacked just-so and that eleven knives sit snugly in the proper draw, not ten. Lord, deliver us from a library book not properly catalogued, or three minims of oil unaccounted for in its apportioned column.

* * *

Night. My duties now accomplished, I keep vigil over Mr Adamson in the library. The wind has stilled yet further but the waves have risen and great walls of ocean heave against the tower. I have watched them from the lantern: rolling swollen and heavy – fatigued with their own density – and folding about the tower in futile embrace. Like burly boxers in the final throes, they look for anything to hold that will support them.

I cannot sleep for their incessant explosions, expecting

that some envious surge will be the one to crash through a shuttered window, burst in the main door or sweep the column, disintegrating, from its rock. Not a single clock has worked since the lightning strike and so we have little concept of the time. I was dozing at some tender hour when a thunderous impact was accompanied by screaming metal and an awful impact on the reef.

The lantern.

Water was dripping down the stairs as I went up to the light-room. I paused before opening the newly constructed manhole. Would a torrent of freezing brine descend to encompass me?

I pushed. Water dribbled but did not gush. I tentatively raised my head above the floor to see that almost the entire lantern and cupola had been wrenched off by some barbaric wave whose crest had vaulted two hundred feet or more. The lens lay on its side amid emerald and prismatic rubble. The majority of panes and astragals were gone, leaving only jagged metal angles. The lighthouse had lost its crown and become a common chimney. I saw clouds racing through the steel mesh ceiling as water dripped apologetically into the light-room. A strand of seaweed glistened on the table where I had passed so many hours on watch.

What luck that I was in the library when that billow struck! Imagine – the great green sea appearing at the pane, its speckled mane wind-whipped, its concave maw a wall ten times thicker than the thickest course of Ripsaw. Imagine the very instant when it broke against the glass and all went dark before immense pressures blasted every pane to dust and permitted ingress to the beast. In one moment, the one-ton lens was lifted like a pine cone in a river and jerked from its base, before the wave continued out the other side, taking glass and copper with it. Nature had erased the art and science and the will of man.

Further down the house, I found the surge had smashed in shutters and windows, leaving puddles in the lower stores and in the kitchen. They would need to be repaired, but I lacked energy. It would be futile to attempt any work until the waves subsided further.

And so now I wait. Wait for sleep. Wait for light. Wait for Mr Adamson to return from whatever bourn he sojourns in. Wait for the weather to change and for the inevitable cutter. Wait for the inescapable.

Mr Adamson looks as Principal Bartholomew did at the end. Pale. Immobile. His skin is painted with an exquisite filigree of burns and angry venal labyrinths. I envy him. I envy him because he has been touched by God, whose arrow shall go forth as the lightning with whirlwinds of the south, his eyes as lamps of fire, and his arms and his feet like in colour to polished brass, and the voice of his words like the voice of a multitude. Mr Adamson has felt the holy fire of Judgement – a power vast and limitless that leaves mortal man destroyed or purer for its searing Truth. It punishes sin, or eradicates it.

TWENTY-NINE

I awoke cold and damp. The stove had cooled and the atmosphere had entered the lighthouse through the many broken windows. My body was stiff from having slept in a chair.

Mr Adamson was awake and free. Not only free, but reading. He was reading this very volume, my personal journal, that I had left on the marble tabletop after writing.

"You are awake, Mister Adamson."

His hand moved to the hatchet on the sheets beside him. "Aye. I can't hear anything in my left ear. My other arm is almost numb."

"You are untied."

"You'd make a hopeless sailor, Poet. A child could wriggle free of your knots."

"You are reading my journal. My private journal."

"Indeed I am. And what a work of fiction you've written. What a mind you have, Meakes! What lies and fancies! All that stuff about the boy – conversations with him, no less! I think the Commission would be very pleased to take this volume into evidence, don't you?"

"Give me the book."

"These pages are full of calumny and defamation. You say I locked you out on the balcony. Two times, in fact!"

"So you did."

"I did not. I never asked you to go out looking for a shadow or whatever lunacy you wrote about. It's pure fancy and lies."

"Please. It is my property." I held out my hand.

"Then you shouldn't leave it lying carelessly around, should you?"

I stood. "I must insist."

"Are you going to kill me, too, Meakes? The last one. You have killed all the rest, Bartholomew included... Or so I surmise from your account. This is evidence, Meakes. I will have nothing to answer for when the Commission sees *this*."

I snatched at the book in his hand. He swung the hatchet at my head and it glanced off my shoulder. I threw myself bodily upon him, grappling for the book, but he was strong: fired with the divine electricity of his lightning bolt.

I caught another blow, this time on the ear. Another must have hit my temple because all went black for a few moments and I awoke to find him gone. My precious journal lay on the floor.

His footsteps were banging down the stairs to the commissioner's room. I heard the rattle of the lock and the hasp.

"I don't need the book, Meakes!" he shouted. "I know what's in it and I know where it is. When they come, I'll tell them and they'll take it from you. Or you'll destroy it first – and I don't think you'll do that."

I said nothing.

"I'm not coming out, Meakes! You'll have to smash this door before you reach me... And I have all the tools in here. The cutter will come out soon – you know it's true. The sea will calm. They can see we've lost the lantern. We're dark. They'll come and they'll find just you and me and we'll tell our stories and see who they believe: you the madman, or me the drunkard. But *I* never killed a man, Meakes. They're not investigating *me*. I'll tell them about the bark and the sailors. There'll be a record of the missing vessel and crew manifests. I only have to wait, Meakes. I don't need food. I have enough in here. The Commission will be here before I suffer thirst or starvation. I'll not be your final victim, Meakes. But I hope I'll be there when they sentence you to hang."

I said nothing. I sat and thought.

I thought of Nero, of Herostratus, of Titus in Jerusalem and the ire of the Lord who will come with fire, and with his chariots like a whirlwind, to render his anger with fury, and his rebuke with flames of fire, and who rained upon Sodom and upon Gomorrah brimstone and fire from out of heaven.

I thought I smelled smoke.

Perhaps the previous night's lightning bolt had grown and kindled in the coal depots or among the stacks of candles. Perhaps the great lantern-sweeping billow had burst in the windows and fed the nascent embers with the air they sought for life. Perhaps the great quantity of oil spilled by the ruptured cistern was providing a path whereon the infant conflagration might creep slowly up the great flue the house had become.

I went below to investigate and, lo, a small fire had started in the oil store. Coals had been scattered and a heap of splintered manhole-hatch wood piled on that spot as if to encourage flames. The addition of balled newspaper and broken candles only served to give boldness to the growing blaze.

I watched the animal grow valiant, seeking greater territory. Evidently, somebody had taken a canister of oil and dribbled it from the store up the steps to the provision store and among the baskets there; up the steps to the kitchen and around the open draws and cupboards; up the stairs to the keepers' room with its beds and furniture; further to the principal's room and up and up so that the fire had a shining path to follow. Somebody, too, had opened all the manhole hatches.

"Meakes? What are you doing out there?"

I said nothing.

"There is oil coming under my door. Meakes!"

I said nothing.

"Can I smell smoke? What are you doing, lad?"

"I don't know if I can extinguish it alone, Mister Adamson."

"Damn you, Meakes! You will not force me out on this pretence."

"It must have been the lightning. A spark, perhaps."

"Don't do this, lad!"

"I believe it is spreading."

"Put it out! Do it now while you have the chance. Smother it with a blanket. Pour water on it. Meakes – can you hear me?"

I sat in the stairwell outside his room and heard him moving. I heard him opening a window as if to look below for signs of smoke. I saw the shadows of his feet at the bottom of the door.

"Meakes? Are you outside? You have to put that fire out. Don't you know how fire spreads in a lighthouse? It's one massive flue, man! And with the lantern gone... Meakes? Damn you, Meakes! Meakes? We're in this situation together, me and you. We've survived this terrible storm and the many... the many accidents of recent days. We must work together. Meakes?"

The smell of smoke was becoming stronger and was rising past me, curious and questing, on its way to the shattered lantern. The fire was growing as when, on some mountain, through the lofty grove, the crackling flames ascend, and blaze above, the fires expanding, as the winds arise, to shoot their long beams, and kindle half the skies.

The light at the bottom of the bedroom door went dark as Mr Adamson blocked it with a watch-cloak or some other clothing.

I recalled that a sacrifice should properly be attended by an aromatic offering of spice to please the gods. Alexander as a child had been rebuked by his tutor Leonidas for throwing two handfuls of expensive perfume upon the sacrificial fire. But when the youth had conquered Gaza, he sent the tutor eighteen tons of frankincense and myrrh along with a note advising less parsimony with his supplications.

It was difficult to descend with the quantity of smoke and heat now rising. I had to cover my mouth and nose with an arm as I sought the provision store for something that could serve as incense. Time was short, and so I was obliged to grab a can of pepper to cast upon flames that even then were emerging from the oil store and seeking the wooden stairs.

Indeed, I could barely descend past the oil store for the intense heat emerging. I smelled my hair scorching and felt my skin burning beneath my clothes, which shrank and blackened at the fire's touch.

I made for the stone staircase and the water store. This would be my sanctuary. Down here, there are no windows and nothing to burn. All is stone, metal and water. I watched the conflagration walking up the wooden steps from the oil store, sniffing out the flow of air and fuel it needed to rise yet higher. I watched it enter the provision store and heard it consuming bags and baskets, puckered apples, crackling grain and popping bottles. The pyre roared on, finding wind, and now it leapt vaulting up the next stairwell, sucked and beckoned by the flow of air effected by the colossal chimney of the lighthouse.

I descended a few more steps to escape the heat and listened to the hollow-moaning holocaust. Next the kitchen fell victim, plates tumbling and wainscot cracking – an inferno, that place where we had sat so many times: a raging den of flames and smoke sent senseless by the ever-luring sky.

"Meakes! Meakes!" I heard faintly over the bellows of ascending hell.

I started to feel faint and leaned against the lightning-scorched brass rail. The combustion was using up my air, inhaling from the very bottom of its stone lung to feed the fury. I had no choice but to descend into the water store and approach the main door through ankle-deep water.

On opening the first metal door to the vestibule, cool air rushed past me and growled into the fire. It was ravenous. It would burn every breath of air fed to it.

Boisterous waves were still banging at the main door, but what choice did I have? I slid the side bolts. I slid the floor bolts and peered through the crack to grey mountain peaks towering. Restraining the door with a trembling shoulder, I selected the boltholes closest to the brass sill and secured the door with a gap of just two inches.

"Meakes! Meakes!" Fainter now amid the uproar.

Wind blasted past me through the vestibule and up the tower, flames wailing and whooping with the levitation they were offered. A wave crashed against the door and water jetted through the aperture with a force that shook the door and rattled bolts. How long before some immense billow smashed the oak to splinters?

I was in a precarious position: caught between the warring elements of flame and sea. Both would starve me of respiration. Both would consume me in their fatal embrace. The heat was rising and threatening to descend. The flood was high and trying to break in.

The tower was a Cuthite fire beacon, a second Tower of Babel. Soon, sacrificial ecstasy would burst from the ruined lantern crown and shoot into the heavens. Ripsaw would become the London Fire Monument made real.

I could see only one course of action: the massed water tanks.

I took off my boots, put my journal inside one of them and laid them on the cover to one tank. My feet were cold upon the chill and briny stone. I then lifted the cover of the emptiest tank and climbed into the black water before closing the hinged lid over me.

There was no room to stand. I sat and hugged my knees, the water level halfway up my chest. My clothes immediately soaked heavy and frigid. All was darkness.

The bombarding sea was magnified within this metal box, reverberating like thunder immediately overhead. The burning column howled and groaned. The main door rattled in its boltholes. And I, a midnight embryo, shivered waiting for the hell to pass.

How long I waited, I could not say. I felt the iron warming. I smelled the smoke. The water vibrated with striking waves and seismic fire. If only one could re-enter the womb and return to purity and innocence, wiping clean all that contaminates and poisons. From that first screaming entry into the world, we are cast upon the flood and at the mercy of the sky. Darkness pursues us with beguiling whispers and false promises. Light offers sanctuary and salvation. We live amid penumbrae. Burn this house; don't burn this house. Kill this man; do not kill this man. Revenge oneself for horrors committed; forgive others for their sins. Bludgeon, dismember and inculpate – or walk away to fairer horizons and a life of happy routine.

Choices. Choices.

Mr Fowler said we all have choices, but I wonder. The higher mind is a crystal lens that gathers rays and concentrates them in a beam of saving light to pierce darkness and warn sojourners of peril. That light is knowledge. That light is art and science. That light is Socrates' daemon and St Augustine's soul. It is a beacon to all men through history. And yet where does the great and pure refracting lens stand but on a tower? And where is the base of that tower but in the foundations of the earth or amid the sea bottom's wretched jellies? That darkness, that cloaca, is man the animal. Man the hunter. Man driven by black and lascivious urges, man malignant and envenomed with the feral passions in his blood. To conquer. To possess. To annihilate for personal gain. And which of this pair will triumph in the end: animal or anima? Lust or love? Piety or pride?

Without light there is no darkness. But inside these frail columns of flesh, inside these veins, inside this skull, there is only night. Illumination is without, beyond. Illumination burns bright and needs fuel to live. It is delicate and requires nurturing. But darkness needs nothing to exist. It is the essence and the origin of everything.

In the beginning, God created the heaven and the earth, and the earth was without form, and void, and darkness was upon the face of the deep. Before the light? Numberless eons of nothingness to which we all return.

THIRTY

I don't know how long I was inside the water tank. When I emerged, my limbs were stiff and I was shaking. The storeroom was awash, the main door ripped free of its fastenings by mocking billows and carried to my feet. The lighthouse was hot and reeked of incendiary destruction. I went to the stone staircase and put on my boots to ascend.

The oil store was a charred and smoking hell, all coal burned up and the oil cisterns soot-blackened. The ruptured one had been consumed entirely, but the others remained covered and seemed still to contain some oil. It was necessary to cover my face against the harsh and acrid smell.

The staircase to the provision store had burned entirely and I was faced with an impossible leap to reach the next chamber. I dragged an iron coal depot – still hot – from the oil store to use as a step and managed to jump high enough to grasp the edge and hoist myself, soiling my legs and arms black in the process.

The smell there was worse: a compost of burned hessian, soap, vinegar, wicker basket, sundry grains, salt beef and ship's biscuit. The place was a chaos of carbonised detritus and ashes, all reduced to shrivelled debris.

Again, I had to drag a japanned locker – now stripped of its lacquer to the bare metal – to hoist myself up the stairless gap to the kitchen.

Waste. Destruction. Ripsaw had become an empty crucible, its interior scarred and blasted by purifying incandescence.

All that remained was heat-scoured walls and the vestiges of familiar things transformed by fury into shadows. No doors or partitions were left. No wax-cloth covering. No furniture. No staircases. Gehenna's fire had whirled voracious through the house and razed everything that fed it. The keepers' room: a shell of embers. The principal's room: dilapidated heaps of smoking cinders, the leech jar empty and desiccated corpses spread about its base.

The commissioner's room's double-locked door was gone – reduced to ashes by the up-rushing firestorm. I went inside. The heat had been intense in here, fuelled by book and chart. The sheets were gone, the bed a mere charcoal sketch of beams.

No bones. No body.

The library. The poor, blameless library, once so like home, was now a nightmarish Hades. But not all the books had burned. Those stacked closest together had lost their spines to flame, but remained intact: Crusoe soot-smeared but still determined; Achilles and Hector – no strangers to the fires of sacrifice – still brandishing their arms; Macbeth, waist-deep in blood, waded on; Hamlet coached his players undistracted. But Dickens had succumbed, and Scott. Arthur Gordon Pym, too, was lost. They would live on in other books on other shelves.

But no bones. No body.

Up into the light-room store, whose walls showed marks of spirituous explosion and whose accumulated rubble smoked still. Here, so close to the nourishing air of the light-room, the inferno had burned its hottest and most crazed. The vice lay on the ground amid the fragments of the table that had held it.

But no body.

The light-room was still hot, its metal column, cogwheels and mesh ceiling super-heated. Raven flags and tatters of paper and cloth dangled where they'd been left by the tower's hellish expirations. The sky showed as a circle of pale grey.

There was a smell of roasted meat. Not beef or pork or anything I recognised.

The spiral metal staircase to the lantern had buckled and it creaked as I ascended to the open air. No glass remained, and only jagged spikes of astragal. The cupola was entirely vanished. This was now the uppermost platform of the lighthouse, exposed fully to the open sea and sky. The lens – the great one-ton lens – lay on its side, charred black on its lower half and missing sections that had fallen and smashed.

Inside and foetus-curled were the remains of Mr Adamson: hairless, naked, black. What impulse had compelled him to seek protection in the lens – the same chamber that had scorched him with heaven's fire? Did he believe in the sanctity and sanctuary of the light? Did he, in his final asphyxiation, see something reflected, something refracted, of a life to come? Of a place to rest? Of a home?

Ripsaw Reef had been his hell. He had lived the full length of his life, travelling the seas and land, traversing friendships, learning, perhaps loving, to finish here – roasted 'midst a lunatic inferno inside a crown-glass coffin. Piteous. Absurd. A man sketched in charcoal on a cave wall.

And so I sit amid the rushing clouds and write and look occasionally at the approaching cutter. If I wished, I could call on Boreas or Zephyrus and draw a squall. I could summon cataracts and hurricanes to blow the world back whence it came. That is within my power. For if the winds rage, does not the sea wax mad? I am the sea. And if calm is upon the flood, is it not a field of tranquillity and a mirror to the vault of heaven?

I am the sea. I am the sea.